THE LOST AND THE BLIND

Previous Titles by Declan Burke

The Harry Rigby Series

EIGHTBALL BOOGIE
SLAUGHTER'S HOUND

Other Titles

THE BIG O
ABSOLUTE ZERO COOL
CRIME ALWAYS PAYS *
THE LOST AND THE BLIND *

* *available from Severn House*

THE LOST AND THE BLIND

Declan Burke

This first world edition published 2014
in Great Britain and 2015 in the USA by
SEVERN HOUSE PUBLISHERS LTD of
19 Cedar Road, Sutton, Surrey, England, SM2 5DA
Trade paperback edition first published 2015 in Great
Britain and the USA by SEVERN HOUSE PUBLISHERS LTD.

Burke, Declan author.
  The lost and the blind.
  1. World War, 1939-1945–Atrocities–Ireland–Donegal
  (County)–Fiction. 2. Murder–Investigation–Fiction.
  3. Suspense fiction.
  I. Title
  823.9'2-dc23

ISBN-13: 978-0-7278-8464-0 (cased)
ISBN-13: 978-1-84751-567-4 (trade paper)
ISBN-13: 978-1-78010-615-1 (e-book)

All Severn House titles are printed on acid-free paper.

Severn House Publishers support the Forest Stewardship Council™ [FSC™],
the leading international forest certification organisation. All our titles that
are printed on FSC certified paper carry the FSC logo.

Typeset by Palimpsest Book Production Ltd.,
Falkirk, Stirlingshire, Scotland.
Printed and bound in Great Britain by
TJ International, Padstow, Cornwall.

ACKNOWLEDGEMENTS

My sincere thanks to my agent, Allan Guthrie, and to the good people of Severn House, and particularly Sara Porter and Kate Lyall Grant; and my love and gratitude, as always, to Aileen and Lily.

The real hero is always a hero by mistake; he dreams of being an honest coward like everyone else.

Umberto Eco, *Travels in Hyperreality*

ONE

S hay Govern strolled into the lobby of the Shelbourne Hotel looking like he'd just bought the place, or sold it. There was something easy and coiled about the way he moved. A bounce in his stride at eighty-one years old that put me in mind of dancers pre-show, stretching it out but not too far, not yet.

He spotted me beside the fireplace and waved a hand to tell me to stay put, he'd come to me. Not a tall man but compact, square through the shoulders. Up close the suit was black pinstripes on a coal-black two-piece, narrow through the hips and legs, a thin black tie and crisp white shirt. The wingtips were shiny black patent leather. He could've been prowling the Sands with Frank and Sammy, still working a look he could have fun with but be serious if he needed to. That first time he was all business.

'Tom Noone?' he said in a flat Boston accent that was half drawl, half snarl.

'That's me.'

I'd been wondering how it might feel to shake hands with ninety million dollars, give or take, on paper at least. It was a firm, dry squeeze. Nothing you might remember.

'Sit down, Mr Noone. Or would you rather I called you Tom?'

'Tom will do grand.'

'Glad to hear it.' A waiter was already hovering. 'What'll you have – coffee? Is it too early for the hard stuff?'

'Coffee's good.'

He ordered a pot of coffee and sat back into the leather armchair with both hands planted on the armrests. His face looked like someone had chipped it out with a fine-bladed chisel, the deep wrinkles around the hooded eyes and thin mouth carved one careful tap at a time. Pale blue eyes over a hawkish nose, the snow-white hair clipped close.

'You want to wait for the coffee,' he said, 'or will we get straight to it?'

'Let's get to it.'

'Great. So I'll start off, then you ask anything you need to know. Then we make a deal or we don't, no hard feelings. OK?'

'Sounds good.'

'Right. So, Tom Noone, you're a journalist, freelance, mostly movies and books, some music reviews, interviews with writers and so forth. Also a writer, with four thrillers published, two non-fiction, a couple of awards nominations, a citation or honourable mention, I forget where. No, don't tell me, it'll come. You're married with one daughter but separated and I'm sorry to hear that, it's never good when there's kids involved. You still seeing her?'

'My daughter?'

'Sure.'

'Most weekends, yeah.'

'Good. So what've I missed?'

I was still wrong-footed by how well prepared he was. 'Not a lot, actually.'

'No? What about the two books you ghost-wrote? Is that the right way to say it – ghost-wrote?'

'I've worked as a ghost-writer, yeah. Close enough.'

'Close enough is a mile wide. You ashamed of those books?'

'Not at all.'

'So how come they're not on your website with all the rest?'

'Because they're not my own work, not the way the others are.'

'And you don't want to take credit where it isn't due.'

'That's about the height of it.'

'Fair enough. You enjoy it, the ghost-writing?'

'It wouldn't be my first choice for work, no.'

'Pays the bills though.'

'It has done.'

'So what would you say to forty thousand euro to ghost-write my story?'

Back then forty grand was roughly my annual income. Which, I guessed, Shay Govern already knew.

'I'd say it was a generous offer,' I said, 'and that it'd probably be a lot more interesting than the others I've done.'

'Cute answer but no cigar.' He smiled for the first time. 'Anyway, it's not me.'

'No?'
'It's Sebastian Devereaux.'
'Who?'
'Exactly.'

The coffee arrived. Shay Govern tipped the waiter a ten-spot and told him he'd pour it himself. As he sat forward, hunched in, he said, 'You write thrillers, right?'

'They're more detective stories. Thrilling in spots.'

'OK, sure. The point I'm making is you've never heard of Sebastian Devereaux.'

'Can't say the name rings a bell.'

'Don't beat yourself up. First I heard of him was four months ago, when I was on Delphi.'

Delphi Island, a couple of miles south of Buncrana on Lough Swilly in northern Donegal.

'Fascinating guy,' Govern said. 'English originally, an archaeologist who came to Delphi in his twenties and ended up staying for the rest of his life. As in, he never stepped off the island again. A recluse, apparently. Wrote these thrillers back in the day, the sixties and seventies, they did pretty well. Then he just stopped.'

'I really should've heard of this guy.'

'Which is why someone needs to write this book.'

'That could be one reason, sure. Mostly, though, the reason people get books written about them is they're famous.'

'I'm familiar with how the publishing business works, Tom. The broad strokes, at least, mainly because it's a business. But listen, I should tell you a little bit about myself before we go on. Maybe it'll make a bit more sense then.'

I'd done a little research on Shay Govern myself and what he told me more or less chimed with what I'd been able to find in the week or so since I'd received his email requesting a meeting. Not that there was a lot of information available. According to his profile on the Govern Industries website, he'd been born in Donegal in 1925 but now very clearly defined himself as Irish-American. His background was in mining, although the Govern Industries portfolio incorporated offshore drilling, high-risk prospecting and property development on a vast scale. He, or the various incarnations of Govern Industries, had interests in Boston,

Florida, Alaska, the Bahamas and South Africa. He was widowed, with three grown children, all of whom were non-executive directors on the board and all of whom kept themselves busy heading up an array of trusts, endowments and charitable institutions.

'So I'm retired now, as you probably know, but sitting around the country club doesn't really appeal. What I'm hoping to do is set up some programmes here in Ireland, along the lines of what we have going back home in the States.'

He'd come over the previous September for what he called a jaunt around the old place. The first time he'd ever been back.

'I'm not an emotional man, Tom. You'll learn that about me if you haven't already picked it up. But yeah, that was an interesting trip.'

He'd fetched up on Delphi after hearing, in Derry, about an interesting project being run on a tiny island in Lough Swilly.

'Seems like the island was an old shooting estate belonging to some English gentry, this is going back hundreds of years, all the way to the Plantation. Anyway, some time in the late sixties the islanders bought it out, started running the place like a co-operative. I'm thinking, OK, how's that work? So over I go, take the ferry, and I meet with this amazing lady, Carol Devereaux. She actually has the old title, so officially she's Lady McConnell. She tells me how she's the daughter of this writer, Sebastian Devereaux, she used his money to buy out the title, ploughing it all back into the island. I'm like you, I've never heard of any Sebastian Devereaux, not that I'm so well read. But Carol fills me in, and we get to talking about what I've just mentioned. Carol says she has plans for an artists' retreat on Delphi, it's ideal for it, the island's so quiet and peaceful. Maybe even a boutique publishing house if they discover any new talent coming through the programme. Naturally she's going to name the programme for her father. So I say, OK, why don't you write a book about him, launch the retreat that way. She says what you're saying, that he's forgotten, why would anyone want to read a book about a writer when his books have been out of print for twenty years? So I say, who owns the rights? I mean, I don't know much about publishing, but business is business, am I right?'

The contracts were already drawn up. Shay Govern was funding an endowment to establish the Sebastian Devereaux Centre for Contemplative Arts ('I don't need to tell you it wasn't me picked the name, right?') and commissioning a biography of the great man himself. Carol Devereaux was planning to republish her father's books to coincide with the opening of the centre and the publication of the biography.

'All going well, the programme's self-funding within five years.' He shrugged. 'Worst-case scenario, a forgotten man gets his due. Anything else you need to know?'

What I was wondering was if Sebastian Devereaux's voluntary exile in a foreign land had touched a chord with Shay Govern. What I said was, 'Why me?'

'You think you're not up to it?'

'It's not that. But you've done your research. You knew before we sat down I'm no expert on Sebastian Devereaux.'

'I've looked around, Tom. No one is. At least, no one with your publishing record. You came highly recommended. Plus you write thrillers yourself, you'll have what they call a real empathy for your subject.'

'Like I said before, I write detective stories. Private-eye stuff.'

'What's the difference?'

'Thrillers sell better, for one.'

'Listen, don't sweat it. Spies, detectives, cops, it's all the same thing when you shake it out.'

'I'd love to do it, Mr Govern. But—'

'Shay.'

'OK, Shay. So yeah, I'd love to do it. But I don't want to take it on under false pretences.'

'I get that. And I appreciate you pointing it out. But look, don't worry so much about not knowing Sebastian Devereaux at this point. You'll be working closely with Carol and she has all the information you'll need. Manuscripts, diaries, first-hand testimony of the man, the works. What I suggest is, you come with me to Delphi this weekend, we'll sit down with Carol and see if you can work together. If she's happy and you're happy, we're good to go. If not, I'll pay your expenses and we say so long, no harm done.'

'Sounds more than fair.'

'You have an agent, right? Good. So we'll get him to look over the contract while you're away, although Carol tells me it's standard stuff. You get paid a flat fee of forty grand, like I said. Ten on signature, ten on delivery, the final twenty on publication. And the standard royalty fees apply. Good so far?'

'Great, yeah. What's the catch?'

'Heh.' He smiled again. 'There's two catches, actually. The first is that I need you to devote yourself exclusively to the project. We're talking about a publication deadline of six months, and you'll need to be onsite on Delphi to work with Carol. Is that doable?'

'It's possible, sure. But it'd depend on how quickly we work and what kind of book Carol has in mind. Lots of factors.'

'Sure. But you'd be available, right?'

It would mean parking a couple of regular freelance gigs, taking a sabbatical and hoping they were still there when I came back. But there was other work I could do just as well while I was based on Delphi, just to keep the freelance side of things ticking over.

'It'll take a few favours,' I said, 'but yeah, it's do-able. What else?'

'You'll understand, Tom, that this is a very personal project for Carol. She's very protective of her father's reputation. So the book will be published under Carol's name. You'll be ghost-writing, like we discussed. I mean, if you want, we can put your name on the cover too. But it'll go out as Carol's book. Is that a deal-breaker?'

The short answer was not really. The longer answer involved a forty-grand fee plus royalties and bills that, as Bruce put it, no honest man could pay.

'I'll have to run it by my agent,' I said, 'just to be on the safe side. But in theory, yeah, it shouldn't be a problem.'

'Terrific. I'm heading for Delphi on Saturday morning, driving up, leaving here around noon. You want to travel with me or make your own way?'

'Whatever suits you best.'

'We'll go together, yeah? Kill the journey.'

'Sounds good. Just one last thing.'

'Yeah?'

'You said I came highly recommended. Who was it?'

'Father Ignatius Patton.'

'Iggy?'

'Yeah. He said if he was the one looking for someone who'd give a dead man his due, you'd be first on his list.'

TWO

R achel and I had this routine where she never picked up when I rang, this on the basis that it was usually bad news and she'd need time to calm down before dealing with the fall-out. So I left a message as I strolled down Dawson Street, saying I wouldn't be able to take Emily this weekend and apologizing for the short notice. I'd call again later to speak to Emily herself, and explain why.

It was almost 11.30 a.m. by then, a sunny, breezy Friday in central Dublin. I rang Jenny, one of the few commissioning editors still taking my calls, to see if she was available for a quick coffee. She said she wasn't, but that if I asked nicely she'd let me buy her lunch. So I asked nicely.

I nipped into the coffee shop on the corner of Anne Street and picked up a couple of lattes. Iggy Patton did good work with homeless kids and addicts, running a soup kitchen out the back of the boxing club he'd put together in a basement off Molesworth Street. All very noble but the coffee budget didn't extend to anything better than powdered instant and there's only so many sacrifices a man can make in one day.

Iggy Patton was a priest and a boxer, and not always in that order. What he'd do was he'd wait until you found out he was a priest who boxed, or used to, then he'd tell you he couldn't decide which vocation had sucker-punched him hardest.

The idea being, presumably, that you'd imagine a bruised heart, a punch-drunk soul.

When he'd tried it on me, I said, 'Iggy, man, if God knocked you around any more than whoever it was busted in your face, you should skip pope and go straight to saint.'

He had eyes the colour of prunes which were prone to melancholy. He was somewhere in his late forties now, the sandy-blond hair getting thin, the face battered to a dull shine and not entirely unlike the old leather punch-bag in the corner of his office oozing horse-hair stuffing from a split seam. I'd interviewed him a couple of years before, working on a book about a Magdalene survivor,

Rose and the Thorns. He'd played it straight and I'd done him the same favour. We got on just fine.

His office was the club's storeroom. There was a scarred plywood desk wedged in against the far wall under a window that was opaque with grime, reinforced with wire and mossy on the outside. Iggy offered me his seat behind the desk but I took a pew on the punch-bag in the corner, its cracked leather pickled from booze-soaked sweat he'd pounded out in pre-mass dawn sessions.

He sucked down about half of his latte in one go, closing his eyes to privately savour the bitter sin of its extravagance, then unlocked the bottom drawer of his desk and topped us both up with a couple of Jameson bracers.

'The sun's over the yardarm somewhere,' he said.

'*Sláinte.*'

He had himself a sip and situated the cardboard beaker just so on the desk and said, without looking at me, 'A book about *who*?'

'Sebastian Devereaux. Used to write thrillers back in the day. I never heard of him either.'

It was odd. Iggy had been expecting me – it had been obvious from his expression when he'd opened his door. But I could tell that he'd been expecting something else entirely. 'What is it, Iggy?'

'He came to me for confession, Tom. Sorry.'

'Shay Govern, you mean.'

'Aye.' He had another sip on his Jameson latte.

'When was this?'

'Late last week. Thursday, I think.'

'So what can you tell me?'

'Not much.'

'But you recommended me, right? Thanks for that, by the way.' I toasted him with the latte. 'Much appreciated.'

'No bother.'

'So what was it you were recommending me *for*?'

'I got the impression,' he said after a minute or so spent staring at the cardboard beaker on the desk, 'that he wanted his own story told. That was my sense of it.'

'This story he told you in confession.'

'Yes.'

'But that story had nothing to do with Sebastian Devereaux.'

'This is the first I'm hearing that name.'

'Doesn't make sense, does it?'

'Well, it obviously does to Shay Govern.'

'Should I be worried?'

'I honestly don't know, Tom. I mean, he's bona fide when it comes to the money side of things, if that's what you're asking. He cut me a cheque for this place after we talked. Liked what we were doing for the kids. It wasn't a fortune, exactly, but it didn't bounce.'

'Good to know,' I said, 'but I'm not asking about the money. Govern said you recommended me because I'd give a dead man his due.'

'That's right.'

'Did you tell him about my father?'

'Don't be daft, Tom. All I meant was, you're conscientious to a fault.'

'A fault?'

'Jesus wept.' It was his only profanity, although he was fond of it. 'It was a compliment, Tom. And hey – it got you the job, didn't it?'

'Not the job you thought I'd get, though.'

'Maybe not, but then God isn't the only one who works in mysterious ways. But listen, Tom?'

'What?'

'If it does work out with you and Shay Govern, I'll be expecting a finder's fee. A donation to the boxing club, we'll say five per cent. What d'you say?'

THREE

I met Jenny for an early lunch in the Happy Bean at the bottom of South William Street. As always, we ate fast and then lingered over the coffee, despite the calypso-styled jazz wibbling through the Happy Bean's speakers.

'Sounds horrendous,' she said after I'd filled her in on Shay Govern's offer. 'Six months' paid leave, they're putting you up on some island retreat, you'll probably have time to work on something of your own. *And* you get another book on the shelf. What's not to hate?'

'I wouldn't be able to do the movie column.'

'I know. Don't sweat it. We're coming into blockbuster season anyway, it's not like you'll be missing much.'

'You can hold it for me?'

The weekly movie column was my one regular gig, the central plank of my monthly income. It was also my favourite. Time-consuming, sure, getting along to the morning preview screenings, all of which took place in Dublin city centre, but it was enjoyable and it paid well. It pretty much covered my big outgoings, which were rent and my contribution towards keeping six-year-old Emily in the style to which she was accustomed.

Jenny was the first friend I'd made when I moved to Dublin, a comrade from the days of scuffling around the barricades of freelancing who was now tucked up in a velvet coffin as the editor of *Night in the City*, the *Independent*'s weekly magazine supplement that covered movies and books, theatre and music, fashion and food. Her hair had never really recovered its shape from the Rachel she gave it back when *Friends* was still hot, and I'd never really recovered from the first time I saw her heart-shaped face, those violet-tinged eyes peeking out from behind a ragged fringe, both of us covering the Pixies at the Point in 1991 – Jen for *Hot Press*, me for *In Dublin*. She'd had a raspy voice, a filthy sense of humour and a healthy instinct for self-preservation that had kept me at arm's length for nearly two decades now.

'It won't be an issue, Tom. If anyone asks I'll say you've taken a sabbatical; it sounds more official that way. Being honest, though, if anyone even notices I'll be shocked.'

'Thanks.'

'Don't mention it. So how is Emily these days? Seen her lately?'

'Last weekend, yeah. She's great.'

'Still keen on Disneyworld, is she?'

'I think it's Disneyland, actually. Which is the Florida one?'

'You don't know?'

'Do you?'

She didn't. 'The difference being,' she said, 'I'm not the one who's supposed to be bringing my six-year-old daughter to Disney heaven. So you might want to read up on that.'

'Actually,' I said, 'we might have missed the boat for Disneyland. All she was talking about last weekend was the pyramids, the Sphinx.'

'It'll be Machu Picchu next.'

'Could easily be.' With Emily you never knew.

'So this guy, Shane Govern,' she said.

'Shay Govern.'

'Shay, right. He's eighty years old—'

'Eighty-one and still dressing like Dean Martin. You'd love him.'

'Sounds like my kind of man, all right. What's the hitch?'

I told her about Iggy's recommendation, the dead man's due. How he'd been expecting me when I called around to see him, but then baulked when he heard what Shay Govern was commissioning.

'Sounds a bit weird, yeah,' she said. 'And because it was a confession . . .'

'He can't tell me anything.'

'Not even off the record?'

'I don't think priests are allowed off-the-record briefings, Jen.'

'You think?' She grinned, evil. 'Here's a newsflash, journo-boy . . . Crap, hold on.'

Her phone had started chirping. Almost literally, as it happens – Jenny's ring-tone was Woody Woodpecker. She answered it getting up, mouthing 'Martin' to me and spiralling her forefinger at the table.

'Hey hon,' she said as she walked away. 'What's hot?'

I caught the eye of the waitress mopping the table alongside, ordered another couple of coffees. She'd dropped them off by the time Jenny came back. 'Martin says keep your hands on your own side of the table,' she said, sitting down. 'Also, he can't wait to read the Sebastian Devereaux book.' She rolled her eyes at the Martin–Tom mutual appreciation society and ripped open a sachet of sugar and sprinkled half into her fresh coffee.

'He's heard of him?' I said.

'You're surprised?'

I shouldn't have been. 'What are you doing tonight?' I said.

'I am out and *about*,' she said grandly. 'Which means Martin's babysitting tonight.'

'I don't think it qualifies as babysitting when they're your own kids, Jen.'

'Yeah, well, with our pair there's sometimes some actual sitting on kids required.'

'You're a hard woman, Jenny Boyle.'

'Be nice,' she said, 'or I'll kidnap a chimp from the zoo, get *him* to write your movie column for the next six months.' She sipped on her coffee and got herself settled in for some hardcore gossip. 'So what's the latest on Rachel?' she said. 'Is the custody hearing still going ahead?'

'Week after next.'

'Anything we can do?'

'Other than offer me a full-time job with pension and health benefits, not really. But thanks.'

'If it was my call,' she said, 'I'd do it in a heartbeat. If I thought you'd take it.'

'I'd take it.'

The freelance life is fine when you're still a kid, scrabbling from month to month to pay for booze and dope, making sure there's enough left over for rent and bills. When you're a married man with a baby and a mortgage, the thrill of not knowing what you'll earn next month tends to lose its appeal.

That wasn't the only reason Rachel had finally given up on me. But there was a reason why her new guy, Peter, was a life assurance broker.

Life assurance. The guy was peddling snake oil, sure, but he was getting well paid to do it.

As far as I could make out, from quizzing Emily on weekends, Peter was actually a decent guy. He was nice, she said. Uncle Peter. Told her funny stories. He didn't sound particularly flash, either. He'd buy her books, or a football, or a DVD once in a while.

The trip to Disneyland, or Disneyworld, had been Rachel's idea.

I had ten days before I stood up in front of a judge to try and persuade him, or her, that I was financially competent, that Emily's long-term interests wouldn't be best served by awarding custody to Rachel and Peter.

It'd be a tough one. Mainly because lies only ever really work when you believe them yourself.

FOUR

I sent Martin a text as I walked up George's Street, heading for home.

You receiving gentleman callers this evening? Looking to pick your brains on S. Devereaux. Will bring beer.

Martin Banks was an accountant, which meant he tended to stress over details that most people, the taxman included, considered excessively petty. Or so I tried to convince him on an annual basis, usually late in November and a week after deadline, when Martin was sweating the small stuff on my tax return.

He was a good bloke, though. Solid. At the time I'd presumed Jenny was taking the soft option in marrying him, like buying a Volvo, safe and reliable and something you could learn to respect and maybe even love if you hung on to it long enough.

Martin was quiet and ran well, for sure, but he was funny too in a dust-dry way, and he always got his round in. In his twenties he'd looked too old for his years, with his sensibly short haircut already going grey at the temples, the square-rimmed specs that might have been retro-hip if it weren't for his penchant for suits and ties, rugby shirts and pressed jeans. He was a slow burner, though. Over the years he'd even managed to turn me on to the finer points of rugby. Where we overlapped was Jenny and crime novels. There wasn't much to be said about Jenny without saying too much, so we talked a lot of crime fiction. The first time we met we'd bonded over Alistair MacLean's *When Eight Bells Toll*, but where we really got on was with the old hardboiled stuff: Hammett and the Cains and Chandler, for sure, but McCoy and Burnett too, Edward Anderson, Goodis and Brewer.

His reply arrived as I let myself into the apartment.

Sounds good. Leave it till after 9 though. Anything new?

By which he meant new writers, or at least writers who were new to us. I put the kettle on and then hunted out the Kem Nunn I'd come across, *Tapping the Source*, and put it to one side for later. After making a pot of coffee I went up the hallway to the smaller of the two bedrooms, which I'd converted into an office back in the grand old days when you could still claim for the costs of running a home office on your tax return. Handy, and a nice commute too. That day I was putting together a feature, twelve hundred words, on good movies adapted from bad books. Good fun, and I was about seven hundred words in when my phone beeped to let me know I had a message from Jenny.

Your friend Govern? IT pg 7. xx J

I put another pot of coffee on to brew and went downstairs and around the corner for an *Irish Times*. The piece on page seven was a short one, below the fold:

Morrigan Mining, a division of Govern Industries, has tendered for a prospecting licence for Lough Swilly, Co. Donegal.

If approved, the licence will cover gold, silver and copper. Archaeological excavations have revealed that copper was mined on Delphi Island in Lough Swilly as early as 2,500 BC, although it is believed that the seam identified by Morrigan Mining lies offshore.

The licence is dependent on a survey which will determine the commercial viability of the proposed mine.

In a statement, Morrigan Mining said: 'Geological records of the Donegal area offer anomalies consistent with gold. The evidence to date confirms the presence of gold, although it remains to be seen whether it occurs in sufficient quantity to justify a full-scale mining operation. There is also evidence of other base metals on the proposed site but our main exploration will focus on gold.'

A significant gold mine would be the first in Ireland for 2,000 years, and would offer a considerable boost to the beleaguered local economy. Morrigan Mining was unwilling to commit to a precise figure, but conceded that a viable mine offered 'potential measured in millions'.

'If the survey brings back positive results,' said Morrigan spokesman Hugh Conroy, 'we will be applying to the Department of Enterprise for funding in a public-private development.'

The Minister of State for Natural Resources, Donal Daly,

has promised the people of Donegal that the government
will do all in its power to assist Morrigan Mining in its
endeavours.

A *gold* mine? Shay Govern obviously wasn't a man for half
measures. Give him six months and he'd be building a launch
pad on Delphi Island for a rocket aimed at Mars.

I was a little pissed at missing the scoop, but the good news
was that Shay Govern wasn't messing about. If he could afford
to waste money prospecting in Lough Swilly, then the forty
grand for a ghost-writing commission would be coming out of
petty cash.

It did make me wonder, though. About how much Shay Govern
was committing to Delphi, and why. He'd described Carol
Devereaux as an amazing lady, and he'd been protective of her
interests, adamant that the book would be hers regardless of how
much work I put in.

He wouldn't be the first widower to fall for a younger woman
late in life, of course, but neither would he be the first rich guy
to belatedly realize he was being strung along, and pull the plug.

Call me a cynic when it comes to affairs of the aging heart,
but I needed to sign a contract to put myself on a legal footing,
and fast.

I went back to my desk, finished the feature and filed it. I was
three days early, which would probably give the sub-editor a
fright, get him thinking he was two days late putting the section
to bed. Couldn't be helped.

Then I pulled up a fresh Google search and went looking for
Sebastian Devereaux.

It didn't take long. No, scratch that – I spent about an hour
or so, but everything there was to find I found in the first five
minutes, and virtually all of it courtesy of a short bio from his
last book, *Endgame on Cyprus*.

> **Sebastian Devereaux (b. 1915)**, the son of a Presbyterian
> minister, was born in Norwich and grew up in Edinburgh.
> He attended Edinburgh University, studying archaeology. In
> 1939 he went to Delphi Island off the northwest coast of
> Ireland, where he has lived ever since.
>
> Sebastian has published four novels to date: *Rendezvous*

at Thira (1968), *The Corsican Affair* (1971), *Two Days to Malta* (1973) and *Endgame on Cyprus* (1977).

In 1984, Sebastian Devereaux was awarded an honorary degree by Edinburgh University.

His books, as Shay Govern had said, were out of print, and his publisher had nothing about Devereaux on its website. I tried searching for *Sebastian Devereaux literary agent* but all the news fit to print there came from an obituary published in 1988. Wikipedia pretty much rehashed the info from the bio, and apart from some mostly positive reviews scattered here and there, none of which contained any personal information, that was as good as it got.

After an hour of feeling like a fifth-rate Beckett, sitting there telling myself nothing twice, I decided that the lack of information was actually a good thing. That everything Carol Devereaux and I put into the book would be new and freshly minted and utterly fascinating.

Provided, of course, we could find anyone who was even remotely interested in the life and times of one Sebastian Devereaux, the ex-archaeologist, forgotten author and, by the sounds of things, Olympic-standard hermit.

It was looking more and more like the best bit of writing I'd be doing in the next six months was penning my signature to that contract.

I was rooting around in the fridge for something that might constitute a dinner when my phone rang. I checked the caller ID, picked it up and said, 'Jack B. How're they hanging?'

Jack liked that kind of thing.

'I'm in the Butchers,' he said, 'and buying.'

'Sorry, Jack.' I needed to eat and then get back online to find out what I could about Carol Devereaux and Delphi Island. 'I'm up to my tonsils over here.'

'Let me guess. Right this second you're working on Shay Govern.'

He was close enough to make it worrying. 'Put me on a stout. I'll be there in five.'

'It's already settling,' he said.

There were rumours, unproven, that Jack Byrne's retirement

from the illustrious ranks of the detective branch of An Garda Síochána had been hastened by allegations that Jack, being something of an electronics whizz, had facilitated the tapping of phones, some of which may or may not have been regularly used by senior government ministers during a public inquiry into the possibility that certain members of the Gardai might have exceeded their powers of restraint and persuasion while investigating a Tallaght-based gang suspected of having a financial interest in funnelling cocaine from South America through Alicante and Amsterdam and onwards to the not noticeably mean streets of south County Dublin's leafy suburbs.

Anyway, Jack took early retirement, a pension and a lump sum, and went into the security business. He ran a stable of nightclub bouncers and nightwatchmen, and offered private consultations on best practice for business owners concerned that an insurance company might find a damning loophole in their security arrangements. Now and again the private consultations tiptoed over the line into private investigations, which was how I'd first met him, when I'd tracked him down and picked his brain for realistic detail in the private eye novel I was writing at the time.

'First thing you want to do,' he'd told me, 'is forget about that realism shit.' Try writing a realistic crime novel, he said, and it'd run to ten thousand mind-numbing pages and fall apart on the last page halfway through the court case because some overworked tech mislabelled a piece of evidence in the lab three years ago. As far as Jack Byrne was concerned, the most realistic crime novels ever written came out of Czechoslovakia courtesy of the boy Kafka.

All told, Jack Byrne's literary advice, garnered from his own extensive reading in the genre, had amounted to not letting the language get in the way of the words, and to read the Ross Macdonald book, he couldn't remember which one, where Macdonald has Lew Archer say money costs too much.

The Butchers was just around the corner from my apartment block off Patrick Street, a dimly lit pub of gleaming wooden surfaces and mismatched furniture, its walls decorated with the tools of its insalubrious past as an abattoir. That day Jack was in jeans and Timberland boots and a creased pastel-pink shirt worn untucked, and took up half the old church pew along the pub's back wall. He had a square-ish head, wide blue eyes and the kind of abrupt and jagged features that suggested his face had very recently detached itself from the side of an iceberg. A fresh pint of Guinness sat on the table in front of him, alongside a half-drunk fruit concoction conspicuously lacking straw and umbrella. Which meant Jack was on the wagon, and things were serious.

He folded up his newspaper as I plonked myself down on the stool opposite him and observed the pleasantries.

'Story, Jack?'

'All right, yeah.'

I had a long, cool pull of stout. It slid down bitter and easy.

'So,' Jack said, 'Shay Govern.'

'The very man.'

'What are you doing for him?'

'He's commissioning me to write a book.'

'About himself?'

'No.'

'So what's it about?'

'Need to know, Jack. How come you know I'm working with him?'

'*With* him?'

'With him, for him. What's the difference?'

'About ninety million dollars, roughly speaking.'

'Point taken. So how'd you know?'

He'd seen me with Govern in the lobby of the Shelbourne earlier that morning. Jack had been commissioned by Govern too, a couple of months ago now. 'Called me from Boston, said he was coming over, wanted an old friend tracked down.'

'I only met Govern for the first time this morning, Jack. And I don't know him well enough to—'

He held up a shovel-like hand. 'I already found the friend.'

The way he said it, I got the distinct impression he hadn't mentioned that fact to Shay Govern. I said as much.

It was complicated, he said, although I suspected that the main complication was the fact that Jack was working on a juicy per diem and Shay Govern was worth ninety million dollars, give or take.

He'd had a meeting scheduled with Govern for this morning, then walked into the Shelbourne's lobby and saw me talking to him.

'So I'm wondering,' he said, 'what's Tom Noone hearing? Maybe he knows something about Shay Govern's friend that might be useful.'

'I doubt it, Jack.'

'Gerard Smyth,' he said, watching me intently.

'He didn't mention the name.'

'Gerhard Uxkull.'

'Sorry, no joy.'

'You sure?'

'Certain.' I drank some more of the Guinness, sucked the froth from my upper lip. 'Get it out, Jack. How come you're not telling Govern you found his friend?'

'Because this friend, Gerard Smyth, he's never even heard of Shay Govern. Also, Gerard Smyth wasn't born Gerard Smyth. Or in Ireland. He's Danish, was born Gerhard Uxkull. You think it's likely Shay Govern out of Donegal had a Danish friend?'

'Maybe they go all the way back,' I said, 'to the Vikings. Had themselves a moment during one of the raids.'

'That's one possibility, sure. Except Shay Govern, right, he went to the States in 1940, when he was fifteen.'

'So I'm told.'

'And Gerard Smyth, back then calling himself Gerhard Uxkull, only arrived in Donegal in 1940. Sailed into Lough Swilly on a German submarine. The politics and language barrier aside, I'm thinking that didn't leave them much time for developing this life-long bond Shay Govern's talking about.'

'You wouldn't have thought so, no.'

'So when I hear what Gerard Smyth has to say, I'm a wee bit peeved. Y'know?'

'Maybe Govern thought it was none of your business. I mean, he hired you to find this guy Smyth. Which you did. The why isn't your problem.'

'In one of your books, maybe.'

'Touché.'

'But if it comes out I'm the guy who somehow missed the fact that his client was mixed up in a massacre of six kids, it's not going to look so good for me. Either I'm too blind to notice or I've turned a blind eye. Either way I'm not seeing as much as I should.'

'A massacre?'

'A Nazi war crime, yeah. On Delphi Island, early 1940, just before Shay Govern takes off for the States. I'm guessing he hasn't mentioned it to you either.'

'It never came up, no. So what happened?'

'It's Smyth's story, I'll let him tell it.'

'To me?'

'Correct.'

'Why would he want to tell me?'

'Because I've promised him I'll help get it published.'

'No chance. Are you shitting me?'

'Last I heard, you were still trading as a journalist.'

'Nice try, Jack. But you'll have to find yourself some other sap.' If Jack Byrne thought I was going to screw with a book commission to chase some lunatic's story about Nazi war crimes in Donegal, Jack Byrne was due a radical rethink.

'Mind if I ask,' he said, 'what Govern's paying for this book of his?'

'It isn't his book. And yeah, I do.'

He reached for the fruity concoction and slurped some down, then slumped back against the hard frame of the church pew. 'You know what he's worth, don't you?'

Now we were getting there. 'Say it, Jack.'

'The man's worth ninety million, Tom.'

'And?'

'I just think,' he said, 'it might be interesting to see how Govern reacts when he realizes Gerard Smyth's been talking up a storm.'

'So now I'm a go-between.'

Jack grinned. 'That's right, Tom. A cut-out.'

'Sorry, Jack.'

'You're not curious,' he said, 'about why Govern wants Smyth found?'

'Not particularly.'

'The old-buddies routine doesn't fly; Smyth's never heard of him. So let's assume there's another reason.'

'It could be anything.'

'Sure, but let's assume for now it isn't. Let's just assume, for argument's sake, Govern wants Smyth found so he can be sure he stays quiet.'

'You think he's planning to buy off Smyth.'

'Makes sense, doesn't it?'

'Not really, no. I mean, Jack, Nazi war crimes in Donegal? You think, if that shit actually happened, we wouldn't have heard about it already?'

'Listen to Gerard Smyth before you go making up your mind.'

And that was the kicker. Jack Byrne, ex-Garda detective and alleged phone-tapper and subverter of the democratic process, had many faults. Gullibility wasn't one of them. If Gerard Smyth had convinced Jack, he had a hell of a story to tell.

'OK,' I said. 'I'll listen to Smyth.'

'That's all I'm asking.' Smyth, he said, had documents he wouldn't release to Jack, would only hand over to a journalist. 'So don't forget to flash your press card.'

I drained the last of the Guinness. 'Does Smyth know anything about this?'

'Not yet, no.' A cynical grin. 'Between you and me, all Smyth wants is for the truth to come out.'

'He hasn't mentioned money?'

'Not once.'

'Seriously?'

'He's one of a kind, Tom. So what do you say?'

I shrugged. 'I'll talk to him, yeah, hear him out. But Jack, there's no way I'm trying to sting Shay Govern. If that's your game, you're on your own.'

'*Sting* him? That's harsh, Tom. All I want is for Gerard Smyth, if he's going to be bought off, to get a fair price.'

The sentiment was sound but the grin on Jack's face told another story.

'You know it can't work,' I said.

'Why not?'

'Because even if all this massacre stuff is true, and Govern was somehow involved, Govern's the one with the money.'

'That's the whole point, Tom.'

'Come on, Jack, you've been around. Govern'll have an army of lawyers. Try twisting his arm and you'll get swamped with gagging orders, injunctions. He'll bury you in paper. And that's providing he doesn't just call in your old mates, have you hauled up for extortion.'

'Sure.' Jack slurped down the last of his fruity drink. 'Against all that,' he said, tapping the folded newspaper, 'is the fact that the first thing this guy'll do is shit himself a plank if he thinks this crap's likely to break. I mean, now? When he's talking up a gold mine, looking for investors, a public-private partnership with government?' He shook his head, plonked the glass back on the table. 'This guy's a businessman, Tom. He'll cut a deal.'

FIVE

I t was well after ten that night when Martin ushered me through
into the sitting room.
'Sorry I'm late, man, but it's been a hell of a day.'
'No worries. The kids aren't long down.' He muted the TV, what
looked to be a documentary on Krakatoa, and pointed me towards
the armchair beside the wood-burning stove. He took the bottle of
vodka I'd brought and went through the arch into the kitchen.

I put the manila folder on the coffee table and lowered myself
into the armchair, soaked up the room. I'd always liked it. Cosy
and comfortable, the carpet and couch and armchairs a little
battered, there being no point getting anything new, or so they
reckoned, until the kids were older. The lights always seemed to
be low, with a warm fire of turf or logs in the stove, although
that was possibly because it was always late or getting on for it
whenever I was there.

What I most liked about the room was that the bookshelves
in the opposite corner to the TV had one shelf devoted to my
books, some of them with the spines broken and pages turned
down, others pristine – Martin made a point of picking them up
in any edition they appeared in. A good guy, yeah. I wasn't his
favourite writer, not even his favourite Irish crime writer, trailing
in there a long way behind Connolly and McKinty and Eoin
McNamee. What he said was that I was the best writer he knew.
As in, personally. Which was why he put in the extra effort.

Or so he said. I believed it was more to do with Jenny and
me, and the fact we had history, and Martin in his quiet way
letting us both know it wasn't an issue, that I was just one of
Jenny's stories from way back when. He was one of those rare
men with no interest in fencing off his wife's life, in drawing a
line between pre-Martin and now. She was who she was, all in,
and if I was her friend, and a writer, then he'd support the writing.
Not that I was the only one to benefit. There were paintings and
bits of sculpture all over the house – there was even a triptych
wool-weave tapestry – that told the same tale.

He came back in from the kitchen with a couple of vodka-tonics. He held up his glass in a silent toast and had himself a hefty swig. 'Christ, but I needed that,' he sighed, pushing the square-rimmed specs back up on his nose. Then he remembered why I was there and toasted me. 'Nice work on the Devereaux book, by the way.'

'Cheers. There's been, ah, some developments since.'

'Oh?'

I told him first that it was a ghost-writing commission. Martin winced.

'That's not the issue,' I said.

'It's worse than ghost-writing?'

I told him about Jack Byrne, his theory about Shay Govern and a Nazi war crime on Delphi Island, and his plan to maximize Gerard Smyth's hush money.

'As an accountant,' Martin said, 'I can only applaud Jack Byrne's ambition. It's only fair to warn you, though, that monies earned through blackmail are liable for tax in the highest bracket.'

'It'll never happen.'

'Glad to hear it. I'd hate to think of Jenny not visiting you in prison.' He had another sip of vodka-tonic, then abandoned the levity. 'What is it, Tom?'

'Gerard Smyth,' I said.

'You think he's genuine?'

'I honestly don't know,' I said. 'But he's either deranged or sincere. And possibly both.'

Martin winced again. 'I'll go get the vodka,' he said. 'Sounds like this could take a while.'

Gerard Smyth had lost two children, a girl and a boy, to an Allied bombing raid in February 1944. He tapped ash as he spoke, a saffron thumbnail flickering against the mouth of his cigarette holder.

'Time heals,' he said, 'but it cannot cure.'

Some part of him, he said, still believed that the authorities had misidentified the tiny mangled corpses in the rubble, because he still dreamt of them occasionally and in his dreams they'd grown up. The girl had children of her own. His son, an engineer or an architect, had never married.

'I do wonder at times if they're not real,' he said. 'If they are not living in a parallel dimension, with my craving for them exerting a gravity that pulls them close enough to sense if not actually see. The mind is a curious and unusual thing, Mr Noone. It is stronger at rest than when fully aware.'

He lived now, he said, for those dreams and little else.

'I am not a religious man, Mr Noone. Nor am I spiritual in any way. Even so, if there is even the remotest possibility that I might soon be seeing my children again, I would prefer to do so with a clear conscience.'

He had that look, the one a boxer gets when he's been hit so hard he doesn't even know he's been hit. Eyes like the sky in the wake of a storm, watery blue and wild, his gaze intense but far away and lost, vaguely startled. A feeble octogenarian, or maybe even older, thin to the point of emaciation and lost inside the overcoat that had flapped like dark surrender as he came shuffling into the park.

The cigarette holder looked to be plastic, an onyx-effect job. I wondered how he'd got the yellowing nails. Maybe from smoking the roll-up cigarettes he wedged into the holder, which rather undermined the genteel effect and left his trousers flecked with ash.

Jack Byrne had made a call from the Butchers, asking Gerard Smyth if we could meet him to sit down and talk through his story. At first Jack had suggested we go to Smyth's home but Smyth said no, he'd meet us somewhere public. Par for the course, apparently. The way Jack told it as we made our way across town, he got the impression the old man was a little ashamed of his poky basement bed-sit. Which was maybe the case, but if I was Gerard Smyth I wouldn't have wanted Jack Byrne in my home either. Or me, for that matter.

So Merrion Square it was, at the corner of the American College, near where Oscar Wilde sprawled on a boulder in his green smoking jacket with pink trim at the cuffs. The traffic hissed by slow behind us on Pembroke Street, a fine drizzle falling. Gerard Smyth was already waiting when we arrived, huddled into his grubby olive-green overcoat. I wondered if he realized or cared how he appeared to the world, sitting there and looking like that just fifty yards along the path from the kids' playground.

He gave me the creeps.

At first I thought it was the need in his eyes and the dandruff speckling his shoulders. The greasy hair, glistening under its fine sheen of drizzle, that made me want to scratch. Then I'd noticed his frayed trouser cuffs, and the dull brown shoes, oddly swollen, that put me in mind of rotting puffballs in a far corner of some dank wood.

Eventually, though, as he talked on in his tremulous rasp, I had to admit the truth: that he reminded me of my father, in the last days when the cancer finally surfaced like an algae bloom. He was that gaunt. The skin melting back into bone and so tautly stretched that when he smiled it was the smug leer of bare skull. In the few remaining shadows his pallor had the same dull olive sheen as his coat. A disgusting yellowy tinge in the corners of the rheumy blue.

I glanced down at my notes to break the spell of those half-wild eyes. Hypnotic, almost, in their mute pleading. Desperate to be believed, to be taken seriously, for one last chance at seeing this one thing through.

'A dying man,' he said, 'if he is any kind of man, will live beyond the law.'

He shifted in his seat as the words tailed off, uncomfortable perhaps with the pompous tone. Then he subsided into an awkward posture, angled towards me along the bench, slack and hunched over, favouring his right side. Haunted but not yet entirely resigned. Those rheumy eyes searching mine.

Right around then, yeah, I felt pretty bad about myself.

It was when we were crossing town, walking up Grafton Street, that Jack tried to justify his decision not to tell Gerard Smyth about Shay Govern. At first it had been standard client confidentiality. 'Also, you don't want to just dive in there and tell a guy, a pensioner who looks like he's on the ropes, that there's this American multi-millionaire searching for a long-lost friend. You tell him that, he'll tell you anything you want to hear.'

Finding Gerard Smyth had been a relatively straightforward affair. He was of a certain age, so Jack availed himself of the information on the Department of Social Welfare and focused on those Gerard Smyths in receipt of a state pension. After that it was a matter of time and shoe leather. Keen to string out his lucrative per diem as long as possible, and curious as to why Shay Govern wanted to track down Gerard Smyth in a clandestine fashion, Jack watched Smyth for a couple of days before finally approaching him in a bookies. It wasn't long before he started to hear the archaic formality of Smyth's speech, the odd inflection on certain words. So he dropped it in casually, asking Gerard Smyth where he was from, originally.

Denmark? Really? And how long have you lived here . . .?

This was when he realized Shay Govern wasn't playing it entirely straight, was keeping a few cards back. So Jack, with Gerard Smyth already in his pocket, decided to play it the same way.

'I don't know,' Jack had said, 'maybe he wasn't used to talking to people any more. But once he started, he just wouldn't quit.'

Which was how we ended up sitting in the park on Merrion Square with Gerard Smyth, an old man under the impression that his new friend, Jack Byrne, had persuaded a journalist to tell this story he'd kept bottled up for most of his life.

'Let me first say thank you, Mr Smyth, for trusting me with your story. It's a fascinating—'

'It is not a story.'

'No, I understand that. What I mean is—'

'It happened, Mr Noone. Many years ago, yes, but it did happen. Those children were murdered. But if no one is prepared to say what they saw, then it's as if it never happened at all. Do you understand me?'

'Of course. You want to see justice done.'

'Justice? No.' He leered, although I believed he meant it as a smile. 'Jack tells me that you also write detective novels. I am afraid, Mr Noone, that this is not a fairytale.'

Now he looked away, rubbing his hands in the fretful way old people do, those frail hands of spidery blue calligraphy that had been whisperingly dry when we shook. His grip had been no stronger than a child's. The probability that his mind was the same had grown with every word he'd said.

Now I wasn't so sure.

'There was a time, Mr Smyth,' I said – his formality was infectious – 'when I was arrogant enough to believe I knew more than fairytales can tell. These days I'm not so convinced.'

That brought the rheumy eyes back up to meet mine. They weren't so wild now.

'I do appreciate,' he said, 'why you might find it difficult to believe.'

'It's not a matter of belief, Mr Smyth. It's a matter of proof.'
I nodded at the manila folder on his lap. He had offered it to me
as soon as he'd arrived but I'd asked for a verbal synopsis, which
he'd delivered in that quivering rasp, the words carefully chosen,
his grammar so precise it would have betrayed him if I hadn't already
known English wasn't his mother tongue. 'Is there anything in there
by way of independent corroboration?'

He shook his head. I waited for the 'but' and the standard
justification, that the very absence of proof was itself testament
to the extent of the conspiracy, how high into the shadowy corri-
dors of power the cover-up went.

'I am afraid,' he said, 'that you will have to take my word
for it.'

From his tone I understood that he was of a generation of men
who offered something precious when they gave their word,
precious and possibly even profound. He placed his shaking hand
on the manila folder and in his eyes I saw my father as he slipped
away, a yellow stain against those crisp white hospital sheets,
his hand a chicken claw as it reached out for mine.

I am afraid, Mr Noone, that this is not a fairytale.

I'd met Gerard Smyth so many times before. Him and his
kind. Iggy once told me they recognize a kindred spirit, that they
sense me out there in the ether. Lost souls so desperate for any
kind of recognition, even just the acknowledgment that they are
still alive and worth talking to, that they'll spin any yarn they
think might fly.

Maybe Iggy's right. They tell their tales, I tell mine. Maybe
the only difference is that behind it all, no matter how old and
bitter, how wild their eyes or how close to the sun their flights
of fancy soar, they've somehow retained that heart-twisting innocence in the belief that the truth matters, that it is both real and
pure, a tangible that belongs on the table of elements. That it
can be excavated like diamonds or palladium and, being rare, can
be wonderful.

Martin fixed another brace of vodka tonics.

'You don't suppose,' he said, 'that Jack Byrne coached him?
I mean, if this guy Smyth is on the ropes, like you're saying,
and prone to hanging around in bookies, then all Byrne has to
do is set him up with a story that—'

'I get it, Martin.'

'I'm just saying.' He sipped on his drink. 'You believe him, though.'

'You're hearing what I heard.' I'd recorded the entire conversation on the digital recorder in my jacket pocket. If Jack Byrne hadn't been doing the same, he was a much changed man. 'What do you think?'

'He sounds the part,' Martin said, 'but then I'm no expert. Are you playing the whole thing?'

'If you want to hear it.'

'Why wouldn't I?'

'You mightn't want to get involved.'

'It's a bit late for that, Tom. Have on.'

The recorder's Pause button was blinking its red light. I pressed Play.

'So, just to clarify a few details. You're saying you're Danish.'

'I was born in Denmark, then served in the German navy. But I've been Irish since before you were born.'

'Any supporting documents? A birth certificate?'

'Everything was lost during the war.'

'Of course. What about identification papers? Surely as a sailor you'd have been issued with some kind of ID, dog tags, something along those lines.'

'They took everything away when I was interned. And I was moved around every few months. I wasn't what you might call an ordinary internee.'

'I suppose not. And at this point it's unlikely there's anyone who could verify that they served with you.'

'Unlikely, yes. Our mission was a covert one, to land an agent on the Donegal coast. Those missions were classified as special operations, during which all crew were sworn to secrecy. You may smile, Mr Noone, but such things were taken rather more seriously in those days, especially as the penalty for a security breach was a firing squad.'

'But even now? Nearly seventy years after the fact?'

'You are more than welcome to try, Mr Noone. The operational details are all in the file.'

'OK. So what about the rest of your family? Can we trace you back to Denmark?'

'Perhaps. I really don't know.'

'You've never tried?'

'I joined the German navy in 1938, Mr Noone. My welcome in Denmark would have been on the cool side, or so I would imagine, had I ever returned home.'

'You weren't conscripted?'

'No. But the actions of that young man are irrelevant in the context of our discussion.'

'Some might say otherwise.'

'They are entitled to their opinion.'

'They certainly are. Look, you have to understand that your behaviour then, the actions of the young Gerhard Uxkull, will colour the story. You can't expect people to ignore the fact that you volunteered for the Nazis.'

'You are still a young man, Mr Noone. But you are old enough to have made many important decisions in your life. Tell me, have you ever made a choice, a truly crucial decision, on the basis that it was the *wrong* thing to do at that moment in time?'

'Firstly, this isn't about me. More to the point, retrospective justification won't fly. That old excuse about only obeying orders is—'

'I was a U-boat sailor, Mr Noone. In the Kriegsmarine.'

'Just one of the millions of blue-eyed boys who made it all possible.'

'Have you always been so perfect, Mr Noone? Always acted as you should?'

'Again, it's not about me. No, I'm not perfect—'

'Thank you.'

'But if I do take this on, your whole life becomes fair game. All of it. I'm not, as you say yourself, in the business of writing fairytales.'

'I accept that. I welcome that.'

'It's also only fair to warn you that Jack and I have access to resources you wouldn't. I'm talking about search programmes that can think laterally when cross-referencing. You'd be surprised at what we can do now.'

'Pleasantly surprised, I hope. But Mr Noone, you must understand that there was a time when I could have been shot rather than allow for the possibility that I might some day do what I am trying to do. Even now the material is considered sensitive.

They told me it would be best if they conducted an official investigation, and that I should not speak to anyone until it was concluded.'

'Sorry, what?'

'They told me it would be best if—'

'Who told you? Who's this *they*?'

'I was given no names.'

'OK, but who were they? Who did they represent?'

'It was not a conversation of introductions and how-do-you-dos. They did not ask my name. They simply said—'

'This was where, at home?'

'No, they came walking up beside me. On Molesworth Street. I was on my way home after collecting my pension. I can only presume they waited for me outside the post office.'

'And?'

'The younger man was young enough to be my grandson, perhaps even my great-grandson. He sounded reasonable. Patient, even. The way the young sound when they speak to old men and pretend to respect them. But then he offered to carry my shopping home. It was the older man who told me that the information I requested would not be forthcoming via the conventional channels. That there was a blockage, as he put it. He said it would be best if I allowed for an official request to be submitted in the government's name, and that in the meantime I should not speak to anyone about the incident.'

'You put in an official request?'

'That is correct.'

'And you interpreted this approach as a warning?'

'I appreciate politeness and a prompt response as well as anyone, Mr Noone. But if these gentlemen, or more likely their superiors, had wanted me to know that the information I requested was not available and that an official investigation would follow, a letter or even a telephone call would have sufficed. In this day and age, what government department can afford to send two men out on a social call to an old man who may very well be deluded or senile? Or perhaps you're naïve enough to believe that these two men were simply on their way home after work, together, and decided to detour to the post office where I collect my pension in the hope of saving the cost of a stamp.'

'I wouldn't have thought that was standard procedure, no.'

'No. I should also point out, Mr Noone, that I made my request to the German and British embassies. The two men who came to see me were Irish.'

'That wouldn't be unusual in itself.'

'Except for the fact that they came to speak with me in person.'

'Except, as you say, that they came to see you. When was this?'

'Almost eight months ago. I do appreciate, Mr Noone, that you believe my story improbable. I can only assure you that it is true. You have no reason to trust me, or take my word as given, but all I ask is that you read what I have to say before you decide not to investigate further. Is that too much?'

'No. But tell me this – aren't you afraid we're being watched right now?'

'I know we are being watched. The young woman behind the counter has been glancing this way ever since we sat down, perhaps because you look like the type to run off without paying. And of course God, or so they tell us, is eternally vigilant. But if you're asking me if I'm paranoid enough to believe that I am the subject of a covert operation, Mr Noone, then my answer is no. Who could justify that expense? The idea is ridiculous. I am hardly a threat to national security.'

'But you still believe these guys were sent to warn you off.'

'I believe "fob off" would be more accurate.'

'OK. Well, I'm afraid I can't read your file right now. Would you mind if I took it with me?'

'Not in the least.'

'You have your own copy?'

'That is the only copy.'

'In that case I'd suggest you print off another copy and—'

'I used a typewriter. And before you ask, there are no photocopies resting in deposit boxes or gathering dust in the offices of some unnamed solicitor, to be revealed to the world should I trip down the stairs or fall in front of a train.'

'Did you burn the typewriter ribbon?'

'I'm afraid not. You may not have noticed, Mr Noone, but some commentators believe we are on the verge of an economic crisis.'

'I've been told, yeah.'

Click.

*   *   *

'I was always given to understand,' Martin said after a moment or two spent contemplating the silent recorder, 'that the Irish government couldn't afford to run a secret service.'

'You and me both.'

'Except that,' he nodded at the recorder, 'sounds a lot like spooks to me.'

'That does seem to be the implication.'

'And he's involved the British and German embassies?'

'A feisty chap, our Mr Smyth. Doesn't like being pushed around.'

'Or fobbed off. Jack Byrne knew about this?'

'According to Jack, this is the first he's hearing about spooks or semi-official warnings and threats. I believe him. Afterwards he was talking about hacking into the Department of Foreign Affairs, tapping emails and so forth. See if he could get a fix on any mention of Gerard Smyth. Sounded to me like he was out of his depth, thrashing around.'

'Did he sound anything like you do now?'

'Maybe a little bit, yeah.'

'Then I'd be worried.'

'I *am* worried.'

'Good. I hope you put the kibosh on him hacking into Foreign Affairs.'

'I told him, yes, it was a bad idea.'

'And?'

'He said he'd back off, for now anyway.'

'You think he will?'

'No idea. For all I know he's cracking firewalls right now.'

'It's safes that get cracked, Tom. Firewalls are a different deal.'

'Right now would be a bad time for semantics, Rain Man.'

As far as Jack Byrne was concerned, Gerard Smyth was his toy, to play with as he saw fit. And Jack, tracking down Smyth in the first place, had already wormed his way into the Social Welfare files.

Martin was sitting hunched forward on the couch, elbows on his knees, his glass cradled in both hands. He took another nip, then reached out and tapped the manila folder with the tip of his forefinger.

'Have you had time to read this yet?'

'Skimmed it, yeah.'

'And?'

'You're sure you want to know?'

'Christ, Tom. Don't leave me hanging now.'

'OK. So basically, there's a German submarine, it sails into Lough Swilly, drops off this spy who's headed for Derry to do a deal with the IRA. He gets blown, I guess his contact was a double agent, and the next thing there's a party of German soldiers – or sailors, I guess – rounding up the locals on Delphi Island, wanting to know where the double agent is. Morrigan they're calling him, his code name. Anyway, the locals don't want to play along, so the Germans line up a group of six kids and force them into a church and . . . What's wrong?'

'Hold on,' Martin said. He got up and went to the bookshelf in the corner, took down a book that was lying horizontally across mine. 'I dug this out earlier, when Jenny told me your news. Thought you might find it useful.'

The book was a paperback, nicely battered, one corner torn off the cover on the bottom right. The image featured an artist's impression of the island of Santorini, smoke billowing in a plume from the village of scattered white dice on the cliff-top. In the foreground a submarine was fountaining spray, having just breached at a rather improbable 70-degree angle.

Rendezvous at Thira by Sebastian Devereaux.

'You've read it?' I said.

'Sure. That and another one, it was something to do with Cyprus. I can't find that one though. If memory serves it wasn't as good as *Thira*, so maybe I chucked it. You've never read him?'

'I'd never even heard of him before this morning.'

'He was good, yeah. Alistair MacLean stuff but a bit more stylish, like Joseph Hone.'

'Who's Joseph Hone?'

'For shame, Tom. Anyway,' he nodded at the paperback, '*Rendezvous at Thira* is set on Santorini, during the Second World War. There's a British spy on his way to the Greek mainland from Crete, the Germans get wind of it, they run him to earth on the island. But they can't find him.'

'Go on.'

'The Germans, they round up a crowd of kids, threaten to shoot them all if the locals don't hand over the spy.'

'Shit.'

'Except then the kids are bundled into this tiny church, which is set on fire.'

'Fuck me,' I said.

'Can do,' said Martin. 'Although it looks like I could be waiting a while for my turn.'

SIX

S hay Govern opened his hotel-room door dressed in a white towelling bathrobe and a Red Sox baseball cap, still chewing.

'I've got jet-lag,' he said. 'What's your excuse?'

It was early. I'd got to the Reception desk at the Shelbourne just after 7.30 a.m. and asked the guy in his natty purple hat to put me through to Shay Govern's room, it was urgent.

Shay told me to come on up, he was still eating breakfast.

Now he waved me through. 'There's coffee in the pot, Tom. Help yourself. Or do you need to eat?'

He went back to his breakfast, grilled kidneys and sausage and toast, orange juice and coffee. His table was in the bay window overlooking St Stephen's Green, the sun streaming through. I was still struggling to cope with too many vodka-tonics and about four hours sleep the night before. The smell and sight of the grilled kidneys turned my stomach.

'Coffee will do it,' I said, taking the seat opposite him. He poured me a cup and gestured to the sugar and milk, apologizing for the fact that there was no creamer.

'I take it black,' I said, and sat back in the seat, angling myself so that my line of sight bisected the messy plate of kidney and sausage and the daggering sunlight.

'So you're early, right?' he said. 'Or did I get the time wrong?'

'No, I'm early. But listen, I need to apologize because I can't travel this morning. I got a call late last night, a commission I can't turn down from a client I've had for years, and the deadline's this afternoon. But I can follow on once it's filed, fly up to Derry airport. I should catch up with you by eight, nine o'clock at the latest.'

'No problem, Tom.' He forked home a mouthful of grilled kidney. 'You could have just called, though. There was no need to come see me.'

'Actually there was. Is, I mean.'

'Oh, yeah? What's up?'

'Well, I wanted to confirm, in person, that I'm taking on the book.'

'Great news, Tom. Carol will be delighted to hear it. Of course, it's all contingent on her approval, you understand that.'

'Absolutely.'

'But I'd be very surprised if you two didn't hit it off right away. She's an amazing woman.'

'I'm looking forward to meeting her. But Mr Govern, there's—'

'Call me Shay, Tom. I'm not usually that formal with people this early in a hotel room.'

'Sure. Well, I wanted to talk to you about this personal situation I need to deal with. As in, a financial situation.'

'Right.'

'So I was hoping, and this is presuming that Carol gives us the green light, that we click together, like you say, that—'

'An advance, right?' He laid the knife and fork on his plate, crossed with the tines down. 'A retainer.'

'Something like that, yeah.'

'Before we even sign contracts?'

'Sure, it sounds off. But what I'm asking for is a post-dated cheque. For next week, say. If it turns out Carol doesn't want to work with me, then you just cancel it.'

'So this financial situation, it's not an immediate one.'

'No.'

'And if I cut you a cheque right now you're not going to run off to the race-track for the afternoon.'

'I'm not much of a gambler, Mr— Shay. I never really got the thrill of making bookies rich.'

'Richer,' he said. Then the right corner of his mouth twitched, and he relaxed. 'Me neither,' he said. He gave his hands a cursory wipe with the cotton napkin and dropped it on to his plate. 'Tell you what, Tom. You tell me why you need the money right now and if I think it's a good enough reason I'll write you a cheque for the first five grand. That sound fair?'

It was a lot fairer than I'd thought likely.

'Sounds reasonable to me.'

'OK. Shoot.'

If you want to be cynical about it you could say that writing a post-dated cheque for five grand wasn't exactly a grand gesture for a man worth ninety million bucks, give or take, on paper at least.

Still, I thought it was pretty decent of him.

And now things were getting a little bit tangled.

The last thing I wanted was to betray Jack Byrne, as dirty as his scheme was, mainly because Jack had pulled in a few favours with some of his ex-colleagues when I was still trying to clear my father's name.

I'd said as much to Martin the night before, when we came to the conclusion that the similarities between Gerard Smyth's eye-witness account of a war crime on Delphi and Sebastian Devereaux's *Rendezvous at Thira* made for a remarkable coincidence.

On the basis that it wasn't a coincidence, that left us with two options. One, Gerard Smyth was a pathetic fantasist, an old man so desperate for attention that he'd ripped off a tragedy from some forgotten thriller and passed it off as his own experience.

Two, Gerard Smyth was genuine, and Sebastian Devereaux was the one who'd appropriated a real-life tragedy and used it for a novel.

Martin, being a fan of Eoin McNamee and James Ellroy and David Peace, found it all fascinating.

I took his point, and sure, the second option could make for some very interesting conversations with Carol Devereaux at some point in the near future. But I was about as interested in the literary implications as Jack Byrne. Because Jack didn't care if the story was true or not, if Gerard Smyth was a senile old fart or the last living witness to a horrific crime. All Jack cared about was Smyth's story standing up strong enough to imply that Shay Govern had somehow benefited from the massacre of six young children, and persuade Govern of the merits of shovelling hush money into Jack's pockets.

The trouble there, leaving aside for a moment the morality or otherwise of helping Jack to sting Shay Govern, was that it was now in my best interests, or Emily's interests to be precise, that I protect Shay Govern's name.

'So that's us,' Shay said, handing me the cheque and recapping what looked to be an unusually understated Montblanc fountain pen. 'Five thousand euro, post-dated and made out to Emily Noone, as requested. Don't spend it all in the one shop.'

'I really appreciate that,' I said, folding the cheque and tucking it into my wallet.

'OK, so I'll see you later this evening on Delphi. Although, Tom, you might want to double-check the ferry times. I don't know how late they run.'

'Will do. Listen, Shay, there's one more thing.'

'What's that?'

'Jack Byrne.'

'Jack? What about him?'

'I know him, we've worked together before. Anyway, he came to see me yesterday evening. Said you hired him to find an old friend of yours.'

A bleak smile. 'Friend would be putting it a bit strong. So what'd he say? He told me yesterday morning he reckoned he had a good lead on the guy.'

'Well, he's found him. Gerard Smyth.'

'Is that a fact?'

'Yeah. Jack brought me to meet him.'

'Sounds nice. Meanwhile the cheapo fuck's charging me by the day.' Govern pushed back his chair, stood up from the table and cinched his bathrobe tighter. 'Where's my phone?'

'Hold on a second, Mr Govern. There's a bit more.'

'Spit it out, Tom.'

'Jack had Gerard Smyth tell me his story. About this massacre on Delphi back in 1940. A Nazi war crime, he's calling it. Six kids burned to death in a church.'

He was nodding as I spoke. 'Yep,' he said.

I'd wanted him to rubbish the story, or say he'd never heard of it. But he just stood there with his hands loosely tucked into the pockets of the fluffy bathrobe, waiting for me to continue.

'So Jack's under the impression,' I said, 'that you left for the States not long after it happened.'

'That's a matter of historical fact, Tom. Is that all?'

'Not really. Jack's running a theory that the two things are connected. That you left because of what happened on Delphi.'

'Come on, Tom. Cut to the chase. What's Jack's plan?'

'Well, with the gold mine and everything, the publicity, Jack reckons you might be happier if the story stayed buried.'

He was nodding again, his eyes flinty. 'A clown, this guy.'

'Who, Jack?'

'Yeah.'

'I warn you now, Mr Govern, that he's very serious.'

'Well, I do appreciate the warning, Tom, and I told you already to quit calling me Mr Govern.' He took one hand out of the pocket of his bathrobe to tug on his nose. 'And our friend Jack can be as serious as he likes, but he's still a goddamn clown.'

'So he's got it wrong.'

'Wrong?' He considered that. 'Until I hear what Gerard Smyth has to say, if our friend Jack ever brings him around, I can't say for sure. But the broad strokes? What you're telling me now?' He shook his head. 'No. He's right on the money.'

A man worth ninety million dollars, on paper at least, is not put together like everyone else. If he was, we'd all be billionaires.

He's got something most people don't, like a relentless drive or a ruthless streak a mile wide. Or luck. Or maybe his brain isn't wired right, and the only people he feels comfortable with are dead and famous enough to get their portraits on rectangular pieces of paper.

For Shay Govern, the intangible was survivor's guilt.

Aged fifteen, he'd been considered too old to qualify as a child.

'So they round up these kids,' he said, 'and they line them up in front of the church.' He was sitting on the bottom of the unmade bed, legs splayed, his feet in fluffy white flip-flops, horn-nailed toes peeking through. It was his feet he was addressing, not me. 'What freaked me out at the time, still does, I get night-mares on and off, night terrors . . .' He paused then, looked up. 'These days I'd go straight into therapy, right?' He tried a grin but it didn't take, slid away. 'Not a lot of therapists around back then.'

I was guessing that this was the story Iggy had heard in the confession box.

'Shay . . .'

'No, it's right you should know. This way, if Jack Byrne starts cutting up, you're ahead of the game.'

'That's not my issue.'

'You were going to hear all this anyway, Tom, once you were locked in and committed to the book.' He tried a smile this time, a sad one, and this time it stuck. 'Carol has her own reasons for wanting it written,' he said, 'and I have my own. And this is mine. We on the same page now?'

'It's your call. Mind if I record this?'

'Knock yourself out.' He waited until I'd got the digital recorder out, then started talking again, in the slightly stilted way people do when they're aware their words are being preserved for posterity. 'So yeah, I was telling you about what was spooky, I mean at the time. It's these kids, OK, they're worried, standing there in their nightclothes, it's the middle of the night, they're shivering – but it's not like they're terrified. Not like they'd be if they were you or me. I mean, sure, they're crying, some of them calling out for their mothers, what you'd expect from kids, they've been dragged out of their beds and lined up facing these guys wearing balaclavas. Right? Pointing these big machine guns at them. You're three years old, OK, but you still have a pretty good idea this isn't the way things are supposed to be.'

'So they're scared but they're not terrified?'

'I guess it's because they don't know enough to take it too seriously. Like, they're *kids*. Even if they'd done something wrong they don't realize yet, the way it sometimes goes when you're a kid, they'll get a smack on the ass, maybe a crack across the ear. Right?'

'I suppose, yeah.'

'You're five years old, six or seven – you're not expecting at any time to get ripped apart by machine guns. I mean, one of them, one of the little boys, he pisses himself, he's standing there with a puddle at his feet, it's steaming because it's so cold – *this* is when he starts bawling. Because *now* he knows he's in trouble, pissing himself in public in front of the church, all the grown-ups looking on.'

I'd heard some strange stories in my time, conducted a couple of interviews that qualified as fully bizarre. But sitting in a suite of the Shelbourne listening to a millionaire talking about a kid fouling himself in front of a church during a Nazi massacre on Delphi Island in Lough Swilly, Donegal, on the night of 4 April, 1940 pretty much topped the bill.

His account was consistent with virtually everything Gerard Smyth had said. Which meant, of course, that it also tallied with Martin's bullet-point account of Sebastian Devereaux's *Rendezvous at Thira*. German soldiers, coming ashore from a submarine in pursuit of a British spy. A group of children herded into a church, which was then set on fire.

'So we're talking an actual war crime,' I said.

'What we're talking about,' Govern said, 'is kids being murdered.'

'And this is the story you want to tell.'

'That's right.'

All evidence to the contrary, Shay Govern was insane.

I said, 'Mr Govern, I'm from Sligo. Originally.'

'Oh, yeah? So we're both from the northwest. Originally.'

'Sure. But what I'm saying is, if a Nazi death squad had come in off a submarine and massacred Irish children in 1940, in Donegal, I'd probably have heard about it before now. That kind of thing, it gets talked about.'

'It was covered up,' he said. He was looking at me now like he didn't want to be the guy who had to point out the straw in my hair. 'Obviously.'

'Who'd want to cover *that* up?'

'Jesus, something like this? Who wouldn't?'

'Well, I'm thinking the parents for starters.'

'You're making it too personal, Tom. Not factoring in the times, the place.'

'You said it yourself, children were murdered. I'd imagine that was pretty personal for the parents, the families.'

'Sure, yeah. Except this is 1940, right? April. The Germans are blitzing through Europe, Churchill's over in London sweating on the Nazis crashing in through Ireland, his back door. Especially with De Valera cocking a snoot, telling Churchill to take a running jump, eight hundred years of oppression, no way the Brits are getting back in even if it's to keep us safe from Hitler's boys. Right?'

'That's hardly the—'

'No, wait. The kids get murdered on Delphi, OK. What's De Valera going to do, tell the world how the Germans can just swan in any time they feel like it, shoot whoever they want? Next thing you know Churchill himself would've been steaming up the Swilly, planting Union Jacks all over. And then there's the Germans. Why would they go shouting about an atrocity like that? So Churchill spreads himself a little thin taking back Ireland, the ports? Maybe. But is that worth crapping on the Irish-American lobby in Washington, get them screaming about the murdering Hun, with Roosevelt already doing his level best to stay out of Europe?'

The problem I had, the main problem, was squaring away what sounded like the ravings of a lunatic with the fact that the guy had made himself ninety million dollars. Not many loonies get to amass that kind of fortune from construction and mining. Inherit it, sure. Happens all the time. But I had to presume Shay Govern was a hard-headed businessman. And that kind of man isn't generally given to flights of fancy, especially when they involve incriminating himself in the cold-blooded murder of children.

He was eighty-one years old, sure. But the guy was still as sharp as his suits.

And anyway, why would he want to make up something like . . .

'So what do you say, Tom? Think you can handle it?'

'If it's been covered up this long, it'll be a tough one to prove.'

'That's where Gerard Smyth comes in. Jack tell you where this guy can be found?'

Shay Govern, fifteen years old, slipped on board a merchant ship in Belfast and arrived in the United States of America on 15 August, 1940. Gets processed and tells them he's eighteen, otherwise they won't let him in. He's a minor, unaccompanied.

No one waiting to vouch for him, to say Shay's their own, they'll put a roof over his head. So he gets put in uniform, sent off for basic training.

'Which wasn't the plan but not really an issue, not at the time,' Shay said. 'It's a job. And there's no way Roosevelt's going to war. Like, no one's even *heard* of Pearl Harbor at this point.'

Shay, he was already talking. I was there with my digital recorder, so he decided to have a fresh pot of coffee sent up to his suite, then settled in for the long haul. Ten minutes later I was wondering whose story I'd been commissioned to tell, Sebastian Devereaux's or Shay Govern's.

'So they train me up,' he said. 'I'm a killer, they send me to Sicily.'

Three confirmed kills on Sicily, nothing in Italy, one more in southern Germany.

'I took a couple of bangs myself, shrapnel, but you'll have to take my word for it. I'm too old to be showing off scars.'

'That's no problem.'

'So anyway, we get back Stateside and there's the GI Bill. Which is, I'm taking the long way round, but you asked how I got into construction.'

'You take your time. This is all good.'

1949: Shay graduates as an engineer.

1950: Shay marries Marie.

1951–57: Shay has three kids – Donal, Shay Jr and Margaret, aka Mags.

'Marie, I should mention, she's a smart woman. Except for marrying me, right? But yeah, she's a thinker. She's the one who suggests Florida, they're building like they want to front the whole coast with hotels. I mean, you couldn't live there, the humidity, Christ. But Marie is Big Dan Mullaney's daughter. He came over in 1912, a Corkman but no one's perfect, am I right? Anyway, Dan's Boston Irish, made his pile after Prohibition running Scottish imports for one of Joe Kennedy's booze companies. Now he's looking for fresh potential. So the three of us sit down and have a look around and Marie says, "Florida". So off we go.'

1962: Shay makes his first million.

1963: Shay makes his second million.

'After that you're diversifying, mainly to keep the IRS honest, so they don't steal every damn thing you pull in.'

1967: Big Dan Mullaney dies of a stress-induced heart attack.

'A real shame. Two Kennedys at the funeral. Cousins, OK, but the point was made.'

1969: Shay moves back to Boston. Building skyscrapers now, up into Maine, across into Pennsylvania.

1976: 'Marie says, "Alaska". What am I going to say, no?'

The big diversification, into mining. Gold, sure. Zinc too; uranium. 'One time,' Shay Govern said, 'Marie said she believed God meant to keep Alaska back for himself, that He buried all the good stuff there. She died four years ago.' His fingers a blur as he blessed himself. 'May she rest in peace.'

The foundation was Marie's idea. 'The tax breaks aside, she was genuine. About giving back, I mean.'

Irish students, graduates in engineering, the sciences, computers, getting a two-year deal with Govern Enterprise, bringing in new ideas, fresh blood. Sports scholarships, funding for innovation, the works. Then, they go back home, they're skilled up, have a whole new outlook on the world. 'That's the theory, anyway,' said Shay. 'In the eighties and nineties, most of the kids just worked out their contract and jumped ship, went illegal or married a Green Card. Better than coming back here, right?'

Shay's big plan for Delphi: 'The old copper mine, it's looking like there's a chance there's gold underneath – a seam that runs north up the lough. Not easy to get it out, but if it's there that's an opportunity to give back. I mean, it's not just the gold, if it's there. You're talking about jobs, investment, the boost to the local economy.'

'I saw the story, yeah, in the paper.'

'Right. Any reaction to it?'

I shrugged. 'Surprise, mainly. Gold in Ireland? There was a couple of leprechaun jokes. But most people, I'd imagine, would see it as a good news story.'

'Isn't it? Marie, it's just a pity she can't be here when it opens.'

'But what I'm wondering, Mr Govern . . .'

'Yeah?'

'Well, I'm just not sure how talking about the atrocity helps here. Or why you need to mention it at all.'

'You don't get it?'

'Being honest, no.'

'Christ, call yourself a writer?'

'That's kind of my problem.' I flicked back through my notes, gave up. 'Usually, when you're writing a story, there's stepping stones. Something happens, so then something else happens, and on you go. But I'm missing a piece here, the one that bounces us from a massacre into opening a gold mine.'

'Use your imagination, Tom.'

'I've been trying, don't think I haven't. And about the best I've come up with is if the massacre doesn't happen, you don't leave Ireland, and if you don't leave Ireland you don't make ninety million dollars, and without that there's no investment in a gold mine, no happy ending.'

'That's actually true,' he said.

'But not what you had in mind.'

'Not really. I mean, it's only true now we're looking back at everything that happened. At any point along the line, though, no, that was never the plan.'

'So what *was* the plan?'

'There was no *plan*, Tom. Christ, what are you, five years old? We were making it up as we went along, trying this, doing that. What most people call life. Now I'm here, I have the money. There's a mine on Delphi? Great. Now, at last, I can make it right.'

He was serious. 'With all due respect, Shay, that's crass.'

'Is it?'

'It is, yeah. These kids, you can't just buy them back. You're not running a balance sheet here.'

'You're talking,' he said, 'about how it looks, what people might think.'

'Sure. That's the whole point of telling your story, right?'

'For me? No. This is personal, Tom. This thing's been on my conscience more than sixty years, so mainly it's between me and me. I mean, yeah, I'm Catholic, not a believer but I still know the rules. I could do the confession thing, sit down in a quiet box for a nice long whisper with Father Ignatius and get ten Our Fathers, a Decade of the Rosary, you know the drill. But I want to do this public. Here's what I did, this is what I'm doing now. Expiating my sins, Tom. Does that still sound crass to you?'

'Mediaeval, more like.'

'Oh, yeah? Great, I'm an old-fashioned kind of guy.' He sat back in the wicker armchair, cinched his robe tighter. 'But maybe you're only realizing that now.'

'Or maybe it's that you're a bit more old-fashioned than you look. More Catholic than you seem to believe.'

'Heh. You think?' A flash of the perfect teeth. 'That's worth considering, Tom. It really is. But listen to me now.' He sat forward, the neck of his robe falling open, revealing a thin chest dusted with white hairs. 'This is all part of the book. And our deal is, I tell you what happened and you write it down. If it gets to where I need you to make moral judgements, work in some philosophy maybe, then we'll have a chat and rework our arrangement, make sure your extra effort is taken into account. Meanwhile, and before we go complicating things unnecessarily, how about we put it to the people of Delphi, this idea I have. Let *them* decide what's right and what's crass.'

There was no edge to it. No malice. If it'd been pretty much anyone else, you'd have known he was putting you in your place, reminding you of the hierarchy of the boss–peon relationship.

Shay Govern, he was just laying it out there.

I gave him more, or better, than he believed he needed? OK, that was worth paying for.

The Delphi islanders? They could take their blood money or not take it.

I left the Shelbourne thinking there were maybe two stories going on. The first was Sebastian Devereaux's, mixed with a little of Shay Govern's, however the hell he wanted to tell it, or have it told.

The second was about how too much money deadens the soul.

That line from Ross Macdonald running through my mind.

Money costs too much.

SEVEN

It was nine forty by the time I made Enniskerry and pulled into the car park behind the football pitch in the bowl of the Bog Meadow. A beautiful morning, still a little crisp, the sun warm on your back when you moved from the shadows. I got out of the car and rang Rachel, watched as she fumbled in her pockets on the sideline, finally got the phone to her ear.

'What is it, Tom? I'm busy. As you should know.'

Saturday morning football practice was usually my responsibility, mainly because I'd been the one to persuade Emily to take it up. This week, with the planned trip to Delphi, I'd had to tell her I couldn't make it. Which meant Rachel had had to step up, again.

'I'm behind you,' I said. 'In the car park. Can we talk?'

She turned, scanned the car park. 'You can't come over here?'

'I don't want Emily to see me. She might get distracted.'

Emily had been disappointed – yet again – when I couldn't make football practice. To see me on the sideline, then watch me walk away, would be a total crusher. And not just for her. I'd been one of those parents who'd held their swaddled baby for the very first time with a vague sense that that moment was the whole point of the universe to date, that all of infinity and eternity had somehow peaked and was already starting to roll back, the process of entropy inexorably set in train. And despite all the scientific evidence to the contrary, and a full awareness of how illogical that kind of thinking was, especially as virtually every other parent felt the same about their own kids, I still couldn't shake the feeling.

Every time I disappointed her, told her I had to work, or needed to reschedule until next weekend, her little face would take on that serious expression, not quite a frown but as if she were contemplating an idea that remained irritatingly just beyond her ken, and then she'd blink twice or three times, and say, 'That's OK, Dad. I know you're busy.'

And then, like some heart-scorching version of Einstein's

spooky action at a distance, her six-year-old sadness would detonate inside me. I'm not a man who believes in the soul, which is just as well, because if I had one it'd look a lot like a smouldering white flag.

'Christ,' Rachel said now. 'Tom, this better be good.'

'It's important,' I said. 'I wouldn't be here if it wasn't.'

Rachel rang off and started marching in my direction. I watched Emily run her drills, dribbling awkwardly around the little orange cones, passing it off to the next girl in line then jogging to the back of the queue, laughing at something one of the other girls said. Felt the pang, the bitter squeeze of the heart, and had a moment of clarity – this was it, and this was how it would always be. Standing back, out of sight, watching Emily grow up from so far away that I'd need binoculars to keep up with the details . . .

No way.

'What is it, Tom?'

'Rachel. Nice to see you, too.'

She had her hands jammed into the pockets of her puffa jacket, a woollen cap tugged down over her ears. Her cheeks were ruddy from the morning chill but even so she looked wan, the eyes red-rimmed and dull. From the looks of things she'd had one toke too many the night before, and her expression suggested that this, too, was somehow my fault.

'What is it this time, Tom?'

I handed her the cheque. She glanced at it, then looked again. 'What's this supposed to be?' she said.

'It's a cheque for five grand.'

'I can read, thanks. What I'm asking is, how come it's made out to Emily?'

'Because it's hers. For a college fund. You can tell her it's so she can go to the High School Musical school.'

'She doesn't watch that, Tom.'

'What're you talking about? We watched it a couple of weeks ago.'

'She told me, yeah. Because you put it on and she hadn't the heart to tell you it was, and I quote, "a little bit old-ish".' A shake of the head. 'She's six years old, Tom. Try to keep up.'

'Will do. Only it's hard to keep up,' I said, 'when I'm chasing her through this obstacle course that gets a few more obstacles, some more brick walls, every time I make it through.'

'Tom—'

'It's not going to happen, Rachel. I'll be lodging a copy of that cheque with my solicitor first thing on Monday morning.'

She shrugged, handed back the cheque. 'Why don't you just give him that? It's post-dated until the end of the month anyway.'

'Which isn't a problem, seeing as Emily won't be off to college for another twelve years or so. I'd imagine the judge will see the bigger picture.'

'I'd imagine she will. A loving family home, a father who knows how much he'll be earning next month, and the month after that . . .'

'A mother who likes the occasional toke, had an affair with her boss when her daughter was three years old . . .' I held up the cheque. 'Rachel, you can open a bank account for Emily or I can do it, I really don't mind. But here's what you need to get your head around – I'm not going away. If Emily decides otherwise at some point when she's old enough to make those kind of decisions, then that's her call. But if you think I'm just going to sign her away on some piece of paper, tell the most beautiful child that was ever born she's just this thing adults can play swapsies with, then you seriously need to lay off the Burma Gold or whatever it is you're smoking these days.'

She stared at me, dead-eyed. I don't know; maybe it was a Gorgon vibe and I was supposed to just fossilize right there in the car park, keel over and shatter into a million pieces. The cheque fluttering on the breeze.

'I love her, Rachel. I mean, you know that, right? I love her like I've never loved anyone. And there is nothing, literally nothing, she could do to change that. All she'll ever have to be with me is whoever she is. You think she'll get that from Peter, no matter what a piece of paper says?'

'Brave words,' she said, 'from a guy hiding from his daughter in a car park and waving a piece of paper around.'

Then she turned and walked away, shoulders hunched, hands jammed again into the pockets of the puffa jacket.

I drove back to town with one eye on the rear-view mirror. Not entirely sure who I was watching for, but alert to the possibility that someone might be keeping tabs on my movements, who I was meeting. It had been a wake-up call yesterday, when Jack

Byrne mentioned in passing how he'd seen me in the Shelbourne with Shay Govern. Something of a shock, and a slightly chilling one when it became obvious that Jack was playing a long game, to realize just how visible I was to anyone who might be trailing me, keeping tabs, especially when I'd had no reason to suspect they were there.

For all I knew, Jack was having me tailed right now, or was doing it himself.

Rachel's last line had burned, especially the bit about my skulking back in a car park hiding from my daughter. Given the way the conversation was going, though, it probably wasn't a good time to tell her that I didn't want Jack Byrne – or anyone else he'd dragged into my life – seeing me talk with Emily, or knowing where she lived.

Which reminded me. I put my phone on speaker, rang Jack Byrne again.

This time he answered, on the fourth ring, whispering, 'Tom?'

'Yeah.'

'What's up?'

'I need to talk with Smyth again. There's a couple of points I want to clarify.'

Mainly I wanted to look in those rheumy eyes and say the words *Sebastian Devereaux*, see if he flinched.

'When?' he said.

'Today. This morning.'

'Sorry, man. No can do. I'm on a job.'

'You don't have to be there. It's just a couple of details I need to clear up.'

'Like what?'

'Dates, mostly.'

Silence, or rather a faint hiss, on the other side. 'Text me the questions,' he whispered. 'I'll see what I can do.'

'Not good enough. I need to talk to him myself.'

'Is there something you're not telling me?'

'Plenty, yeah. We're on an unsecured line, right?'

'Yeah, right. Shit.'

'But Jack, you should know the clock's ticking.'

'How d'you mean?'

'I talked with Govern this morning. Fronted him up about Gerard Smyth.'

'And?'

'He admitted it. Says he was involved in the massacre.'

'Seriously?'

'Yeah. But Jack, the guy wants to go public with it himself. He doesn't want to keep Smyth quiet, he wants Smyth to confirm his story.'

'You're winding me up.'

'Wish I was. But according to Govern, it's the whole point of the gold mine. I mean, he actually used the phrase *expiating my sins*.'

'Shit.'

'So you can see,' I said, 'why we need to crack on. Look, text me when you get wrapped up at your end, we'll sit down and talk. In the meantime, send me Smyth's address. His phone number too. I'll buy him a coffee, we'll have a chat, get these dates fixed. Then you and me, we can talk about getting this out there before Govern does.'

'All right.'

He rang off. A minute later my phone vibrated with a text message alert.

I was in business.

I was going north across the canal on Leeson Street, turning right for Fitzwilliam Place, when the phone rang. Martin.

I got parked in jig time – one of the joys of Saturday morning in the city – and rang back.

'Can you talk?' he said.

'Go ahead.'

'More problems,' he said.

'Shit. Plural?'

'Looks like it. Are you at home?'

'Not right now. I'm in town, on the way to talk with our friend.'

'Who, Govern?'

'No,' I said. 'Our *older* friend.'

'Smyth?'

Not a great man for the code names, our Martin.

'Why don't you shout a little louder? There's an old married couple out on the Aran Islands who didn't catch that one.'

'You're worried about being tapped?' he said.

'Not any more. So what's up?'

'Maybe I should come meet you.'

'You can't just tell me?'

'Not now,' he said. 'Now you've got me worried we're being bugged.'

'We're very probably not being bugged, Martin.'

'If you're sure, Mr Bernstein . . .'

'Fire away.'

'All right.' A rustling of paper being reorganized. 'So I was up early with the kids, Jen being out last night, and I started reading through the, uh, paper. Anyway, I did a little bit of, ah, *other* reading, and I couldn't find any trace of this hoo-hah our friend's talking about. And here's the thing – there was no sign of the, um, spaceship he was travelling in when he—'

'Martin?'

'Yeah?'

'Can you get away now?'

'Sure. Why?'

'You know the Paddy Kavanagh bench on Grand Canal?'

'I do.'

'I'll see you there, soon as you can.'

I strolled up the canal along Wilton Terrace, pacing myself with the swans gliding along, the reeds conducting the faint hissing sighs they were sifting from the breeze. Dandered back down along the not quite leafy-with-love bank again, trying to remember if we'd agreed that Martin would work on Gerard Smyth's file. As far as I could remember, all I'd asked him to do was make a copy and stash it in his office safe. By the time I got back to Paddy Kavanagh's bench, Martin was waiting, trying to work out how we'd all fit – him, me and Paddy – on the seat.

'Pity he didn't ask to be commemorated with a Ferris wheel,' Martin said, which was when I knew he was a lost cause. We turned back up towards Baggot Bridge and cut left into town. I told him about Shay Govern's confession, how he was planning to go public with his guilt and pay it off with a gold mine.

Martin, I could tell, was conflicted. Fascinated by Shay Govern's personal tragedy but agog at the mine's potential for tax breaks.

He'd been up half the night trawling the web, put in another couple of hours this morning while the kids watched TV.

'So Govern's theory,' he said, 'is the massacre was covered up.'

'That's what he's saying.'

'Sounds juicy. Except here's the thing – I couldn't find any trace of this so-called special mission Gerard Smyth says he was on back in 1940.'

Which was hardly surprising, given that it was a top-secret mission.

'Sure. And at one point,' he flicked through his notes, 'here, yeah, he says a lot of Germany's war-time records were destroyed. Which is true. The building housing a chunk of German military records burned to the ground during an air raid on Berlin early in 1945.'

'Yeah,' I said, grabbing Martin's elbow and tugging him towards me, this to prevent his walking into a lamppost. 'Here, let's duck in for a coffee. Less chance of you concussing yourself that way.'

We were tempted to sit outside, on the basis that the weak sunshine was at least sunshine and there was no telling when we might see Baggot Street so prettily dappled again, if ever. Common sense and a creeping sense of paranoia prevailed, though, so we took a table at the back of the coffee shop, both of us turning our chairs so that our backs were to the wall. Once the coffees were delivered, plus a couple of almond croissants, Martin said, 'Let me read out this bit, OK? This is Smyth's own testimony.'

'Have on.'

'Right. So Gerard Uxkull, as he was then, was a Danish-born sailor serving in the German Kriegsmarine when the submarine U-43 sailed into Lough Swilly in northern Donegal on March twenty-ninth, 1940. On board the U-43, along with the usual crew, was an OKW operative.' He looked up. 'The OKW was the—'

'Unless I ask, Martin, presume I already know.'

'No problem. So the operative called himself Klaus Rheingold, although Uxkull, along with the rest of the crew, assumed that this was an Abwehr cover name. The U-43 was on a special mission, which meant the sailors weren't told the operational details, but Smyth says that a submarine is a difficult place to keep secrets and everyone knew from an early stage that the plan was to land Rheingold in Donegal close to a beach just north of Buncrana. Kitted out as a British sailor, Rheingold would then hike southwest along the Malin Peninsula and cross the border into Derry, there to rendezvous with another agent, who was coming from London via Belfast. The U-43 was due to return to Lough Swilly a week later, to evacuate both agents and return to its base in Kiel. This is where it gets interesting.'

'I had an early start. Just nudge me if I start to snore.'

'There was a U-boat base at Kiel in 1940, all right. The first and seventh flotillas were operating from there.'

'But?'

'There was no U-43 based at Kiel during that time.'

'No?'

'Not officially. In fact, I couldn't find a record of *any* U-boat called U-43. That said, I'm no expert on U-boats. Maybe they got different names, or numbers, every time they left base.'

'That seem likely?'

'Not to me.' He shrugged. 'But I don't know. And with this being a special mission . . .'

I chewed slowly on some almond croissant. 'You'd have to say it puts a dent in Smyth's story. From the get-go, like.'

'You'd be wondering about the consistency, sure. But look, it was sixty-odd years ago, maybe he got confused about that particular detail.'

'It's possible. Although, if he's not certain, why put it in?'

Martin had a sip of his Americano. 'The other way of looking at that,' he said, his devious accountant's mind filtering the options, 'is why would he make it up, knowing it was bullshit, when it could be easily checked out?'

'This is true. But no, you're right. That's good to know.' I polished off the croissant while Martin shuffled his notes. 'I don't suppose you came up with anything concrete?' I said. 'Anything that might confirm his story?'

'Well, there's Delphi, we have that.'

'It didn't sink into the sea or disappear into the mist?'

'Not unless it happened since early this morning.'

'And we'd probably have heard about that. So what do we know about Delphi?'

'I'll spare you the geology, although that's—'

'Spare me. No massacres, right? We've established that.'

'No massacres, atrocities or war crimes. What it has is a small enough population, couple of hundred at most. During the tourist season that can treble or quadruple in any given week; there's plenty of attractions.'

'Really?'

'It's not the Côte d'Azur, sure, but not everyone loves casinos and yachts.'

'Or sunshine.'

'Still, there's plenty to see and do. The copper mine, it dates back a couple of thousand years BC. There's beehive huts, an ancient monastery of sorts. There's also a pretty impressive water sports centre, and apparently the island is top of the pops with hikers and walkers. And then there's the bird sanctuary.'

'Hold me back. An actual bird sanctuary?'

'Yep. Roughly a third of the island, the northern third, is private property, given over to this bird sanctuary. Right around now the place is white with Arctic geese on their way home for the summer.'

'Good for them. They don't happen to feed on red herrings, do they?'

'They might. But listen, here's what *isn't* an attraction on the island of Delphi. Or who, I should say. There's no mention in the official material, I mean on the island's website, of Sebastian Devereaux.'

'Really? They somehow neglected to mention some dead guy who wrote third-rate thrillers no one read about a million years ago?'

Martin shook his head, had himself a slug of Americano. 'At the risk of repeating myself, Devereaux's books were good. At least, the two I read were. Smart, although maybe too quirky for their own good. The point is the island's website is raving about water-skiing and hill-walking and so forth, scraping the barrel when it comes to what they call attractions of interest. So why doesn't it mention the only half-famous person ever associated with the place?'

'Well, he was English, wasn't he? They're still a bit touchy about the whole Flight of the Earls bit up in Donegal.'

'Maybe they are. Except it's not a case of was.'

That took a second or two to process. 'Devereaux's still alive?'

'I can't find any record anywhere of his death. Also, when you drill down into the bird sanctuary's own website, Sebastian Devereaux is listed as the honorary president of the foundation that runs the sanctuary.'

'An *honorary* president? What's an honorary president good for?'

'No idea. But listen, I did a bit of digging on Devereaux too.'

'Did you sleep at all last night?'

'Not much, no.'

He'd found nothing more on Sebastian Devereaux than I had, but presented his bare details with a kind of flourish.

'What am I missing?' I said.

'You don't think it's odd? A guy like that, this writer-hermit who lives in the back of beyond, and there's sweet FA on him out there?'

'The answer's in the question, Martin. The guy's pulled a Salinger, except I'm guessing *Rendezvous on Thira* isn't exactly *Catcher*. And he wrote his books, what, forty years ago now? Why would anyone be interested?'

'You know how it is, Tom. There's always *some*one.'

'These days, sure. But try thinking pre-Internet. If the guy was living in the wilds of Donegal, off on some island for Chrissakes, and was doing no interviews, any of that rot . . .'

'Maybe he couldn't.'

'What, he's a mute?'

'Be serious, Tom.' Martin the cautious accountant riffled back through his notes again as he built his case. 'I want you to have a think about this English spy Smyth talks about. The one who wouldn't give the Germans what they wanted, so they started herding the kids into the church.'

'You think they're the same guy?'

'Tell me it's not possible.'

'Christ, Martin. Anything's *possible*.'

'Sure, yeah, but listen. We have Sebastian Devereaux writing a thriller about a Nazi massacre of children and setting it on Santorini. We also know that Devereaux came to live on Delphi in 1939, as an archaeologist' – he gave the word some air quotes for effect – 'where two different sources have told us there was a Nazi atrocity in which a group of children burned to death.'

'Which means what?'

'Well, now that Shay Govern is confirming Gerard Smyth's story, you're looking at Sebastian Devereaux being cheeky enough to write a thriller about an actual war crime, one he was actually involved in, and responsible for, and disguising it by setting it in the Greek islands.'

'That's a bit of a stretch,' I said, although even as I said it I had to admit to myself that Martin wasn't usually prone to anything that might be confused for lurid exaggeration. 'I mean, if it all really happened, and some English spy *was* involved? We're talking about Donegal, Martin. Those boys take no prisoners. They'd have burned him out long ago, wild geese or no fucking wild geese.'

'Sure, yeah. Except it looks like he's still there.'

EIGHT

Gerard Smyth's address turned out to be a basement bed-sit on Fitzwilliam Lane, where steep slick steps led down to a tiny courtyard with its stone flags swept bare. There was paint flaking and rust showing on the iron bars at the single window, but the window itself was clean, the curtains inside drawn back. Yellow marigolds in pots either side of the front door gave a splash of colour.

The doorbell was working, and I could hear the phone ring inside when I called his number, but the marigolds remained the only sign of life. I gave the door a hefty thumping, in case Smyth was sleeping late, then went back up to the street and along to the Quiet Americano and took a high stool at the window counter, sipping a decaff latte and staring up the street towards Smyth's bed-sit.

An hour later there was still no sign of Smyth and even the thought of another coffee, decaff or otherwise, was turning my stomach. I got out my notebook and scribbled a note.

Mr Smyth – I dropped by to let you know that I'm interested in taking on your story. I'd like to ask some follow-up questions, if that's OK with you. Give me a call when you get this. Yours, Tom Noone.

I glanced up to check on the street, wondering if I should add a PS about Sebastian Devereaux, and saw a woman standing outside on the footpath in a knee-length grey wool coat. She was looking straight at me and didn't glance away. Instead she nodded – not a greeting; a confirmation – then turned towards the door. She ordered straight away and pointed at the window counter and made her way through the maze of tables and chairs, slipping out of her coat to hang it on the high stool beside mine, leaving that one empty as she eased herself up on to a seat two stools along.

She was tall and slim. The eyes were smoky-grey, accentuated by black eye-liner, and she wore her blonde bob in a ragged mess of a bird's nest that probably took no longer than most birds' nests to get just so. It was the nose that stood out though, long and narrow from the bridge but swelling wider than it should have over the full lips. I'd hate to know what Freud might have made of it, but I've always liked a woman with an interesting nose.

She nodded at the notebook and said, 'Please don't tell me it's a screenplay.'

I took my time ripping out the page and folding it up, making a point of tucking it into my back pocket. She wore no ring on her wedding finger, and I was guessing her to be late thirties, so she'd probably earned the right to the sardonic drawl, the cynical appraisal in the watchful grey eyes.

'Is there something I can help you with?' I said.

The barista arrived with her coffee. She nodded her thanks, gave the barista a flash of a warm smile, and turned back to me. She left the smile where it was, which gave her the look of sun glinting on frost.

'Gerard Smyth,' she said.

'What about him?'

'You were kicking in his door just now. How come?'

'Kicking, no. Knocking, yes.'

'Why?' she said.

'What's it to do with you?'

'I'm concerned,' she said. 'Mr Smyth didn't come home last night, which is by all accounts highly unusual behaviour for Mr Smyth. Or by one account, at least. His neighbour, an admirably concerned citizen, is worried that Mr Smyth may have come to some harm. According to his neighbour, Mr Smyth is not, and I quote, "a man to run off on the lash with some floozy".'

'I wouldn't have thought so, no.'

'So when the neighbour rings up and says someone's having a good old batter at Mr Smyth's door, and the man who did the battering is now sitting up the road in a coffee shop, I thought I'd have a word.'

No uniform – if she really was a cop – meant a detective. I'd always thought you needed to be missing for twenty-four hours before the cops got involved, but then and there didn't seem to be the right time, if there ever is a right time, to ask stupid questions.

'He's missing?' I said.

'His neighbour is concerned,' she said again, 'so we're concerned. I don't suppose you'd have any ID on you?'

I did, but I was entitled to see hers before I showed her mine. She dug into a coat pocket and flipped open a battered black leather wallet that said she was a Garda detective sergeant called Alison Kee. It looked bona fide, so I took out my wallet and gave her my driver's licence.

'Would you mind,' she said as she handed it back, 'if I had a look at your phone?'

'What for?'

'Clues,' she said. 'Bloodstains and semen traces and suchlike.'

I gave her the phone, trying to remember if it was detectives or uniformed gardaí who generally pursued missing-persons cases. She scrolled down through my contacts, the list of calls made and received, the text messages. Then she placed it on the counter, slid it across. 'What do you want with Gerard Smyth?' she said.

'I want to talk to him. He wasn't at home, so I thought I'd hang around and see if I could catch him coming back.'

'And this chat,' she said. 'What might that be about?'

'A book we're working on.'

'You're a writer?'

'That's right.'

'And what's the book about?'

'That's confidential.'

She grinned at that. Then, when she realized I was serious, she said, 'Maybe he told you something in confidence, but that's not really the same thing, is it? And anyway, the man's missing. So it's all in play now.'

'Look,' I said, 'I don't want to be difficult, but—'

'Have you paid?'

'What?'

'For your coffee,' she said. 'Have you paid for it?'

'Sure, yeah. Why?'

She ducked in so fast I nearly wound up with a mascara smear on my nose.

'Do *not* fuck me around,' she hissed from about three inches away. 'There's an old man gone missing who could be wandering around right now not knowing who or where he is, and that's probably our best-case scenario.' She tapped the counter three times with her forefinger. 'So you tell me exactly what you know right fucking *now*, or I'll drag you out of here quick fucking smart.'

She made a compelling argument. It was unlikely she'd pull me into some dark alleyway and start punching, even if she looked plenty capable, but once she'd dragged me out of the coffee shop she'd have to take me somewhere. Which meant delays, and possibly even a holding cell, and multiple conversations that could well become an interrogation. All to protect a man I didn't really know, and certainly couldn't trust.

So I told her what I knew of Gerard Smyth, and why I was sitting in the coffee shop watching his basement flat. As a goodwill gesture, I even gave her the note I'd written him.

She sat back on her stool and read it, then placed it on the counter and had a hearty slurp on her black coffee. 'Nazis in Donegal,' she said.

'So he says.'

'And he was one himself?'

'Not a Nazi, no. A sailor, he says.'

'And you believe all this?'

'I honestly don't know.' I gestured at the note. 'That's one of the reasons I'm here.'

'If you didn't think there was something in it, you wouldn't be hanging around.'

'I'm giving him the benefit of the doubt. For now, anyway.'

'OK,' she said. She drained her coffee, then announced she was giving me a lift home. I told her I was fine, I was driving myself, had my car parked up on the canal. She was persistent, though. In the end she dropped me at my car – she drove an unmarked maroon Renault Mégane, the radio tuned to Classic Hits FM – and followed me home. I zapped the security gates and drove on through into the car park, leaving Kee to park on the double-yellow lines outside the apartment complex. By the time I got back to the gates she was propping a 'Doctor on Call' card on her dashboard.

'You won't mind if I come in,' she said, 'on the off-chance you've left any clues lying around.'

'Or semen traces.'

'We're all human, Tom. I promise not to judge.'

Once inside I put on the central heating, got the kettle going and asked if she'd like another coffee. She said she would, and instant was fine.

'Mind if I have a quick look around while the kettle boils?' she said.

'Should I ask to see your search warrant?'

'If you have some reason I shouldn't look around.'

'No, fire ahead. But the only cupboard big enough to stash a body is in the master bedroom.'

'I'll start there so.'

Maybe she did, but I found her in the other bedroom, the one I use as an office. She was hunched over my laptop, scrolling down through my Gmail account. I stood in the doorway sipping my coffee.

'Is there anything in particular you're looking for?' I said. 'I'd hate for you to be in breach of the constitution for nothing.'

She only shrugged at that. Another couple of turns on the mouse wheel and then she minimised the window. 'Just doing my job, Tom. And I do appreciate your cooperation.' She stood up, jamming her hands into the pockets of her coat and rummaging around. She came up with a tattered card. 'Right so,' she said, 'I'll be off. If you hear from Mr Smyth, or remember anything you might want to tell me, give me a call on that number.'

I couldn't see where she'd put it, but for all I knew the grey wool coat had been tailored with all kinds of secret pockets. 'Are you going to put it back?' I said.

'Put what back?'

'The folder. Manila, beige, containing Gerard Smyth's testimony. Which I left lying on top of the printer.'

She hadn't gone the Botox route just yet. An eyebrow rose slowly towards the ragged fringe. 'There was no folder when I got here,' she said.

'Come on, Kee. It's the only copy I have.'

By way of answer she pulled her overcoat wide open. No inside pockets big enough to hold a manila folder. No worn beige folder tucked under her armpit. 'I'm not going to ask if you want to search me,' she said.

'You didn't touch it?'

'There was nothing to touch. You're sure you didn't lock it away?'

I was sure, but Kee had me pull out all the desk drawers anyway, root through all the files on top of the bookshelves. Then we moved to the master bedroom.

All told we spent more than an hour going through the apartment. If the floors weren't bare wood she'd have had me pulling up the carpets.

The folder was gone.

NINE

Detective Alison Kee was a thorough cop with a particular flair for asking questions and presuming the answers were lies. When she asked me the same question for a third time, or maybe the fourth, tossing in a threat of having me up for wasting Garda time, I'd had enough.

'You're the one mooching around my apartment,' I said. 'Seriously, who's wasting whose time here?'

Given that I'd already told her I had the folder, and the gist of what was in it, I had no good reason to hide it from her. For that matter, I'd had no reason to hide it from anyone else. Which was why I'd left it sitting on top of the printer.

'Only,' she said, 'if you're not playing silly buggers, we know someone wanted it.'

'All I know is that it's not here now.'

'So who took it?'

'I don't *know*.'

'Does anyone else have keys to the apartment?'

'The landlord, yeah.'

'No one else? A girlfriend, say?'

She'd seen the framed picture on my bedside locker, Rachel with Emily clutched to her lap, the pair of them laughing on a swing in a playground.

'No one else has keys,' I said.

'See, my problem there,' she said, 'presuming that's all true, is that there's no sign of a break-in.' She'd checked the door, the windows back and front. 'And you're saying there's nothing else missing.' I nodded. 'Which means the folder evaporated or whoever swiped it knew what they were doing.'

'Folders don't evaporate.'

'Science, right. But let me ask you this,' she said, sitting forward on the couch, elbows on her knees, hands joined and forefingers pointed at me. 'Say you were a pro, breaking in to steal one particular thing. Would you take it and go, or would you trash the place, lift some valuable stuff, and leave it looking like an amateur job, some junkie on the prowl?'

'I'd probably go the junkie route. Unless I was trying to make a point.'

'There's that,' she conceded.

Which meant they knew who I was, what I was doing and where I lived. My first thought was Jack Byrne, working his latest angle, although I found it hard to believe that Jack would be subtle enough to slip in and out without leaving any sign of his being there.

My second thought was that Gerard Smyth had been very badly mistaken when he'd laughed off the idea that he was being watched.

'It's possible,' I said, 'that they didn't actually break in.'

'That they got the keys from the landlord? Sure. You have a number for him handy?'

The landlord was a she, and I did. While Kee made the call I wandered back up the hallway to the office, had a rummage through the coat she'd left hanging on the back of the chair when we started our search. No secret pockets, and no folder or loose pages. Unless she'd eaten it while I was making the coffee, Kee knew nothing about the folder.

What I did find, in her inside breast pocket, was a couple of ballpoint pens and a small hard-backed notebook. More interesting was the mini tape recorder in the deep outside pocket on the left side. I rewound for a couple of seconds, pressed play. Heard Kee's voice first:

'*Put what back?*'

'*The manila folder. Smyth's testimony. Which I left lying on top of the printer.*'

'*There was no folder when I got here.*'

'*Come on, Kee. It's the only copy I have.*'

Then a click, and silence.

All of which made sense of the moment, earlier, when she'd opened her coat wide – '*I'm not going to ask if you want to search me*' – and I'd thought for a second she was flirting, undercutting the flasher's dirty-mac routine with a little crackle in her voice, a slow burn. I wondered if she'd accidentally knocked off the recorder spreading her coat wide, or if the gesture was a magician's misdirection, so I wouldn't notice her switching it off.

I put the recorder back in the coat pocket, trying to guess what it was she'd been after. Proof that I'd had the only copy of Smyth's testimony, or that I no longer had it?

When I heard her end the conversation I went back down to the living room. Her expression was sour.

'She says no,' Kee said. 'No one has asked her for keys to access a tenant's apartment.'

'You don't believe her.'

'I've no reason not to. But she'd have been warned, wouldn't she? And if anyone who was asking had the power to force her to hand over keys . . .'

'I know they weren't worried about getting caught,' I said.

'How do you make that out?'

'The laptop. It's still there.'

'And?'

'The folder, Smyth's story, it was the only copy. But they'd have assumed I'd made another copy. You would, wouldn't you?' A terse nod. 'So they'd have checked the laptop, to make sure I hadn't typed up a version or scanned one in. And they couldn't have been sure I didn't bury it somewhere, so they'd have been thorough.'

'How long were you out?'

'Since early this morning.'

'Plenty of time, if they knew what they were doing.'

'Especially if they weren't particularly worried about me coming back and barging in.'

Kee sighed and thumbed her nose. Not a happy woman. She'd started out this morning following up on some doddery old geezer who might have been missing or who might have just taken a wrong turn on the way home. Now, if I was telling the truth, and especially about the friendly chaps who'd offered to help Gerard Smyth carry home his shopping, she was tiptoeing around the edges of something that looked to be way beyond her pay grade.

'Kee,' I said, 'there's not a lot of people who know there's only one copy. Me, Jack Byrne and Gerard Smyth.'

'And you're thinking this is out of Jack Byrne's league.'

'Well, maybe I don't know Jack as well as I thought.' A bad time, I gauged, to mention that Jack Byrne had been planning only yesterday evening to hack into the Department of Foreign Affairs. 'When I rang him this morning he told me he was on a job. Maybe he was here, filching the folder.'

'But he's the one who brought you to Smyth. Right?'

'Correct.'

'So there's no good reason for him to break in and steal Smyth's story. I mean, he already knows what's in the file.'

'The general gist of it. But Smyth wouldn't give him the testimony, he wanted it to go straight to a journalist. Maybe Jack wants it for insurance. So I don't try to gip him.'

'It's possible.' She was shaking her head. 'Although there's also the possibility that Byrne told someone else . . . Why don't you ring him, see what kind of mood he's in?'

'I don't know if that's likely.' I pulled up Jack Byrne's number, hit redial. 'Jack didn't strike me as the kind of guy who'd run around cutting anyone else in on his deal.'

'You're presuming he had a choice in the matter. Then again, the same scenario applies to Gerard Smyth.'

The call went straight to voicemail. 'Jack? It's Tom. Give me a buzz back when you get this. We need to talk.'

I hung up. Kee beckoned for the phone, made a note of Jack Byrne's number, tossed it back.

'There's a couple of options here,' she said. 'One, there's some kind of clean-up going on; someone wants Smyth and his story taken out. The other is they've suddenly decided to take him seriously, investigate his story, and they don't want you making a balls of it by putting it all in the public domain before they're ready to roll it out.'

'They could've just told me that.'

'Right. Because that's how journalists make a living, sitting on stories to keep them warm until they're ready to hatch out.'

If her theory was sound, then whoever had broken in had made no more distinction than Kee between investigative journalists and guys who reviewed books and movies for a living. So I didn't bother pointing that out.

'If these boys,' I said, 'have the power we think they have—'

'We're making a lot of guesses here, Tom.'

'I know. But if you're right about the keys *or* you're right about the break-in, and if we believe Smyth about the spooks, then we're dealing with serious people. The kind who'd have no problem getting an injunction against me. Or maybe pull out the Official Secrets Act.'

'Possibly.'

'Meanwhile, you're still at square one. As in, where's Gerard Smyth? Skulking around the Four Seasons under a fake name while these guys get their ducks in a row?'

She sat a while and thought about all that. Or maybe she was trying not to think about it. For all I knew she was wondering about what she'd be having for dinner. Eventually she said, 'You're entitled to report the break-in.'

'I know.'

'Do you want to?'

Make it official, she meant. 'Might be smarter not to,' I said.

'I'd have thought so.' A shrug. 'They took something you can't prove is gone. And there's no sign of forced entry.'

'Sure. But what I mean is if they wanted to make a point it might be better to let them think it's been made. That they've put the frighteners on and I'm letting it go.'

'I wouldn't imagine you've anything to worry about in that department,' she said. 'If they wanted to throw a scare into you, they'd have been waiting when you came home.'

I'd worked that much out myself.

'So what happens now?' I said. 'With Smyth.'

'We'll take it to the next level, get a team in play. Public appeals, the works. He's a priority now, he's at risk.'

'And what about the spooks? Are they in play too?'

'Not my decision to make, Tom. I'll have to send that one upstairs.'

'Just so long as it doesn't get stashed in the attic.'

'What's that supposed to mean?'

'It means I don't want him forgotten about, deliberately or otherwise. And if I don't hear that Gerard Smyth has been found safe and well in the next couple of days, I'll be asking why, and how much your bosses know about these guys who helped Smyth with his shopping.'

'Tom,' she said, 'you really don't want to take this personally.'

'They broke into my home, Kee. Made their point, some power-play bullshit. I'm not the one who made it personal.'

'You're not thinking this through. You're pissed off they broke in, I can understand that. And you're worried about Smyth, sure. But you'd be causing yourself all sorts of problems if you get involved here.'

'Because they told me to back off? Fuck 'em. Listen, you go

ahead and write up your report, and you let the boys upstairs
know about the spooks. While you're at it, mention that the
break-in put me in the mood to cause *them* problems. What are
they going to do, blacklist me? Lift me off the streets like they
did Smyth?'

'We don't even know that happened.'

'In that case I have nothing to worry about, do I? But on the
off-chance they did lift Smyth, you might want to mention in
your report that I was planning to send an email to my good
friend Father Iggy Patton just as soon as you left. It's a new
service he's running: online confessions.'

'I can do all that,' she said. She stood up, looked around. 'But
Tom, think about this. If we're right about Smyth, and he hasn't
just wandered off somewhere, you kicking up a shit storm could
put him in a very bad situation. Where's my coat?'

I told her I didn't know, and then she remembered she'd left
it in the office. While she was gone I conceded that she made a
good point about not causing any more trouble for Gerard Smyth,
much as I grudged admitting it. By the same token, if Kee was
a stooge, sent along to persuade me not to follow up on the
burglary, then that's exactly the kind of thing she would say.

Except when she came back she had the grey coat folded over
one arm, the tape recorder in her other hand. She tossed the coat
on to the couch, sat down and placed the recorder on the coffee
table between us.

'You know what's in the folder,' she said. 'You've read it, right?'

'A couple of times, yeah.'

'OK.' She pushed the record button. 'Tell me everything you
remember. And please, spare me the confidential bullshit.'

'Why?'

'Because if I'm in this, I need all you have. Any little thing
you can remember.' There was no humour in it this time. 'You
never know what might turn out to be a clue.'

'OK, so my name is Tom Noone, I'm a journalist and author. I
had a meeting yesterday morning with a man called Shay Govern,
he's an Irish-American—'

'Hold up.' Kee, on the couch, had her notebook on her knee,
pen poised. 'Who's this Shay Govern?'

'That's what I'm about to tell you.'

'What I mean is how come I'm only hearing about him now?'

'He didn't come up before.'

'But he's important enough now that you're starting with him?'

'I can leave him out if you want, go straight to Smyth.'

'Leave nothing out, Tom. Leave no one out.'

'That was the plan, yeah, before you interrupted me.'

She took a moment to pinch at the corners of her eyes, massage the eyelids. Then she exhaled, slow. 'Go on,' she said.

So I told her about Shay Govern and how he'd commissioned me to ghost-write a book about Sebastian Devereaux, a forgotten thriller writer who lived on Delphi Island in Lough Swilly, Donegal.

'Except then, this morning, Govern told me that he was an eye-witness to the murder of six children during a Nazi massacre on Delphi Island in 1940, shortly before he left home for America.'

'Why is that name familiar?' Kee said.

'Shay Govern? Maybe you heard about this gold mine he wants to open.'

She nodded to herself, scribbled a note.

'So it's bad timing for Govern,' she said, 'if this story comes out now.'

'You'd think so, wouldn't you?' I gave her Govern's spiel, the mine as a philanthropic gesture, the expiation of sins.

'Jesus. Go on.'

'So then Jack Byrne comes to see me. He's tracked down Gerard Smyth for Govern, except he—'

'And Jack Byrne is . . .?' Kee said, nodding at the recorder.

'Oh, yeah.' I cleared my throat. 'Jack Byrne's an ex-Garda detective, now a private investigator, hired by Govern to find Gerard Smyth, his long-lost friend. When Byrne locates Smyth, he realizes Govern's not telling the truth. So he has a chat with Smyth, gets the gist of his story, and decides Govern might pay more than a finder's fee to keep Smyth quiet.'

'Not realizing that Govern wants Smyth to corroborate his story,' Kee said.

'Exactly. Anyway, he takes me to meet Smyth, which is when Smyth gives me a folder with his testimony of the atrocity, one he'd typed up himself. That original and only copy is now lost, possibly destroyed, so this account serves as a secondary source.'

'Relax, Tom. You're not testifying here. Just tell me what Gerard Smyth told you.'

I couldn't see how it could hurt, so I told her everything. Kee was either genuine or she was going through the motions so that I wouldn't suspect she was a stooge – and if she was, they already had Smyth's account. Telling her the story could only keep it fresh for when I came to write it down.

If I was ever allowed to write it.

So I told her about Gerhard Uxkull, Danish-born, who'd joined the German Navy in 1938. I told her about the secret mission to land a German spy, Klaus Rheingold, in Donegal, and that Smyth claimed to have been sailing aboard the U-43, a U-boat operating out of Kiel that appeared to have left no record of itself behind.

According to Smyth, the U-43 surfaced into poor weather not long after 3 a.m. on the night of 26 February. Smyth was one of four sailors who climbed down with Rheingold on to a slippery deck, where they began inflating a dinghy while Rheingold attended to a number of last-minute checks on his equipment. Conditions were difficult, not least because the covert nature of the mission meant a full black-out. Heavy rain driven by a gusting south-westerly further hampered their efforts, while the narrow deck pitched and bucked on the choppy swell and a fast-turning tide.

'What's funny?' Kee said.

'You'd have to meet him to find it funny. Smyth's a serious guy, very precise. Anyway, he said that while the conditions were difficult for launching a dinghy, they were perfect for launching Gerhard Uxkull.'

He had been kneeling on the deck, struggling to keep the dinghy's bow steady, when a wave slapped the dinghy's keel and sent the bow crashing into his face.

'He has no memory of going into the water. One second he was there on the deck of the sub, the next he was sinking. He was wearing a life preserver, so that pulled him back to the surface, and the first thing he remembers is lying on his back staring straight up at the stars. The cold was brutal. A killer. But he was still stunned. If he hadn't puked he'd probably have just drifted until hypothermia got him. Anyway, he started to swim. Or tried to, anyway. Basically he was just tossed around on the waves while he thrashed his arms and legs.' A nightmare. 'He began to panic when he realized the U-43 was nowhere to be seen, that he'd been abandoned in pitch dark on a stormy—'

'You can skip the poetry, Tom,' Kee said. 'Just tell us what happened.'

Smyth's knowledge of Lough Swilly was of the most basic kind. He knew that it angled northwest to southeast, that it was no more than two miles wide where they had surfaced north of Buncrana, and that he was closer to the Malin shore than the western – or had been at the time of the drop, although he had no idea of how far he had drifted since then. He understood that being picked up on the eastern coast would compromise the special mission and the agent's cover, but by then Gerhard Uxkull had very little interest in special missions and the greater good of the Third Reich.

He was no swimmer. Had it not been for the preserver he would have long since drowned. In any case, the strength of the current was such that even a champion would have struggled to make headway against it. He was swimming only to stay warm, all the while trying to gauge the fine line between expending enough energy to retain his core temperature and working so hard that he exhausted himself entirely. His hope was that the southerly current would deliver him to the eastern shore before the tide began to turn again. If it didn't, he would be swept north again and out to sea, and he would be dead long before exiting the lough into the North Atlantic. When he could swim no more he rolled on to his back and drifted, and then he swam—

'We know he didn't die, Tom. What happened?'

'He was picked up by a fishing trawler about two hundred yards off the coast of Delphi. He'd been in the water nearly three hours by then, was damn near deranged and pickled and frozen to death.'

'So they thawed him out and . . . Hold on,' she said, scrabbling for the phone that was ringing somewhere on her person. She found it, took the call. 'Kee,' she said.

I sat forward and pressed Pause on the recorder.

'When?' Kee said. She listened again, then said, 'OK, I'm on my way.' She ended the call, then looked at me. The corners of her mouth turned down. 'They've found a body,' she said. 'Pulled out of the canal over at Grand Canal Dock.'

Which wasn't very far from Fitzwilliam Place.

'They think it's Smyth?' I said.

'They don't know – the body's been in the water a while and

there's no wallet or any identification. But it – he – looks to be the right age.'

'Be a hell of a coincidence if it's not him.'

A too-bright smile. 'Coincidences happen all the time, Tom.' She was already standing, shrugging into her coat. She retrieved the recorder from the coffee table, switched it off. 'Even if it isn't Smyth, we'll still need to finish this conversation.'

'Sure, yeah.' I got up too, and then just stood there, not knowing what I should say. 'Look, if there's anything I can do . . .'

An icy smile. 'Identify him, you mean?'

'Well, I don't know. But I suppose, yeah, I was one of the last people to see him.'

'Maybe the last, Tom. So don't go rushing off anywhere, taking any trips. If it is Gerard Smyth, and if it looks like he didn't go into that canal under his own steam, you'll be the first person we'll want to talk to.'

'That's bullshit. Why would I go looking for him today, hang around outside his flat, if I'd done anything like that?'

'You might be smarter than you look. Or think you are, anyway.'

'Kee . . .'

'Tell you what you could do,' she said. 'Just to show willing, that your conscience is clear.'

'My conscience is *crystal* fucking clear.'

'Great. So you won't mind leaving your passport with me for now. Unofficial, like. Just until we know you have no reason to do a runner.'

'That's ridiculous.'

'Maybe so. But imagine how stupid I'd look if I walked away and you disappeared.'

I could see her point. So I stomped off back to the office and rooted out the passport, and stomped back down the hall again. Kee asked for the tattered card she'd given me, and scribbled a number on the back. 'That's my personal phone,' she said. 'If you hear anything, ring me straight away.' When she offered the card I refused to take it, so she put it on the table. Then she took one last look around. 'I take it you'll be staying here tonight?'

'Fucking right I will.'

'Good. I'll be in touch,' she said, and left.

TEN

I went to the bay window and watched Kee as she walked out of the car park, opened the Mégane, tossed the Doctor on Call sign on to the passenger seat, drove away.

Then I went up the hallway to the bedroom, dragged the khaki duffel out of the wardrobe and set it on the bed. Threw in some T-shirts and jeans, a couple of sweaters, boxers and socks. If Kee thought I was going to hang around an apartment where guys could break in whenever the mood took, some crew good enough to leave no trace of themselves behind, she was bat-shit insane.

The last thing to go into the bag was the laptop. The plan I'd agreed with Shay Govern that morning was that I'd catch him up by flying to Derry, make my own away around to Delphi Island via Letterkenny. But even as I brought up the Aer Lingus website (the vomit-comet internal flights were always half-empty, so there'd be no problem booking a seat) I was wondering if that was such a smart move. If the crew had been good enough to break in and leave no sign, and had spent time on the laptop, then there was every chance they were tech-savvy enough to bury a tracer on it that would track my every keystroke.

So, no flight.

I was packing away the laptop when I remembered telling Kee I'd email Iggy, let him know the score. So I dug it out again, fired up Gmail and sat on the bed with the laptop on my actual lap for the first time in years.

Iggy –

I hope all's well. Not so good at this end. That thing with Shay Govern has gone wide.

I interviewed a guy yesterday, Gerard Smyth, who told me a story that confirmed what I'm guessing Govern told you in confession. Now Smyth's gone missing and there's a body in the canal and the cops think it could be him.

Bad enough, but now it looks like there was someone in

*my apartment this morning, some bastards who took a file
Smyth gave me and left no sign they were here.*

*I'm expecting them back, Iggy. If they got Smyth, why
wouldn't they come for me? Wait until night, make sure I'm
asleep, then come sneaking in, making no sound . . .*

Me right there in the dark with a baseball bat.

Good plan, right?

*Or might be, if the closest thing to a baseball bat I own
wasn't a proofreading ruler. And even if I did have a bat
or knuckledusters it's no kind of plan. If it ever comes to a
scrap between me and professionals my money's on the
other guys, because at least that way I'd collect on the bet
when I got out of hospital, maybe pay off some of my bills.
That's presuming I ever made it as far as a hospital, didn't
wind up in a canal . . .*

*I'm taking off, Iggy. Getting out of Dodge until this settles
down, whatever the fuck this is. Heading for that place in Cork,
near Kinsale – remember I told you about it? I'll call tomorrow
at noon, check in. If you don't hear from me, call some cop
you know you can trust and then duck for cover.*

Tom

I clicked Send and the email disappeared into the ether. I shut
down the laptop, packed it away and zipped up the duffel.

Ready to go.

Ding-dong.

Raymond Chandler has this line, advice for writers, where if
you're ever stuck for something to happen, have a guy come
through the door with a gun in his hand.

Chandler was notoriously picky, though, was always rewriting.
So maybe in an earlier draft it read: 'Have an ex-wife come
through the door with a six-year-old by the hand.'

There was a time when I'd have given anything to have Rachel
in my bedroom. Now wasn't such a good time.

'It's only two nights, Tom.' She kept it low but urgent,
whispering. Just the way I'd always liked her in the bedroom.
'And OK, I know it's short notice and you'll need to rearrange
your Monday, but she'll be in school most of the day and she
gets picked up after, gets driven to after-school. So all you

really need to cover is tomorrow and Monday morning. We'll be back that evening. Or I will, anyway.'

'I know, yeah. That's not the issue.'

'I can't take her down there, Tom. Peter's a mess, he can't even drive. You know how close he was to his mother.' I knew nothing of Peter's relationship with his mother, and cared about as much. 'And I can't look after *both* of them,' she said. 'I'm stressed enough as it is.'

I could hear the sound of cartoons blaring from the TV in the living room, *Scooby-Doo*, Emily parked about two feet from the screen sitting on her lettuce-green Trunki carry-on. Peter, apparently, was outside in the car, having himself a meltdown in the passenger seat.

'I can't do it, Rach.'

'You *won't* do it.'

'It's not that simple.'

'It never is, Tom. Not with you.'

I could have told her what I was involved in, I suppose. Nazi massacres and spooks breaking in. Old guys gone MIA, presumed drowned. All of which would play beautifully with any judge presiding over an application for custody of a six-year-old girl.

Blanking Rachel, refusing straight up to look after Emily in a family emergency – that wouldn't play too well either.

But if I had to make a decision, then it'd have to be . . .

Ding-dong.

Rachel didn't stick around long after Kee walked in. I guess she thought Kee was the reason I couldn't take Emily for a couple of nights. She was right in a way, just not the way she thought. I was a man, Kee was a woman, and Rachel was hot stuff when it came to basic math. Not that she was pissed about Kee per se, the slow up-and-down look she gave Kee notwithstanding. It was that I was putting Kee before Emily.

By the time I'd worked up a line that might have put her straight, Rachel was long gone, although not before going down on one knee to wrap Emily in a hug and warn her to take care of Daddy, he looked like he was having a mid-life crisis.

She didn't know the half of it.

Kee, bemused, said, 'Who was *that*?'

'Rachel. My wife, technically speaking.'

'OK. But she's coming back, right?'

'To me? No, she's hooked up with Peter now.'

'I mean here. Soon.' An edge in her tone. 'For the kid.'

'She is, yeah. On Monday evening, all going well.'

'Daddy?' Emily said, eyes on the TV as Shag and Scoob plunged headlong down a mineshaft.

'Yes, love?'

'What's a mid-life crisis?'

'It's what happens to daddies when they realize their little girls don't love them any more.'

'Oh.'

'Tom?' Kee was nodding towards the hallway. 'A word?'

I followed her out, up the hallway to the office.

'She can't *be* here right now,' Kee said. 'Are you kidding me?'

She was right, of course. At least in theory. But there was no getting around the fact that Emily was sitting right there on her Trunki in the living room, watching cartoons.

There being nothing to gain from telling Kee what she already knew, I asked if the body they'd pulled from the canal was Gerard Smyth.

'We don't know. Could be. He's the right age, it's not far from where he lives . . .' She was shaking her head, lips pressed together. She glanced back up the hallway and lowered her voice. 'He had no ID on him. So we'll need someone to identify the body.'

'If you're talking about me, you can forget it. There's no way I'm taking Emily anywhere near a morgue.'

'She wouldn't have to go.'

'Forget about it. Ring Jack Byrne – he knew the guy better than me.'

'Already tried. He's still not answering.'

'Shit. Really?'

'Yeah. What's this job he's doing?'

'No idea. I don't live with the guy, Kee.'

'Well, he's off the grid. Him *and* Smyth.' She had her hands in her coat pockets again. I wondered if she was recording the conversation. 'You really can pick them, you know that?'

'I didn't pick anyone. I was minding my own business, and they came to me.'

She was nodding while I was talking but not really listening, her gaze roving around the office. Then she realized what was missing.

'Where's your laptop?' she said.

'I put it away.'

'Put it away or packed it away?'

'Packed it, yeah.'

'I thought we agreed you were going nowhere.'

'That,' I lied, 'was before Emily arrived.'

She shrugged, conceding the point. 'So where are you taking her?'

'Cork. There's a place near Kinsale, we were there once on holiday. There's a nice beach, it has a Blue Flag, we can do some—'

'Great, yeah.' She leaned past me, toed the office door shut. 'Listen, I'm not supposed to do this but needs must. Brace yourself.' She took her phone out of her coat pocket, brought up her photo album. 'Is this him?'

Maybe it was the light, or maybe her phone's camera wasn't up to snuff, but he looked ghastly. A greeny-blue cast to the pallor that made me think of Paddy Kavanagh again. He must have been in the water for a long time, because the skin that had been stretched taut on his bones was bloated now, gone slack. His puffy eyes, thank Christ, were closed.

'Is it him?' she said again.

'Yeah.' I wanted to puke. 'Are we done now?'

'For now. I can't use this as an official ID, but at least now we know we're not looking for Smyth any more.'

'You think it was deliberate?'

She considered that. 'We don't know. There's no sign of assault, nothing that makes it look like he was forced into the water. The post-mortem will tell us more.' She put away her phone, slipped her hands into her pockets again and straightened her shoulders. 'You know I can't let you just drive off to Cork, Tom.'

'What d'you mean?'

'You're the last person we know who saw Smyth alive. Then, you were hanging around his flat this morning.'

'We've been through this,' I said. 'If I was the one who tipped him into a canal, why would I go banging on his door?'

'Because you might want us to think that you believe he's still alive. Which was why you stuck around after, went to the coffee

shop. Hoping someone like me would turn up, so you could say
something along the lines of what you just said.'

'You're telling me I'm a suspect.'

'Right now you're a person of interest and you'll be helping
us with our enquiries until such time as we decide otherwise. So
Cork's off the agenda.'

'You want me to stay here? With Emily?'

'We can take Emily and place her—'

'No.'

She shrugged. 'In that case, yes. You stay here with Emily.
The other option,' she said as I opened my mouth to protest, 'is
that I arrest you for non-cooperation, obstruction, put you in a
holding cell until we've had a chance to post-mortem Smyth.
That way you get to ring your ex-wife, she swings back around
to pick up Emily. But I get the impression that that wouldn't be
ideal either.'

'I had nothing to do with it, Kee.'

'I don't think you did. But there's no way I'm going back to
the office and telling them I let you swan off into the sunset. Oh,
and I'll need that laptop. Your phone, too.'

'How come?'

'Standard procedure, Tom. Don't take it personal.'

I puffed out my cheeks, let it all go. Nodded at the double
doors of the wardrobe behind her, where I stored my lever arch
files on the top shelf. 'The backpack's in there,' I said. I reached
past her, opened the door. 'Listen,' I said, 'if I'm going to be
here with Emily, we'll have protection, right? Someone watching
the apartment.'

'I can arrange that,' she said.

'Sorry, it's on the other side,' I said, edging around her, reaching
for the other wardrobe door. She stepped aside as I bent down
to reach into the wardrobe and as she moved I shunted forward,
my shoulder shoving her left hip. She reeled back, hands still in
her pockets. One heel caught the wardrobe's lip and down she
went with a startled 'Hey!' that was cut off as I slammed the doors
shut.

All I needed now was a way of keeping them shut.

The ruler was right there on the desk, the one I used for my
proofreading gigs, an old-fashioned chunk of wood, twelve inches
long and two inches thick and seamed with a thin steel edge.

Not enough, maybe, to see off any post-midnight intruders, but just the right thickness to jam between the vertical handles on the wardrobe doors.

In it slid, snugly tight. Kee kicked and shouted, but her voice was muffled and the ruler held.

'Kee?' I said. 'Can you hear me?'

A couple of vicious kicks on the inside of the wardrobe doors suggested she could.

'Don't take it personal,' I said. 'It's Emily. There's no way I'm hanging around and putting her at risk. But I'll be in touch. OK?'

'Don't you *dare* leave me in here!'

I didn't see how I had much choice. Letting her out now would cause me even more problems than I already had, and I had more than enough to be getting on with. So I closed the office door and went into the bedroom and hauled the duffel out from under the bed where I'd stashed it when I heard the first *ding-dong*, went down the hallway to the living room and told Emily it was time to go – Shag and Scoob at full pelt through a cemetery now, a pumpkin-headed ghost in hot pursuit – that we were taking a little holiday, just me and her, a sleepover.

'But this is nearly *oh*-ver, Dad.'

'I know, love, but we can't wait.' I picked up the remote control and switched off the TV. 'We'll see it again.'

She pouted at that, then stood up off her Trunki with an exaggerated sigh. 'Pinky promise?'

We linked our little fingers. 'Pinky promise,' I said.

ELEVEN

Emily and me, we weren't exactly Bonnie and Clyde. For one, Clyde probably didn't have to worry about Bonnie putting her hand up and saying, 'I think I need to wee.' Also, Clyde could very probably get away with saying things like, 'Can you give me a couple of minutes over here, Bonnie? I'm trying to think.' Try that with the average six-year-old desperado and, depending on your tone, she'll likely burst into tears or ask what it is you're trying to think about. Or both.

I hadn't exactly been working to a strategy when I'd barged Kee into the wardrobe. It was instinct, mostly. Kee was standing there in front of an open wardrobe, telling me she was either going to arrest me or leave me sitting there in the apartment with Emily, a pair of sitting ducks if the break-in crew came back for another look-see, maybe a proper chat this time.

Cue the red mist.

So I'd shoved and slammed and wedged the doors closed.

Would I have done it if I'd only had me to worry about? Probably not. But it was done now and it couldn't be undone.

I drove up Patrick Street past the cathedral and down to the quays under the Christchurch arch, my sensible brain telling me that it still wasn't too late, that the best thing to do was turn around and go back, release Kee and apologize and hope for the best.

I turned west along the quays into the late-afternoon traffic, my adrenaline-crazed brain screaming at me to shoe the accelerator and just *do* one.

I was out on the M50, heading south with one eye on the rear-view – the mirror at an angle so I could see the road behind and Emily strapped into her booster seat – when it occurred to me to wonder what might happen if the break-in crew arrived at the apartment and found Kee still in the wardrobe.

That sensible part of my brain reckoned they wouldn't come back, that they'd got what they wanted and made their point, and anyway, there was still a decent chance Gerard Smyth had accidentally slipped into that canal.

Which was tough to hear, given that my crazy brain was screaming that they were already there, hauling Kee out of the wardrobe, and that they'd kill her too.

'Daddy?'

'Yes, love?'

'Why was that lady in your apartment?'

'She's Daddy's friend.'

Silence, Emily gazing out the window. Then: 'Why was she banging the door in your office?'

'It's, ah, like hide-and-seek, Em.'

'She's trying to find us?'

'That's right.'

'Is she counting to one hundred?'

'I certainly hope so.'

'Is that why she was shouting?'

'It is. So we'd know she wasn't cheating.'

She digested that. Then: 'Melanie cheats.'

'Is that right?'

'She never counts all the way. *And* she pecks.'

'That's not very fair, is it?'

'No. Why do people cheat, Daddy?'

'I don't know. Why do you cheat?'

'Because it's easier.'

'Well, there you are.'

I wondered, providing the ruler held, how much of a head-start we were likely to get. If I was Kee, I'd hold off on ringing the station and letting them know I'd been locked into a wardrobe by some civilian and his pint-sized accomplice. I'd be trying to figure it all out first, see if I couldn't kick down the wardrobe doors, maybe screw off the hinges.

Then again, Kee might be made of sterner stuff. Could take the hit, the guys giving her a hard time about being stuffed into a closet like a winter coat. For all I knew they were already co-ordinating a stop-and-search.

'Daddy?'

'Just give me a sec, Em. I'll be with you in a minute.'

'Can we play I Spy then?'

'Of course we can.'

I had to presume the worst. That Gerard Smyth's drowning was no accident. That I was, or would very soon be, the prime

suspect, and that there'd be a personal element to Kee's desire
to track me down, a wounded pride to be salved, a professional
reputation to be repaired.

And that was just the cops.

If the spooks who'd broken into the apartment had had a couple
of hours to play with, there was every chance they'd be tracking
my emails. Which meant, once they read my email to Iggy, they'd
think I was headed south for Kinsale.

Kee would believe otherwise, because I'd specifically mentioned
Cork, but there was no harm in giving her a reason to second-
guess herself. So I cut west off the M50 at the Kilnamanagh
junction, driving out through Belgard and Cookstown, the industrial estates with their security cameras, then north after Whitehall
and back up to the N7 and the motorway to Limerick and Cork.

Except the trick now was to avoid all motorways and toll
booths, anywhere there might be CCTV. Head north through the
midlands, then northwest, to Donegal and Delphi Island. Find
Shay Govern and get him in a headlock and choke the truth out
of him, find out what the hell was really going on, why Gerard
Smyth was going cold on a slab. Then call in a big favour from
Jenny, go public, get Emily and me on to a front page or two.

Spooks thrive in the shadows, sure. But they do tend to melt
away once the spotlight is turned on.

Emily's appetite for I Spy was insatiable. Three hours later she
was still finding new things to spy. In the last half-hour, though,
most of them had been spied inside the car, the light outside
fading fast.

'Clouds?'

'No.'

'Coral.'

'*Daddy*.' She shook a pudgy little fist at me. 'Why I oughta . . .'

She was near enough the right height for the Jimmy Cagney
impression I'd taught her, but she still had work to do on the
nasal whine.

'Sorry,' I said. 'Corn?'

'No.'

'Is it inside or outside?'

'Inside.'

'Crazy girl.'

'*Daddy*. Play properly.'

'Sorry. Cute girl?'

'No!'

'Give me a clue.'

'No.'

'C'mon. I gave you a clue last time.'

'OK.'

While she was thinking about it I said, 'Are you hungry, love?'

'I think so.'

'What would you like, burgers?'

'Oooh, yes, please.'

We were coming up on Letterkenny by then. Say what you want about the Celtic Tiger – and sure, it was going extinct fast and dying a hard death – but it left behind an impressive road network of motorways and dual carriageways and by-passes that means you can pretty much navigate the entire length and breadth of the country without ever driving through a single town. On a long enough journey, say from south County Dublin all the way to north Donegal, that can clip a couple of hours off your trip. It also meant you disappeared off the radar somewhere on the western edge of Dublin's suburbs and didn't show up again until you got careless, or hungry, or ran low on petrol.

I pulled on to the hard shoulder, knocked on the warning flashers.

'Back in a sec, love,' I said. I got out and went around the car to the ditch, grabbed a couple of handfuls of mud and smeared them across the number plates fore and aft. Then I got back in and reached into the back for Emily's Trunki. Rachel being not only a good mother but verging on OCD when it came to personal hygiene, she'd packed, as I'd hoped, a full packet of baby wipes. Then it was on down the long hill towards Letterkenny, and the roundabout at the bottom of the hill and the petrol station on the far side.

I filled the car and paid with cash. Even if we showed up on CCTV it wouldn't be for a couple of days, and by then, all going to plan, Emily and I would be basking in the limelight, and untouchable.

We ate gourmet burgers in the Errigal Inn on the Ramelton Road just outside Letterkenny, where I consulted Google via my phone and discovered that the last ferry to Delphi Island left

Rathmullan pier at 5.15 p.m. The first ferry out departed at 9.30 a.m. the next morning, so I rang ahead to a B&B in Rathmullan and told them I'd be arriving with my daughter in half an hour or so, and staying for one night.

I'd turned the phone off for the journey north, partly so it wouldn't be a distraction, partly because I had a vague idea that doing so would foil any interested parties trying to track me via triangulation, or at least make it a little bit harder for them to do so. When I turned it back on I'd received a text message from Rachel, asking how Emily was doing, to which I now replied that Emily was perfectly fine, and currently enjoying her dinner. There were also a couple of missed calls from Kee, both of which were delivered in a surprisingly reasonable tone given the circumstances, telling me to come in, I had nothing to worry about, and that my safety, and Emily's, were of paramount importance.

She actually used the word paramount. I wondered if it was in the handbook.

At first I was impressed by her professionalism, how calm she sounded, but then I started wondering if it wasn't the other way around – that she was running solo, and trying to get me back in before anyone discovered I'd locked her in a wardrobe.

I was running low on battery, the little red bar flashing 10%, so I turned off the phone to conserve power and called for the bill. Emily, full to the gunwales on burger and ice-cream, was already nodding off when I strapped her back into her booster seat. I eased out of the Errigal Inn's car park and headed north towards Ramelton. It was almost dark by then, so I gave the road my full attention for a couple of minutes, got my night-sight going. When I glanced again in the rear-view mirror Emily was already asleep, head lolling left and right as we followed the dark and winding road. I was taking it handy, easing into the bends and taking my time coming out, and the set of headlights maybe a couple of hundred yards back was doing exactly the same.

A careful driver, maybe. Or just a guy like me who didn't know the road, was using the car in front as a pathfinder.

I took it slow going down the steep hill into Ramelton, cut left and came up out of the sharp turn after the bridge towards Rathmullan in second gear.

The headlights behind did the same.

I eased up into third, trundling along until I was out of sight around a long left-hand bend, then floored the accelerator. Ten seconds later the headlights appeared in the rear-view, and picked up the pace until it was barrelling along. I laid a soft foot on the brake, dropped down to sixty kph. The headlights gained on us for a second or two, then dropped off again.

By then I was sweating cold. If I'd been on my own I might even have been tempted to pull in, see if he'd drive past. But with Emily in the back I was taking no chances.

The good news, or the best possible spin on very bad news, was that I was being followed – the guy wasn't trying to ram me, or force us off the road. Everything else, yeah, was bad news. I didn't know the area, had no rat-runs I could disappear into. And the road was dark, ditches on one side and the silvery Swilly on the other.

The only option, as far as I could see, was the old fall-back – get somewhere public, a place with people and lights, and see if the guy wouldn't just melt away. So I pushed on along the road towards the orange glow up the coast that I was hoping was Rathmullan.

It's a pretty little village, Rathmullan, and it wasn't exactly a ghost town when we arrived. There were the orange street lights, and plenty of yellow glows in the windows of the terraced houses facing out across the lough, and nary a tumbleweed to swerve around as I drove along the seafront. Of actual people there were very few sightings, apart from one old guy on a corner gesticulating at the stars, which appeared to have done something to displease him.

I was almost through the village – it took about forty seconds – before I found what I was looking for. A pub with its front door open, a splash of buttery light leaking across the street to a low wall where a group of smokers huddled together, one or two of them sitting on the wall. Behind and below them was a mostly empty car park, a children's playground beyond, the pier away to my right. I drove down into the car park and made a wide turn so that I was facing back the way I came, almost directly below where the smokers perched on the wall. One of them glanced down, incurious, as I got out and went around to the trunk and opened it, pulled up the floor and found the tyre jack. Then, as the headlights appeared, nosing down into the car park, I got back into the driver's seat and closed the door.

The sound of the closing door, or maybe the blast of fresh air, made Emily restless in the rear seat, turning her head and muttering something I couldn't hear, mainly because the blood was pounding in my ears.

The plan, if plan wasn't too grand a word for it, was to sit tight and let the guy make the first move. If that move looked like it might become an aggressive or threatening one, I'd crack him fast with the tyre jack and then make another plan.

Like I say, not exactly Napoleonic in strategy. Not that it mattered. The headlights rolled down into the car park and eased up flush with the driver's side of my car, top to tail, so close I couldn't have opened the door. By then I could see that the driver was smiling and that he had an unusually large and squarish head, a shock of curly hair that put me in mind of a clown's wig, and a face that wasn't practised at smiling. Maybe it was because I was expecting the worst, and maybe the size of his head had something to do with it, but that smile looked a lot like how I'd imagine a splitting atom might look.

He winked.

Then, still grinning, he placed a huge paw flat against his window, as if saying 'hello', so that only I could see the gun nestling there snug in his palm.

TWELVE

M y instinct was to floor it, put distance between Emily and that gun.

But there was nowhere to go. I was facing the right way, sure, and the guy would have to get his Peugeot turned before he could start following me, but the village was so quiet that he'd have no trouble picking me up again, and after that it'd be a pursuit in the dark along narrow roads I didn't know. And he very probably wouldn't be still smiling when he finally ran me to earth, or off the road.

The only thing in my favour – possibly – was that I had a nearly full tank of petrol, and could maybe outrun him that way.

Somehow it didn't seem likely. And anyway, I didn't fancy trying it with Emily flopping around in the back seat.

He was still smiling, gesturing now, pointing at the gun – some kind of automatic, a stubby little thing but lethal-looking all the same – and then shaking a forefinger. Telling me, I believed, that he wasn't planning on using it. Then the gun went away and he made a spiralling motion with his hand, telling me to roll down my window.

When we were face to face I could see he wasn't really smiling. At some point in the past he'd had the corners of his mouth slit and then been punched or kicked, so that he'd screamed or groaned and the cheeks had split a couple of inches on both sides, leaving pinkish scars. Which was why, probably, he gave off the clown vibe.

'I know you have a wee girl in the car,' he said. 'What I'm hoping is that means we both behave, do nothing stupid.'

'Then put that shit away.'

'No problem.' He nodded at my lap, where the tyre jack lay. 'I saw you go to the boot of the car, didn't know what you might be carrying.'

He was keeping his voice low, so as not to wake Emily. Or maybe he was more concerned about not attracting attention from the smokers perched on the wall above.

'What do you want?' I said.

'There's a man who'd like a chat.'

'What about?'

'He'll tell you himself. He's not too far away from here.'

'I kind of like it right here. It's bright, there's people around . . .'

'Seriously, all he wants is a chat.'

'Sorry. Like you said, my kid's back there. I'm not taking her anywhere.'

He thought that over. 'Can't say I blame you,' he said. 'Hold on.' He reached a phone off the passenger seat and dialled a number, then held his hand over his smiley mouth so I couldn't hear what he was saying. By now the smokers on the wall above were openly curious, looking down at the two cars parked top-to-toe in the nearly empty car park, both engines still running.

'OK,' he said. Then he passed across the phone.

'What?' I said.

'Tom Noone?'

'Who's this?'

'I could give you a name, Tom, but why would you think it was genuine?'

A Boston accent, this one harsher than Shay Govern's, even though he sounded amused at my naivety.

'What do you want?' I said.

'Like the man told you, I'd like to meet. For a chat.'

'About what?'

'Shay Govern.'

'What about him?'

'This gold mine he's planning.'

'I know nothing about it that I didn't read in the papers.'

'I find that hard to believe.'

'There's not much I can do about that.'

Silence. Then: 'I take it you're heading for Delphi, meeting up with our friend Shay.'

'That's the plan, yeah. He's expecting me first thing tomorrow.'

'Is he now?'

'He is.'

Another silence. Then: 'Seanie tells me you've a kid with you.'

'What about it?'

'A little girl.'

'So?'

'I'm only asking, Tom. I have two girls of my own. It's always nice to see a father spending time with his daughter.' A sigh (a *sigh*?) and then he said, 'You always think there'll be more time, don't you? And then you turn around and it's twenty years later and you realize that more time is the biggest con of the lot.'

I couldn't work out if he was turning maudlin or building towards an explicit threat. I said, 'Look, it's late and I need to get my girl to—'

'Sure, sure. But Tom? Listen, this chat – I'm talking about an exchange of information. OK? By which I mean, an exchange of information about Shay Govern.'

'That sounds fine by me. But there's no way I'm doing it now.'

'No, I understand, it's way past the girl's bedtime. How about we meet tomorrow, have some breakfast. I'm guessing you're taking the early ferry?'

'I haven't decided yet.'

'Well, there's a café not too far from where you are now, Belle's Kitchen, Seanie'll show you where it is. Say eight thirty? They do a fine Irish breakfast.'

'All right.'

'See you then. Put me back on to Sean.'

I handed the phone back, checked on the rear-view. Emily was wide awake and staring at Seanie, her eyes huge and round, wondering what was going on.

I said, 'Hon? Daddy's friend is going to show us where we can have breakfast in the morning. Isn't that nice of him?'

She nodded, but she didn't take her eyes off Seanie. She'd always been wary of clowns.

You couldn't accuse the Swilly View Guesthouse of false advertising. It was a house that took in guests, and when I looked out the window of our upstairs room the view was nothing but Swilly. I'd passed it almost as soon as I'd arrived in Rathmullan, one of a row of terraced houses facing across the road to the lough, which was now calm under a fat moon. Over on the other side Delphi was hunched in somewhere against the darkness of the far shore.

Mr Elliott, bald and stocky, had a broad Yorkshire accent as he welcomed us in, waving off my apology for arriving late – I'd got lost, I said, on the road from Letterkenny – and ushering me up the stairs. He'd put a camp bed in the room for Emily, but after he'd left, a little nonplussed and possibly even offended at the idea that we wouldn't be staying for breakfast in the morning, she asked if she could sleep in the double bed with me.

Not a problem. I got her teeth brushed and her Pet's Parade pyjamas on, then tucked her in under the heavy quilt.

'Is there time for a story?' she said.

'It'll have to be very quick.'

'That's fine.'

So we raced through a tale of princesses and dragons and zombies and laser swords – quite the postmodernist, our Emily, as most six-year-olds tend to be – and ten minutes later she was breathing deeply, lost in the pillows with the back of her hand thrown across her eyes.

Once I was sure she was asleep I locked the door and wedged a chair under the handle. Nothing that would keep out anyone who really wanted to get in, but at least it would work as an early-warning system. Then I took the laptop from the duffel and turned it on, sat on the bed. Checked Gmail first, and found I had seventeen emails, very few of which needed to be replied to immediately – a couple of movie screening invites, some PR stuff from book publicists, an upgrade offering from an Internet security firm, a short line from McFetridge in Toronto wondering if I was thinking of getting along to Bouchercon this year. In among them was a message from Martin.

> Tom –
> Quick one . . . I'm rereading Rendezvous at Thira and just got to the massacre part. There's four kids murdered in the book, not six. Not sure if this matters, and it probably doesn't, but thought you'd like to know.
> Cheers,
> M

The words popped into my mind before I had time to process them: *At least it's going down.*

I glanced across at Emily, fascinated as always by the moth-wing delicacy of her violet eyelids. At how fragile she was. I wondered how many, or how few, children needed to be murdered for an act to qualify as a massacre. One, certainly, was too few, but would two be enough? Would it need a minimum of three dead children before we could start calling it an atrocity?

I was being flippant, sure. Call it a defence mechanism, a way of putting distance between the sordid tale of murdered children and the sleeping beauty faintly snoring by my side.

I'd seen a photograph once, not long before Emily was born, a black-and-white taken somewhere in Russia in 1941, just after the Germans invaded. A perverse family portrait, in part because they were all women – two older women and three or four girls, from teenagers down to a little kid who couldn't have been more than four years old, who was staring back over her shoulder at the camera even as she clung to her mother's thigh. They were all undressed to their underwear, the older women and the teenagers visibly embarrassed, the expressions of the younger girls more curious than anything else. Behind them the rough ground was strewn with corpses, a handful of German soldiers standing around holding their weapons. A pitiful, horrifying sight. But what stayed with me long after I'd clicked the photograph closed was the one thing that wasn't in the picture: the man who'd taken the photograph, who'd ordered the women to strip, and then posed them just so, against the backdrop of their murdered fellow villagers or townspeople, knowing they only had moments to live.

What kind of man behaves that way?

The easy answer, I knew, was that he was insane, a sociopath or perhaps an ordinary soldier temporarily frenzied by blood-lust. Or an exceptionally motivated disciple of the Nazi doctrine, doing what any good Aryan son would do when confronted by the *untermensch* from the east.

The trouble with easy answers, of course, is they're too easy. The way they allow us to go easy on ourselves. There'd been no frenzy involved in creating that tableau. Cruelty, yes, on a scale you might describe as inhuman if you were keen to allow yourself the easy option of believing that the man who took that photograph was not of the same species as yourself. That he had, simply by virtue of being a German adult male abroad in Russia in 1941, sidestepped his way out of the human race and was now peering back through a camera lens at all he had left behind.

No, it was too easy. Whoever took that photograph was as human as I was, had very probably lain down on a bed beside his own children and told them rushed bedtime stories because they were going to bed a little later than usual that night, and had marvelled after at the sight of violet-tinged eyelids and tiny eye lashes on pudgy little rose-red cheeks. And had then gone out and posed a family of women in their underwear for a photograph in a field of corpses, and very likely afterwards put his camera to one side and picked up his gun and ripped those children apart.

Easy answers?

Fact is there may be no answers at all.

THIRTEEN

I must have dozed off because I woke up choking a little before six, when Emily, thrashing around in her sleep as she tried to free herself from the folds of the heavy quilt, caught me with a straight-arm smash across the throat.

I got her settled again, making sure her arms were outside the quilt this time, then lay there staring up at the damp stain on the ceiling that resembled, if you squinted, a skinny Africa. No matter how hard I stared and squinted, though, I couldn't persuade my mind to shut down – it kept jumping to images of a clown-looking goon pulling up beside my car, planting his huge paw against the glass, the stubby black automatic in his palm.

In the end, I got up, careful not to disturb Emily, and unplugged the phone, turned it on. It was a little on the early side, but I reckoned it wasn't a bad idea to ring a couple of contacts back home, see if anyone knew of a solid cop or two in the Letterkenny area who might be useful to touch base with, so I could make myself and my whereabouts known before I sat down to breakfast with Scanie the Clown's handler.

I'd already reconsidered by the time the phone had powered up and located a signal. If Kee wasn't playing it solo, there was every chance she'd put out an APB, which meant walking into a garda station wasn't the smartest move I could make.

The trouble with that kind of thinking was that the longer I mulled it over, the more I realized there *were* no smart moves.

I texted Martin, asking him to call back whenever he got a chance. He rang while I was in the bathroom.

'Tom?'

'Yeah,' I whispered. 'Listen, sorry for the early start.'

'No problem. What's wrong?'

'Can you talk?'

'Sure. Hold on a minute . . . What's that, hon?'

I heard a muffled murmur, and then Martin said, 'Jen says fuck you very much, and she's buying you a ticket for a one-way flight to Mars.'

'Tell her I'll take it.'

I heard the rustle of sheets and realized he was getting out of bed so as not to disturb Jen any further. It seemed like a good idea, so I said, 'Martin? I'll call you back in two minutes, OK?'

I was still dressed from the night before, so I moved the chair away and unlocked the bedroom door, then locked it again from the outside. Tiptoed down the stairs, slipped the deadbolt off the front door and went out into the street, across the road to the low wall on the other side. There were small gardens fringing the foreshore, then a wide beach and the Swilly itself. Beyond the orange streetlights it was still dark, although the sky away to the east was turning pearly grey.

I'd expected it to be cold, but it was actually quite mild. Even better news was the fact that there were no clown-looking goons watching the Swilly View Guesthouse.

'So what's up?' Martin said.

'I could do with someone to bounce a few ideas off.'

I heard the flick-clink of a Zippo, Martin exhaling. It had been nearly three years since I'd had a cigarette, and now I was practically drooling.

'Bounce away,' he said.

I gave it a shot, trying to untangle everything that had happened over the last few days, starting with Shay Govern and his desire to confess to the part he'd once played in murdering children. While I spoke I had a flash of what Jack Byrne's face must have looked like when I told him he'd need to get his skates on if he was planning to blackmail Govern, because the guy was hell-bent on telling the world himself. At the time it had been almost comical, the hardboiled private eye sideswiped by the idea that anyone might want to dish the dirt on themselves. Now it wasn't even remotely funny. Not with Gerard Smyth drying out on a slab.

'He's *dead*?' Martin said. 'The old guy?'

'The cop, Kee, she wanted me to identify the body. But there was no way I was dragging Emily down to the morgue. So then she started in about how I'm a person of interest, I was the last one to see Smyth alive.'

'Christ. So where's Emily now?'

'Upstairs.'

'She's still with you?'

'What else was I supposed to do?'

'You could've rung us, Tom. *We'd* have taken her.'

'There wasn't time.' I explained about Kee and the wardrobe.

'Holy fucking shit,' he breathed. 'So where's this Kee now?'

'I don't know.'

'Hold on,' he said. 'Where are *you* now?'

'It's probably best if I don't say.'

'Jesus.' Another clink-flick, Martin inhaling like it was the last smoke he'd ever have. Then: 'You think it was deliberate? The old guy, I mean.'

'I don't know.' I wanted to believe it was an accident, that an elderly man had simply lost his footing on a slippery towpath and toppled in. The kind of tiny tragedy that happens every day. Sad, yes, but not sinister. Until you start wondering about what an old man was doing wandering along a towpath late at night. 'I mean, he was hardly on the prowl for a tart, was he?'

And then there was the file. Gerard Smyth had gone into the canal before or after the file was stolen, and the sequence of events didn't really matter. What mattered was that unless it was the kind of massive coincidence I tend not to believe in, the two events were connected.

'But that doesn't make sense, Tom. If they already had the file, then why go to all the trouble of taking him out, involving the cops?'

It was a good question. No one had taken Gerard Smyth seriously enough to act on his queries and allegations before now. And even if it was the case that the spooks had heard he'd been waving his file around, that he was talking to a journalist and an ex-cop private investigator, surely all they had to do was throw a scare into him, mention the canal and ask if he'd ever learned to swim after that dunk he'd taken off a submarine into the waters of Lough Swilly.

Taking the file *and* putting Smyth away for keeps – that seemed crude, unnecessary. Not the kind of belt-and-braces approach I'd have expected from a crew that was slick enough to get in and out of an apartment and leave no trace of their coming or going.

'What are you saying?' Martin said. 'That they're *not* connected?'

'The events are, yeah. But if we're agreed that Smyth going into the canal was no accident, then there's two very different approaches here.'

Someone had broken into my apartment and lifted Smyth's file nice and smooth, I told Martin, leaving behind only an invisible warning for me to stay out of it. Then, someone else had gone the more direct route by bringing the hammer down on Gerard Smyth.

I heard him again, although this time it didn't sound anywhere near as pompous as the first time. *A dying man, if he is any kind of man, will live beyond the law*. Maybe at the end he'd decided to live beyond fear too, heard them out as they made their threats and then told them, in that wheezy gasp, fixing them with those rheumy eyes, to take a good long fuck at themselves.

I hoped he had. I really did.

Martin was smoking up a storm on the other end of the line. 'Tom,' he said, 'how come whoever broke in knew to come looking for the file in your apartment?'

'I'm guessing Smyth told them I had it.'

'Right. But how did they hear about it in the first place?'

And that was when I realized that, in among all the missed calls and text messages, one caller was notable by his absence.

Jack Byrne.

We talked it through. Had Jack Byrne tried to hack in somewhere he shouldn't and been tracked down? Possibly. Equally likely was a scenario in which Jack the Player tried to play a few more angles, covering his bets, and dropped a nugget of information in someone's lap that bumped us all up into the big leagues and nudged Gerard Smyth off the towpath into the canal.

'And you haven't heard from him since,' Martin said.

'Not since yesterday morning, when he sent me Smyth's address.'

'Doesn't look good, does it?'

'No, it doesn't.'

I could hear the slappity-slap of Martin's slippers as he shuffled around, the sound of running water as he prepped a coffee. 'The big question,' he said, 'is why it's all kicked off now.'

There was that. Smyth had put in an official request to the British and German embassies months ago, and got no more attention than a brush-off and a pat on the head. What had changed since then to justify the murder of an old man to keep his account of an ancient war crime under wraps?

'Shay Govern,' Martin said.

'Right. Because he wants to go public with it.'

'And the guy's worth a fortune. An American philanthropist. I mean, he'd be missed. So they can't go dunking him in any canals, can they?'

'I don't suppose they can.'

'And the same goes for you, and Emily, if you're standing there beside him. Am I right?'

'That's the theory, yeah.'

'I don't like it,' he said.

'I'm not exactly turning cartwheels myself.'

'I mean,' he said, 'I don't like you dragging Emily into it.'

Martin was a good guy, always keen to avoid causing offence, even accidentally. But he had his principles and I'd crossed a line.

'I didn't have much choice at the time,' I said. It sounded weak even to me.

'I get that, Tom. Heat of the moment and so forth. But now?'

It was a bad time, I believed, to mention that I'd be having breakfast with Seanie the Clown's handler, the guy with the inside track on Shay Govern. 'It is what it is, Martin.'

'OK, but it doesn't have to be. Tell me where you are, I'll come get her.'

'Seriously?'

'Yeah.'

'It's a bit of a hike.'

'Doesn't matter. Where are you?'

The likelihood that Kee or anyone else was listening in was slim. So I told him.

'Grand,' he said. 'Traffic should be light enough on a Sunday. I'll be there in about four, five hours.'

'I owe you big-time, Martin.'

'Yes you do. Just don't do anything else stupid until I get there, OK?'

'I'll try. Oh, and Martin?'

'What?'

'One last favour . . .'

It was after seven by then, the sunrise-pink tendrils creeping in across the eastern end of the lough. I went back inside and upstairs. Emily didn't appear to have so much as moved while I was gone. I showered and changed and got the kettle on and then checked my email.

Martin had been busy. He'd scanned Gerard Smyth's testimony and sent it on as an attachment, as I'd asked, but he'd also
scanned and attached the atrocity chapter from *Rendezvous at Thira*.

'Might be worth cross-referencing,' was his short note.

He was nothing if not thorough, Martin Banks. There and then
I swore I'd never again query his nit-picking on my tax return.

I made a mug of instant coffee and wedged myself into the
armchair, clicked on the first document. I'd already skimmed the
story on Friday evening and given it a closer read later that night,
but if Seanie the Clown's ringmaster was planning to give me
inside dope on Shay Govern and the gold mine, some of it might
touch on the part Govern played in the massacre. I wanted to
have the facts clear in my head, be able to contradict him if it
looked like he was sending me astray.

I flicked down through the first few pages, the David Copperfield
stuff and the voyage of the mysterious U-43 to Lough Swilly,
Smyth taking a header into the lough, picking up his story near
the bottom of the seventh page.

> I remember very little of my first days on Delphi, most of
> which were spent asleep. If I dreamt, I have no memory
> of the dreams. I have recollections of being woken, and
> hauled into a sitting position, and when they moved me I
> thought it was torture and cried out that I knew nothing.
> My voice was hoarse. My muscles were cramped knots, the
> joints seized solid. When I felt strong hands on my legs
> and shoulders, pressing and kneading, and realized they
> only meant to massage me, I wept.
>
> They fed me like a child, bowl and spoon. Porridge and
> mutton broth, and a new stranger's face each time. I grew
> stronger, or less weak. Eventually I was able to walk about
> the narrow room, a stable loft swept bare, head down and
> shoulders hunched so as not to knock my head against the
> steeply pitched rafters. My bed was a mattress of straw ticks
> bound under a tarpaulin in the corner, the blankets soft
> wool. From the high window in the far wall I could see a
> small rough pasture, and beyond that a track that wound
> down the slope to the village below, the tiny harbour with
> its breakwater of massive stones.
>
> They had washed and returned my clothes, the sleeveless

shirt and woollen jumper, the oilskin trousers and sou'wester I'd been wearing when I went overboard. There was a comfort in their familiarity, although I was fully aware that a combatant discovered in enemy territory wearing civilian clothing could be shot for a spy. I knew that Ireland, the Free State part of the island, was a neutral country, but at the time, uncertain of the geography, I could not be sure where I had been pulled ashore. Either way, my war was over for the time being. It was my belief that the islanders would send me off to a prison or a POW camp as soon as I was fit to travel, and the prospect was not a terrible one. If I was to be treated half as well in a camp as I had been treated by the islanders, my stay – temporary, I was sure, given how quickly Europe was falling to blitzkrieg – would be endured without too much hardship.

But those were long and lonely hours. I wondered how my disappearance had been reported, if my wife believed me dead. How my children had taken the news. I had only one mission then, to get a message to my wife that I was alive and being treated well, but the islanders did not make it easy for me. They came in rotation, and I wondered if they did so to suit their own needs and work, or to spread the blame thinly should they be punished for taking me in. I spoke very little English, and when they spoke among themselves – they always came in pairs – they spoke in a language I had never heard before. Gaelic, of course. They were helpful but they were cautious. The woman who treated the wound on the back of my skull had kindly eyes but never smiled. The man with the limp who draped my arm across his shoulders and walked me the length of the loft for the first time remained stiff and awkward throughout. The schoolteacher, heavily pregnant, who told me her name and tried to speak a few words of German, had piercing blue eyes devoid of compassion. I gave her my name and tried to explain what had happened, but I had less English than she had German, and the conversation quickly died. The only islander to come more than once, a thickly bearded man who had to duck to get through the door, seemed to be the man they all deferred to, but he stood back against the wall beside the door, observing, and never spoke.

On the fifth day, in the early afternoon, the bearded man returned, bringing with him another man. He was dressed like the islanders, in a heavy woollen pullover and a collarless striped shirt, and his unshaven face was wind-burnt brown, but the flat cap rested on a thatch of coarse blond hair and when he spoke in Gaelic to the bearded man I heard an accent different to the rest.

Then he turned to me. Between us we possessed enough English and German to hold a stiff conversation.

'Are you well?' he said.

'Well enough. Please thank your friend for me.'

'I will. Who are you and why are you here?'

I gave him my name and explained that I had been washed overboard from a submarine on the night before I had been found by the fishing boat.

'Where?' he said.

'I cannot tell you.'

'Why was the U-boat in the lough?'

'I cannot tell you.'

'What *can* you tell me?'

'I am a sailor. I have no important information.'

'You learned nothing on the journey here?'

'You understand that I can tell you nothing. Yes?'

He patted my shoulder. 'I understand that you are a brave man,' he said. Then he broke away to speak with the bearded man at the back wall, shaking his head while speaking. Their voices were low, the bearded man's a rumble, but I heard and recognized, as I was no doubt meant to, one phrase the blond man used: *agent provocateur.*

He strode back down the room, his head angled to one side. 'These people mean you no harm,' he said. 'But they mean no harm to come to them. If you are found to be a spy, it may go badly for them.'

'I am no spy.'

'But there was an agent on the U-boat. Yes?'

'I can tell you nothing.'

'I think you can tell me something.'

The blond man explained that the islanders' mayor – the bearded man – was conflicted. That there was division between the locals. Some wanted to sail me across to the mainland, put me ashore and leave me to my own devices, so that I could take my chances with the Irish authorities. I would, he explained, be arrested as an illegal alien and interned indefinitely, or at least until my identify could be confirmed.

There were others among the islanders, however, who had bitter stories of how they and their people had been treated by the English, memories of beatings and burnings and murder and starvation. They wanted to help me, their enemy's enemy, to escape and return to Germany.

And there were others still who suggested that I should be allowed to stay on the island for as long as I chose. Two others, the blond man said with a wink and a quick smile, and both were young women.

I told him that I would prefer to go home to my wife and children.

'I understand,' he said. 'If you help us, we will help you. But first you must help us.'

What I understood was that the blond man was not an islander, but that he had taken on the appearance of one. His presence on the island and his knowledge of German, as sparse as it was, and his interrogation of me, as gentle as it was, all pointed to the fact that the man was a British agent.

Up to that point I had been treated far better than I'd had any right to expect, and I further expected that my refusal to answer the blond man's questions meant that it was likely I would be treated more harshly. I was a sailor, not trained to resist interrogation, but I was no traitor, and nor would I easily volunteer information that might result in the capture of my comrades.

'I cannot help you,' I said.

The blond man nodded, as if he had expected nothing less. 'Then let me help you,' he said. 'A man called Klaus Rheingold was arrested in Derry last night. The city of Derry, yes? When he was arrested he was carrying papers identifying him as Sam Davidson, a citizen of South Africa. Have you heard those names before?'

'No.'

'I think you have. When is the U-boat returning?'

'I do not know.'

'I think you do. Please consider my questions again.'

He broke away to speak with the bearded man again. When he returned his tone was sympathetic as he explained that I was in a precarious position. No one knew I was on the island. If what I said about being swept overboard was true, then it was likely I had already been posted as missing, presumed lost.

I understood the threat. All I could do was repeat that I was a sailor and that I had no knowledge of any secret mission. I also said that if I had been captured by enemy forces, I was entitled to be treated as a prisoner of war.

The blond man patted me on the shoulder again but this time he took a handful of my pullover. He explained that I had by my own admission sailed into the waters of a neutral country on a covert military mission and had been wearing civilian clothing when captured. Those actions meant that I was not entitled, the blond man said, to be considered a normal prisoner of war.

I pointed to his own clothes, and reminded him that he wore no uniform.

'No,' he said, 'but I am not at war.'

It was a curious remark, given our circumstance, but then the blond man asked about my family, my children. I said yes, I had a boy and a baby girl.

'Then think of them. Your boy and girl. This war is not being fought between you and I, but against them.'

He told me he would return in two hours. He asked me to search my memory and think very seriously about his questions. If I did not tell him when the U-boat was due to return, I would be taken out and shot.

It was at this point Smyth went wandering a little off topic, talking about how it felt to be threatened with death for not telling what he did not know. It struck him as being in some way an existential dilemma, although whether the notion occurred to him then or when he sat down to write his testimony was hard to say. At the time he was simultaneously 'terrified and enraged' as he paced the loft, trying to decide if the blond man was bluffing. Eventually, helpless and hopeless, he crawled on to the mattress.

As the idea of never seeing his children again crept in on him

Smyth began to cry, at first quietly, ashamed at his weakness, then convulsing in racking sobs. He imagined himself being dragged out of the loft to his death, hands bound, and rather than blink it away he tried to fix the image, to see it and himself clearly, so that he would remember how a man should behave in his final moments. And it was this hopelessness, the understanding that he was so totally at the mercy of the blond man, that allowed, gradually, for a final hope to emerge. He imagined himself being dragged to the very brink, forced to his knees with a gun to his head, the hammer cocked. It was in these last few seconds, he believed, that his only hope lay – that the blond man would accept that Smyth was telling the truth, or more precisely that he had no truth to tell, no knowledge of Klaus Rheingold or the U-boat's movements, and spare him.

It was all moot. Hours passed – each minute a new torture – but the blond man did not return.

I got up from the armchair and checked on Emily, who was now drooling on to the pillow, strands of hair stuck to the slime. I got her turned on to her other side and slipped a fresh pillow underneath her head, knowing that as soon as I stepped away from the bed she would turn back on to her favoured side.

I made a fresh coffee and went back to the armchair. As I picked up Smyth's testimony again I recalled the picture on Kee's phone, those puffy eyes and the greeny-blue pallor, and it occurred to me how bizarre it was to be reading it now – that the first time I'd read Smyth's account, flicking through the pages for the juicy details, Gerard Smyth had been alive. Now that he was dead, and very probably because he had written down those words, I felt as if I should be ignoring his stiff phrasing and awkward syntax and focusing only on his story, the importance of what he had to say. But I was just too exhausted right then, too stressed about needing to watch over Emily and feeling guilty at putting her in the firing line, to be capable of the finer emotions. Instead it all felt pathetic and pointless.

I would be taken out and shot . . .

But he wasn't. Gerard Smyth hadn't died on Delphi Island in 1940, executed in the mistaken belief that he possessed a truth worth knowing. He'd gone on to live to a grand old age and drown in a Dublin canal. His words hadn't mattered a damn to a single soul while he was alive. Now that he was dead, they were the only thing about him worth knowing. And while I hated the idea of owing him anything, he had quite literally put his story into my hands, and at my request. The very least I could do was read it in the spirit it was written.

The first I knew of German commandoes on the island was when one of them kicked in the door of the stable loft and pointed a sub-machine gun at my head. The man was masked, wearing a hood that hid all but his eyes, and for a split second all I saw was the gun barrel. In that moment I believed I was to be shot by the islanders as a brutal but simple solution to the problem of what to do with me.

Then I heard *'Raus!'* and *'Schnell!'*, a muffled bawling from behind the mask. My next thought was that the man was a raider in a rescue party, dispatched from the submarine to take me off the island. Then I wondered why he didn't recognize me.

And then I realized why my first instinct was that I was to be shot by the locals. The sub-machine gun was a Schmeisser, but he was dressed like a local. The black mask and the gun aside, he looked like a fisherman. One thing was certain: this man had not come from the U-43.

Still lying on the mattress, my hands above my head, I gave him my name and rank. The man seemed to stiffen, then beckoned me to my feet, extending a hand to help; but as I was getting up, he stepped in, reversed the Schmeisser and smashed the butt into the side of my head. I collapsed to the floor, then felt myself being dragged up again, shoved towards the door and down the wooden steps. The blow had left me dizzy and reeling, my left eye swelling closed. The man kicked and pushed me down through the rough pasture and into the village, then along a dark alleyway until we emerged into a small square fronting the harbour. A kind of bowl, or amphitheatre, dominated by a massive slab of outcropped rock, at the foot of which was tucked a tiny whitewashed church. I had the bizarre sense of intruding upon a pilgrimage, given the number of people who had gathered in silence near the foot of the steps that led up to the church, but the man in the mask was not one for piety. He marched me straight across the square and past the people to the bottom of the steps, then struck me again with the butt of his gun, this time between the shoulder blades. I went down hard.

I lay there twisted and winded and watched as the masked man went up the steps and touched another man on the shoulder. The second man, also masked, was dressed like the first apart from the knee-length black boots into which he had tucked his woollen pants. Behind them, huddled in the doorway of the church, was a group of six distraught children who were faced by two men with Schmeissers, the barrels pointed at the ground. The whitewashed church seemed to glow in the moonlight, although the square itself was shrouded in gloom. It was only then, as I glanced around, that I realized the crowd assembled in the square were all adults – the parents or older relatives, I presumed, of the children. A pitiful gathering, some supporting one another with arms around shoulders, others staring defiantly, eyes bright and jaws hard. A mother called out in a broken voice to a weeping girl who could not have been more than four years old, and was immediately shushed, although there was little comfort offered in the shushing. Beyond them, at the head of the alleyways that fed into the square, with another holding a position at the head of the pier, were more men, all armed with sub-machine guns. All were masked, and none wore any uniform nor any identifying marks I could see.

Now the second man, the one wearing the black boots, came down the steps. He stood over me and held out a hand. I grasped it and was pulled to my feet.

He gave his name as Richter but otherwise offered no rank or any other detail. As a Dane I often had trouble in differentiating between regional dialects but he sounded thickly Berliner. He was tall, an inch or two more than six feet. The eyes, which were all I could see of his face, were wide-set and seemed dark blue in the strange light.

I gave my name and rank again. 'A sailor?' he said, and I quickly explained how I came to be on the island. Richter nodded and without any discernible change of expression in his eyes told me that it all sounded like a deserter's excuse.

I asked if it was likely, if I was a deserter, that I would

still be wearing the clothes I wore while on duty. He considered that, then said, 'Perhaps not.' Then he asked if I knew when the U-43 would return. I told him that lower ranks weren't given that kind of information. He asked then what I knew about the movements of Klaus Rheingold.

I told him that I had been interrogated by a blond man I believed to be an Englishman and a British agent, who had told me of Rheingold's arrest in the city of Derry the night before.

'Morrigan?' Richter said.

The name meant nothing to me.

'And this blond man – is he in the square now?'

I looked again at the group of adults. 'No,' I said.

'But he was here today?'

'This afternoon, yes.'

'*Gut.*' Richter ordered me to stay close, to stand by to identify the Englishman when he was discovered. He had no weapon to spare with which to arm me, even if his orders allowed for it, but I would be evacuated when they left and my account of how I had come to be on Delphi would be investigated by the appropriate authorities.

The last thing I wanted was a weapon. I was under no illusions as to why the children had been isolated as hostages.

I asked Richter for permission to speak, and told him that the islanders had taken good care of me, and that that should count for something. It was also true, I said, that many of them, according to the Englishman, were sympathetic to the German cause.

'Then they should need little persuasion,' he said. He mounted the steps again, went to the huddled group of children and took a young boy by the wrist. He led the child forward. The adults below seemed to shudder as one, a ripple running through the small crowd.

'Who speaks for you?' Richter called out in English. Heavily accented, muffled by the mask, his voice nevertheless carried through the square. After a moment the large bearded man, the mayor, stepped forward.

'We know the blond Englishman is on the island,' Richter told him. 'If he is not here in one hour, this child will suffer the consequences.'

Shouts and wails, a piercing scream. An older woman collapsed to the cobbles. Two men broke from the group, pushing forward past the mayor, both of them protesting or volunteering to take the place of the children – it was hard to say, because as they did so a harsh chattering broke out, deafening in the enclosed square. When the echoes died away everyone remained frozen in place, staring at the church doorway. One of the men guarding the children had fired into the air, over the heads of the adults, spattering the upper wall across the way and shattering windows.

'If anyone moves towards the children again,' Richter announced, holding the weeping boy's wrist aloft, 'this child will be shot.' He consulted his watch. 'The hour has begun. I advise you to hurry.'

They turned as one on the bearded man and began haranguing him and jabbing accusatory fingers, some of which were pointed in my direction. Where before there had been anger and fear, now there was terror, and panic, the voices shrill. But if the babble was indecipherable, their message was clear: they held the bearded man responsible, perhaps for his dallying with the blond man, the English agent, or perhaps for not dropping me back in the lough as soon as I had arrived. He seemed to accept their verdict, a head taller than any of them, nodding and holding up his hands as if in surrender, palms showing.

At this point I was distracted by Richter, who had gone down on one knee beside the little boy, and had taken a pinch of the whimpering child's nightshirt between thumb and forefinger and was holding it to the boy's nose, encouraging him to blow. His voice was low as he told the boy not to worry, it was simply a game, one that might seem frightening now but would reveal itself as a joke on the adults. Did the boy want to play a joke on his elders? The boy snuffled and nodded, uncertain. It was clear that he did not believe Richter, but was desperate to cling to any suggestion that what was happening was not real. 'Good boy,' said Richter, and ruffled the child's hair. Then he propelled him towards the gaggle of children huddled in the church doorway and stood up, inclining his head at one of the guards.

When I looked back at the group of adults, the bearded

man was gone. Leaderless, with no one to serve as a lightning rod for their rage, they were drifting apart, some
weeping quietly, others shaking their heads or staring
blankly at the children at the top of the steps. Despite all
that had happened they seemed stunned into disbelief, as if
they were somehow experiencing a collective nightmare
from which they would surely awake. An eerie stillness
prevailed. There was hardly a breeze off the harbour to
disturb the stifling sense of anticipation. Even the children
had fallen quiet. I felt nauseous, my throat muscles
constricting. The men guarding the alleyways appeared rigid
with expectation. The man who had found me in the loft
was breathing hard through his nose where he stood a couple
of yards away, knuckles white where they gripped his
Schmeisser, fingers clawed around the barrel and the butt,
all but the forefinger of his right hand, which was tapping
incessantly against the metal, some Morse code message
he appeared to be unaware he was sending out.

He stiffened as a woman stepped forward in the square,
her hands joined and laid flat upon her head. She stood
tilted back, feet splayed, her rounded stomach a kind of
white flag – it was the schoolteacher, heavily pregnant, and
offering to comfort the children. Richter considered this
from the top of the steps, then nodded and went down to
meet her, giving her his hand and helping her to climb. As
she went up the steps she spoke to him in a confiding tone,
so low that I caught only the phrase 'the Geneva Convention'.
He answered her, as he released her hand and ushered her
towards the children, by saying that she might want to take
up the issue with her government in Dublin, if they ever
decided to take a side.

She made no reply, but went to the children with her
arms open, going down on one knee and gathering them in.

It was as courageous and foolhardy a gesture as I had
ever witnessed. She must have known that Richter was
asking for the impossible. If the blond man was, as seemed
now very likely, an English agent, he was duty bound to
refuse the bearded man, even if the man managed to track
him down in the hour allowed. The fate of a handful of
children, perhaps even that of the entire village, was not his

responsibility. In placing her unborn child in front of Richter's guns, was she hoping to appeal to his humanity? To remind him of how truly barbaric his proposal was?

She knew nothing.

Richter now ordered two of his men to round up the remaining adults in the square – I counted fifteen as they passed – and herd them up the steps and into the church. One man, dressed in a shabby bathrobe, stepped out of the line and approached Richter, his arms held wide. He identified himself as the priest, Father Cahill, and offered himself and five other men as hostages in place of the children. Richter declined, telling the priest that his courage had been noted, but that his sacrifice would not be required for now. He told the priest to go into his church and comfort his people as best he could, that his greatest test was upon him. He further told him that he should only pray, that any attempt to overpower or disarm his men resulting from a plan hatched in the church would result in the slaughter of them all, adults and children alike. He understood, he said, that the priest was predisposed to believe in fairytales and unlikely reversals in fortune, but that this particular night would not be a good one in which to put his faith in miracles.

The priest was the last to enter the church. The doors were locked. Then began the waiting.

I have never known time to stand still in that way. It was as if the world had paused to glance this way and now held its breath, shocked into silence by the depth of Richter's depravity. And yet the minutes flew. The men were nervy as they paced back and forth at their stations, clockwork toys with erratic mechanisms, jerky and repetitive as they checked their weapons and adjusted their masks, aiming their guns down the shadowy alleys and doing what they could to take their minds off what was to come.

The only man who did not check his watch during that time was Richter. He sauntered around the square with his hands clasped behind his back, offering encouragement here, a word of advice there. But even Richter was affected by the mood, the sense of dread. Not once did he raise his voice to the point where it was audible at the top of the steps.

It was eight minutes off the hour when the blond man

appeared. We heard him first, announcing his presence as he came down the alleyway closest to the church, calling out that he was unarmed and asking for the senior officer to make himself known so that he could surrender. Richter did so, moving to the centre of the square, then ordered the man nearest the Englishman to search him for hidden weapons. The blond man did not resist, standing with his hands clasped to the back of his head, his eyes on Richter. When they were satisfied he was unarmed, Richter pointed to the house beside the church. This, at least, was a matter of some relief, as it meant that what would happen next would not be witnessed by the children. Then I realized Richter was beckoning me on, that I was expected to join them. A jolt in my lower back from the barrel of a Schmeisser informed me that it was not a request I could refuse.

Inside the house the room was low-ceilinged and dimly lit, a turf fire smouldering in the grate. As the Englishman was lashed to a wooden chair I wondered if I was expected to take part in what was to follow, as a way of proving my credentials. Instead, Richter asked me to confirm that the Englishman – the Tommy, he called him – was the agent who had interrogated me. I said that I had no proof that he was an agent, but that he was the man who had questioned me in the stable loft. Richter then turned to the Englishman.

'Tommy,' he said, 'you know what we need to know. You can save us time and yourself pain if you tell us now.'

I was in no doubt the Englishman was afraid. There was something shrunken about him, as if he was drawing into himself, attempting to protect something valuable at his core. He held himself steady but there was an unnatural stillness to his eyes as he told Richter that he was an archae-ologist living on Delphi since 1939, excavating an ancient Celtic site on the southern tip of the island. Any of the villagers could confirm this fact.

'That may well be true, Tommy. What is also true is that you are a British agent with the code name Morrigan.'

'Not true.'

'As you already know, because you told our friend here this afternoon, Klaus Rheingold was arrested last night in Derry. I assume he has been questioned?'

'I know nothing about any of this.'

'I believe you do but we are wasting time. What I want to know is when the U-boat is returning, and where it will arrive.'

'I don't know that.'

'I find that hard to believe, Tommy.'

'It's the truth.'

'Very well.' Richter glanced up at the masked man standing behind the Tommy. The man placed his machine gun on the table, then stepped forward and wrapped his arms around the Tommy's head, holding him rigid. Richter reached into his pants pocket and took out two simple tools, a pair of pliers and a knife with a serrated edge. He put the pliers on the table and held up the knife. An ugly blade, the kind used to gut fish. 'This is on your own head, Tommy,' he said. 'I give you one last chance to tell us what we need to know.'

The Tommy's eyes were bulging, either in fear or because of the pressure exerted by the man half-strangling him. He tried to shake his head.

Richter stepped forward and pinched the Tommy's earlobe. Then he began to saw.

For a moment I am frozen in place, stunned by the savagery of the act – because an act is how it seems to me now, one staged by flickering candlelight to give it an ancient weight. When the blood starts to spurt the man behind me makes a gagging sound behind his mask, and when I back away towards the door, pushing him aside, he follows.

Outside the air is cool and clear, and in our hurry to leave we have forgotten to shut the door. The Englishman's scream is shrill on the night air and goes shivering through the hushed village. It ascends rapidly to reach an agonized pitch, sharp as gunshot, then fades as quickly in tremulous sobs. Now there is a shocked silence. The masked men ringing the square glance quickly at one another, then begin scanning the cliffs above the village for possible threats and reprisals.

The second scream was louder still, and throbbed with desperation. To endure pain is one thing, because even a child knows that pain is an inevitable consequence of life, and suffering has its own logic. But where there is an awareness of no possibility of relief, when pain, deliberately inflicted, exists for its own sake, then the mind too suffers the agonies. There was in that scream, and those that followed, a note of helplessness that infected the children. Soon the little group was a bedlam of wails and moans and screeching, an anarchic symphony of despair that rose and fell in tandem with the prisoner's, and yet never loud enough to drown him out entirely.

How long did it last? Impossible to say. No one checked their watch to measure off the minutes, because to do so would confirm that the torture had gone on that long, and had yet to end. One of the masked men, the one stationed at the head of the alleyway leading to the harbour, went down on one knee and half-turned away, tugging up his mask to vomit on to the cobbles. The others saw and tried not to see, and took a tighter grip of their weapons. A suppressed rage, sour as barracks sweat, was palpable in the square.

Had the adults not begun to sing inside the church, events might have unfolded very differently. There were many nights, long after the war was over, when I wondered if such a scenario might not have been for the best – if the Englishman, as cruel as it sounds, had died under torture without revealing what he knew. Not simply because the death of one man is preferable to the slaughter of children, but because it might have pre-empted the possibility of the massacre. Richter, had he any experience in the matter, would have known that no one resists torture. Strength and courage might help a man to hold out for longer than even he himself expects, but in the end, and regardless of training or loyalty or love, everyone breaks. Had the Englishman died it would have confirmed that Richter's mission was pointless, that the information he sought was not to be had.

I have wondered many times over the years if Richter would have accepted that conclusion. If at that point he could have allowed for the possibility that his mission was doomed even before it began. If he was even entitled, according to his orders, to cut his losses and depart. It is difficult to say. It was not inevitable that Richter, having failed with the Englishman, would turn his attention to the villagers. But having travelled so far with the Tommy and left so much behind, Richter had very little left to lose. Did the power corrupt him so fully? Was it something as petty as frustration that tipped him over the edge? Was it the stink of blood?

The singing begins hesitantly, with a single hoarse voice.

'*Báidín Fheilimí d'imigh go Gabhla . . .*'

A simple line, repetitive, a sea shanty. Other voices take it up.

'*Báidín Fheilimí is Feilimí ann . . .*'

Low at first, now rising in intensity, the words coming together in a quavering harmony.

'*Báidín Fheilimí d'imigh go Gabhla, báidín Fheilimí is Feilimí ann . . .*'

At first I believe they are singing to drown out the screams coming from the house next to the church, a lullaby to comfort the children, who are now themselves bawling in terror. But as the schoolteacher marshals them, encouraging them to sing along with their parents, I understand that they are singing to support the tortured man, singing in solidarity, employing the only weapon at their disposal: contempt.

The door to the house bursts open and Richter storms out already roaring orders. But it is not his rage that is terrifying: behind him the second masked man drags the Tommy into the square, the pair of them trailing a stench of sweat and blood and singed flesh and fresh shit. One look at the prisoner, before I turn away with bile surging hot and bitter into my throat, confirms that whatever will follow will be terrible beyond my most—

'Daddy?'

Emily was stirring, sitting up with an arm draped across her forehead, blinking as she tried to work out where I was in the dimly lit room.

'I'm right here, love,' I said.

FOURTEEN

'I thought you were gone,' Emily said, sounding nasal and muffled, the way she always does when she wakes.

'Afraid not,' I said, lying down on the bed and cuddling in around her. 'Your stinky old dad is still here, stinking out the whole room.'

'Your *breath* is stinky,' she muttered, but she shuffled backwards into the cuddle and closed her eyes again. When she was fully awake I took her to the bathroom, and we brushed our teeth and then got dressed. She played with her fashion princess Barbie while I got us packed, and then we went downstairs and settled the bill with Mr Elliott, there being no sign of Mrs Elliott, who was – presumably – in the kitchen and responsible for the delicious aroma of Ulster fry wafting through the house.

'Daddy?' Emily said as I strapped her into the booster seat.

'Yes, love?'

'I had a bad dream.'

'Really? What was it about?'

'Clowns.'

I kissed her on the head, for luck, as was my habit when driving with Emily in the car, then went around and got into the driver's seat. 'Clowns aren't scary, are they?' I said. 'They're funny.'

Rathmullan was a little livelier that morning. I counted at least three pedestrians as we drove along the shore road, aiming for the pier.

'Daddy?'

'What?'

'Clowns can't get into *our* house, can they?'

'No they can't, love.'

'If a clown got into our house, what would you do?'

'Well, I'd give him a kick in the butt. Kick him all the way to the moon.'

She giggled at that. 'In a rocket?'

'No, he'd just fly up there.'

'Oh, Daddy,' she sighed. 'Don't you know there's no grabity in space?'

'Really?' *Grabity*. My heart gave a soft kind of twist. 'Who told you about grabity?'

'Mommy's Peter. He went to the sun in a rocket.'

'Wow. I didn't know Peter was an astronaut.'

'Did you ever go to the sun, Daddy?'

'Not yet, love. I was waiting until you were old enough, so we could go together.'

I turned up towards the café, pulled in and got parked.

'Hey, Dad?'

'Yes, love?'

'Jake says if you go to the sun you'll burn into nothing.'

Jake, her cousin, a couple of years older and obsessed with *Star Wars*, Minecraft and doom of all stripes and shades.

'Did he now?'

'Yeah. Why didn't Mommy's Peter burn into nothing when *he* went to the sun?'

'Well, he was probably wearing a special space suit.'

'Jake says he was telling lies.'

I got out of the car, went around to Emily's side and helped her out, then hunkered down in front of her. 'You like Mommy's Peter, don't you?'

She took her time, probably wondering if she should tell me what I wanted to hear, but then she nodded.

'OK,' I said. 'So maybe he was just telling you funny stories about the sun because he knew you'd like to hear them.'

'Are funny stories lies?'

'A little bit. But they're not bad lies.'

'Oh.'

'Listen, Emily?' I stood up and took her little hand in mine, led her along the street towards Belle's Kitchen. 'We're going to have breakfast now, in this café. But Daddy needs to talk to a man while we're eating. Is that OK?'

'The clown man?'

'No, not the clown man. His friend.'

'Is *he* a clown?'

'I doubt it very much, love. Now, what would you like for breakfast? Pancakes?'

'Croissants,' she said. 'But warm ones.'

Emily had two warm croissants with a glass of milk. I had the large fry with extra sausage and a pot of coffee. Francis – 'But call me Franco, everyone else does' – had a cup of Earl Grey tea and a blueberry muffin, which he picked at while I ate.

Of Seanie the Clown there was nary a sign.

Belle's Kitchen had the look of an American diner, longer than it was wide and lined on one wall with cubicles of bright red faux-leather seating, a coffee machine hissing steam behind the counter. Franco hadn't been hard to spot, the only likely candidate, sitting with his back to the far wall at the table farthest from the door, although the fact that he was wearing the gilet favoured by the horsey set caused me to hesitate until he waved me over. Once the introductions were made, and the food was served, I cued up some Adele on my phone and gave Emily the ear buds. She couldn't believe her luck – music and croissants and breakfast in a café. She sat Barbie upright on one side of her plate and tucked in, dabbing her hunks of croissant into a pool of honey.

'You know who I am,' Franco said. The Boston accent, for some reason, was less harsh in person than it had been on the phone. Maybe he'd been forcing it last night, trying to make a point.

'I'm guessing you're Shay's brother,' I said.

The resemblance was unmistakable. He was younger by more than ten years but it was Franco who had the look of a crude prototype to the fully formed man.

'What has he told you?'

'About you? Nothing.'

That didn't seem to surprise him. 'I'm the CFO of Govern Industries,' he said.

I forked home some sausage and toast, chewed it around. When it was down the hatch I said, 'And?'

'I'm just clarifying, Tom.'

'Great.' I lowered my voice. 'So while we're clarifying a few things, let me clarify for you that if anyone ever waves a gun around my child again I'll rip his fucking throat out. Are we clear?'

My father had a phrase when he was talking about a certain kind of man, a serious man, a man not to be messed around. *A hardy joker*, he'd say, the corner of his mouth turning down.

Franco Govern was a hardy joker. Somewhere in his late sixties, with a head that reminded me of the time Rachel and I had taken the three-month-old Emily on a holiday in the south of England and I'd found an arrow flint on Chesil Beach. Blunt and rounded at the back, coarsely struck into sharper points towards the front. He'd shaved his head to a fine stubble, hoarfrost on a skull, but it was the eyes that gave you pause, wide-set and grey, like I imagine an old wolf's eyes should be. They'd seen it all, those eyes, but as calm as he appeared to be as he sat slumped in his seat, both hands in his lap, he never stopped watching, looking, assessing.

I'd met a few of his kind before on my travels. Sat across a table with a tape recorder running and knew, just *knew*, they were capable of doing what they believed needed to be done, and never think of it again.

Which is why I had to put it out there early. Draw a line in the sand about Seanie, or any other clown, playing the pistolero. Franco would have known just by looking at me that I wasn't any kind of hard man. What he had to believe was that I could be, just once, if I needed to be.

'I'll be sure to pass that on,' he said.

I chewed some toast and he worked on pretending he was taking my threat seriously and Emily dabbed up some honey on her chunk of croissant. She had a snotty nose and crumbs glued to the corners of her mouth but I left her to it, waiting for Franco to make the next move.

'Tell me about this book Shay has you writing,' he said.

If he knew that much he probably knew a lot more. 'Are you worried you're in it?' I said.

'Call me curious.'

I considered that as I forked up some sausage, tucked it away. When I'd swallowed I said, 'As I understood it, you were the one who had information for me.'

'Let's just say I hate repeating myself. You bring me up to speed on what he's already told you, it'll save us both a lot of time.'

I nodded, then shook my head, then said, 'Look, Franco, I

don't know Shay at all well. We've only met twice, and briefly
both times. Right now all I know is that he's commissioned me
to ghost write a book about this thriller writer, Sebastian
Devereaux, who used to live on Delphi.'

'And you didn't think to look into his background, this guy
who just shows up and commissions a book.'

'I tried, yeah. But there isn't a lot out there. By the looks of
it, Shay likes his privacy. About all I know is he's worth a hundred
million dollars or near enough, and that he's spent a chunk of
his money on foundations and what-have-you here in Ireland,
and now he's looking to invest in Delphi, this gold mine he wants
to develop as part of the whole Irish-American philanthropist bit.
But that's about it.'

'Maybe we should talk again,' he said, 'once you've had a
chance to chat properly with Shay.'

'Give me a reason.'

'Say again?'

'Shay's paying me good money to write this story. Why would
I want to mess with that, run off behind his back and get cosy
with the guy who stuck a gun in my daughter's face?'

The laughter lines hardened, went thin. 'That's not exactly the
way it played, was it?'

'Wasn't far off, either.'

He was exasperated now, but working to control it. Took his
time, lifting his cup in both hands and inhaling the steam before
taking a sip. 'Has he told you why he went to America?' he
said.

It's a rare conversation where you don't learn more by playing
dumb rather than pretending to be smart. I played dumb.

'There was nothing for him here,' I said. 'So he got out.'

'In 1940.'

'Apparently so.'

'You wouldn't have thought there'd be a lot of emigration to
the States in 1940, would you? With the war going on and all.'

'I wouldn't, no.'

'So what was his hurry?'

'I'm all ears.'

He sipped some more tea, set the cup down on the table. 'I
take it he hasn't mentioned the kids.'

'What kids?'

'The ones that died on Delphi in a massacre not long before Shay upped sticks for the States.'

Playing dumb will only get you so far, and it sounded to me like Franco Govern was all in. 'He told me about it, yeah,' I said.

'Good.'

'How is that good?'

'It means we're on the same page, Tom. That you know where I'm coming from. I mean, a guy who's in control, he's *compos mentis*, like they might say in court – he doesn't usually run around telling people he's just met he was mixed up in some war crime, does he?'

'It wouldn't be my experience, no.'

He was fiddling with his tea cup now, his eyes down. 'We're worried about him, Tom. OK, you've only met him a couple of times, but he comes across as a smart guy, getting on a bit but still sharp. Solid. Right?' I nodded. 'But you don't know him. You don't know who he used to be. The family are worried. Shay hasn't been the same man since Marie died. And it's not just, you know, that he's mourning her. Marie, she was . . .'

'He told me she pretty much made all the big decisions.'

'Well, yeah. And now she's not around any more, God rest her soul, Shay's been a bit flakey for the last couple of years. By his standards, I mean. Making executive decisions, throwing a lot of money around that isn't really his to throw. All very noble stuff, don't get me wrong. It's not like he's blowing it on hookers and coke. But this notion, like you mentioned earlier, of Shay being a philanthropist – he's taking that a bit more seriously than maybe he should. This gold mine on Delphi being a case in point.'

He was worried about Shay, all right. Terrified Shay would blow the family fortune before the CFO and the rest of the family got its hands on it.

I couldn't help but wonder if he was worried enough to put an old man in a canal if he thought the old man could destroy Shay Govern's reputation, the family name, with a story about a massacre, an atrocity.

'You think Shay's being led astray?' I said.

'We do, yeah. To a certain extent.'

'By Carol Devereaux.'

'You've met her?'

'Not yet,' I said. 'Soon as I meet Shay, he's going to put us together. She's the daughter of the guy I'm writing the book about.'

'Sure. But she's also, I'm hearing, the woman who pulls all the strings on Delphi.'

'So Shay said.'

'Yeah. She's working with Shay on this gold mine idea too.'

'I don't know anything about that.'

'Would you tell me if you did?'

'I've told you plenty.'

'What you've done is confirm what I already know.'

By now Emily had wiped her plate, soaking up the last of the honey, and was sitting back with her eyes closed, feet drumming against the seat as she tapped along to Adele.

'Sounds to me,' I said, 'that you know a lot about who I am. Right? So you know what I do.' He nodded. 'Then you'll understand, if I'm working on a story, that I'm obliged to protect my source.'

'Even if your source is the story you're working on.'

'That might complicate things a little, sure. But the principle stands.'

He grinned. 'Principles?'

'That's what they call them, yeah.'

He was still grinning as he leaned in. He spoke so softly I could hardly hear him over the hiss of the coffee machine.

'It's been my experience,' he said, 'that kids and principles don't mix. I mean, in a situation like this.'

Then he folded his arms on the table and tilted his chin upwards a fraction, as if offering me his throat.

Calling my bluff.

'OK,' I said. 'Fair enough.' I nodded over at Emily. 'But not here. I don't want her to maybe hear anything she shouldn't. Is there anywhere we can go?'

He jerked his head towards the fire exit. 'We'll step out there,' he said, standing up and edging around the table. 'Excuse me?' he called to the woman behind the counter. 'Would you mind keeping an eye on the little girl there? We'll be back in a minute.'

'Aye, no bother.'

I held up two fingers for Emily, then pointed at the rear exit and curled my little finger for a pinky promise that I'd be back in two minutes. She nodded, although she wasn't happy about it. Franco went ahead, pushed down the safety bar on the fire-exit door and walked out into a small yard lined with plastic crates full of empty bottles. There was a stink of ammonia and stale urine and cats. Franco took out a pack of Marlboro and a lighter, offered me one, then lit one for himself when I declined. He took a heavy first drag and turned his head to one side as he exhaled, saying, 'Look, all I want to know is—'

He stopped then, because I'd stepped in and pushed the point of the greasy knife up under his chin.

'One more word,' I said. 'Just say one more word about my girl and I'll fucking skewer you where you stand.'

A flash of rage in the grey eyes that drained away fast, leaving behind an Arctic fog.

'Listen to me now,' I said. I gave the knife a little twist, pushed his chin up another inch or so. 'I've had threats before, from boys who'd throw you out of the way to get *at* a fight. And maybe you're Johnny Big-Balls over in Boston, the second coming of Whitey fucking Bulger, but here you're fucking nobody. *Nobody.* You hear me?'

He couldn't nod, but he made a low grunt in his throat.

'I already owe Seanie one for waving his gun around my kid,' I said. 'So go ahead, yeah, call him in. But if you do,' another twist on the knife, 'you won't be in any state to see him or anyone else come through the door. So think on that and mind your fucking manners.'

I lowered the knife and stepped back.

His move now.

He rubbed a thumb on the underside of his chin, then checked it for blood. It came away clean, which wasn't any great surprise, the knife being as blunt as the back of his own skull. Then he took another drag on his cigarette.

Gradually the fog in his eyes seeped away and he came to terms with the fact that I had about thirty years and twenty pounds on him, and was still holding the knife. I'd imagine what tipped the balance in my favour, though, was that he needed what was in my head more than he needed the satisfaction of pounding it off the cat-piss concrete.

When he could trust himself to speak again he said, 'You're a lucky man.'

Maybe it wasn't bluster, exactly, but a man who's talking is a man who isn't doing.

Another drag on the cigarette. The stench of cat piss was so strong now that I wished I'd taken him up on his offer of a smoke. He said, 'So, Shay.'

'What about him?'

'Did he tell you about the gold?'

'He did, yeah. Shay has big plans for Delphi.'

'Not the mine. The real gold.' Franco dropped the cigarette and stubbed it out with his toe without taking those cold grey eyes off mine. 'I don't suppose,' he said, 'Shay by any chance mentioned how he was planning to scrub off the swastikas?'

FIFTEEN

The fire-exit door pushed open with a wheezy sigh. The waitress, her cheeks flushed, stuck her head out. 'Hi, lads? That wee girl's getting restless.'

It had been the same ever since Rachel and I split. If you left Emily alone for more than ten minutes at a time, even watching TV, she started to get anxious, wondering where you were. She'd wander into the kitchen from the living room and watch you chopping onions and peppers, tell you something inconsequential that had happened that day at school, or ballet class, then wander back out again. We didn't need any psychologist to tell us why, although I took it as a positive sign that her anxious moments always seemed to coincide with the ad breaks.

I'd tried to talk her through it. Told her that just because I wasn't with her all the time, that didn't mean I wasn't with her – I'd place my hand over her heart – here. That I'd moved out of our house, sure, but I'd never move farther away than my apartment, and she could see me any time.

None of it worked. She understood what we told her, sure, had a fair grasp of how love can still work at a distance. She just didn't buy it. A child sees what she sees.

When we got back inside she was sitting with her back against the booth, knees drawn up to her chest, her arms wrapped around her shins. No tears, but her eyes were shining.

I ignored the disapproving glances from nearby tables and took the buds out of her ears while Franco went to the counter. 'Sorry, love,' I said. 'I thought you knew we were just going outside for a minute.'

'It was *ten* minutes.'

'I know. I'm sorry.'

'Can we go now?'

'Not just yet. But soon, I promise.' I wanted to get out of there just as much as Emily did, but I needed to know more about this cache of swastika-stamped gold before I sat down with Shay Govern again. 'Would you like another croissant?'

'No, thanks.'

'Is there anything you would like?'

'Apple juice. Please.'

I got an apple juice organized, and watched as she made five or six attempts to spear the straw through the opening in the cardboard carton. Once she was sipping on that I cued up some Arabian Nights stories on the phone – Adele, she reckoned, was too loud – and popped the buds back into her ears.

By then Franco had placed a fresh coffee on the table for me, hot black tea for himself. 'You forget how sensitive they can be at that age,' he said, stirring in a sugar.

'She takes after her father, yeah. So tell me about this gold you're scamming.'

'You think *I* want the gold?'

'You didn't come all this way for the Guinness, Franco. And call me cynical, but if it's stamped with swastikas like you're saying, I doubt you're planning to donate it to any museums. Or maybe, because it'll qualify as salvage, you're thinking of hauling it up and handing it over to the State, get yourself a nice pat on the head. Is that it?'

'Those are options, sure.'

'But they're probably not at the top of the list.'

'No, they're not.'

'Listen,' I said, 'if you're here because you think Shay's told me about any German gold, you're way wide.' Shay hadn't mentioned any gold, and neither had Gerard Smyth. And if illicit Nazi loot had turned up in Sebastian Devereaux's *Rendezvous at Thira*, it wouldn't have been like Martin to miss it.

'You're not wondering why?' Franco said.

'I'm guessing because it doesn't exist.'

'Not why Shay didn't mention it. Why the massacre happened in the first place.'

'The Germans were after a British spy. The locals wouldn't hand him up.'

'Right. But why did the Germans want the spy so badly they'd start killing kids?'

According to Gerard Smyth, Richter had wanted the rendezvous time and place for the submarine. But he hadn't said why it mattered.

'Go on,' I said.

'The gold,' he said, 'was sent over in a German submarine in 1940 to fund an IRA campaign against the Belfast shipyards, the airports, cause a little cross-border mischief. The idea being to destabilize the Brits at their back door, make them think a little harder about the North Atlantic.'

'How much are we talking?'

'Half a million sterling.'

'In 1940?'

He nodded. 'Adjusted for inflation, you're talking about ten million's worth now.'

I gave a low whistle. 'So what happened?' I said.

'What we know for sure is the sub was sunk,' Franco said.

'Attacked?'

'Probably not. What's more likely is that it ran into rough weather, or surfaced into a storm and took a freak wave broadside. Or, what I think happened, it was deliberately wrecked.'

'Scuttled, you mean.'

'I mean the captain was given coordinates designed to send it aground or on to rocks.'

'Let me get this straight. The contact here, presumably an IRA guy, double-crossed the Nazis.'

'That's the theory.'

It was, I supposed, possible. Or at least plausible. Other than it sounded completely ludicrous, a hoard of Nazi gold sitting on the floor of Lough Swilly, a lot of what Franco was saying backed up Gerard Smyth's story. It also went some way to explaining Richter's murderous rage. The guy had been on the hook for a serious chunk of gold, maybe personally responsible for its recovery, its safe passage back to Germany, once Rheingold's cover was blown in Derry.

'You think,' I said, 'Shay's chasing this gold.'

'What we think,' he said, sighing so heavily I gagged on the stink of stale smoke he wafted across the table, 'is someone else is doing the chasing, and using Shay for cover.'

Then he reached for his cup of tea. As he did so, Emily sat forward, handing me the phone. I thought she was fed up with the Arabian Nights, and looking for a new story, or some music, but she was showing me a text message on the screen. It was from Martin.

I'm in Rathmullan. Where you?

He must have left as soon as we'd spoken and burned it up, no traffic on the roads that early on a Sunday morning. I texted back:

Belle's Kitchen cafe. Wait outside. Be there in five.

I gave the phone back to Emily. 'Problem?' Franco said.

'No problem. So who's using Shay? Carol Devereaux?'

He glanced down at the phone again, gave it a half-beat, then decided to let it go. 'Break it down,' he said. 'Why's Shay on Delphi right now?'

'He wants to invest, develop this gold mine he's talking up.'

'Right. So where's the seam?'

'They're not sure.' I was starting to see it. 'But they think, yeah, it could be on the sea floor, running northwest.'

'Correct. And say they strike it lucky, start pulling up raw chunks of gold. What are they going to need on site?'

'A smelter.'

'There you go.'

A neat trick, if true. Shay throws up a smokescreen about investing in a gold mine and then goes after the sunken sub, pulls up the bricks and melts them down, presents the results as raw ore.

'Sounds like a plan,' I said, 'except for one thing.'

'What's that?'

'I've met Shay, we've talked. He doesn't sound mentally defective to me.'

'Why would he need to be defective?'

'Because he'd never get away with it. There's no way you could hide that kind of activity. A con like that, someone would be bound to spot something's off.'

'Would they?'

'Bound to.'

'One of the islanders, you mean.'

'Sure.'

'Not necessarily. I mean, a gold mine is a pretty dangerous place for anyone who isn't supposed to be there. So they'll make sure it's only accessible to designated personnel and so forth.'

'OK, but people talk.'

'Some people like to talk, sure.'

'So it'd get out.'

'Would it?'

'It always does.'

'Not necessarily. I mean, not everyone would know. Just the people who need to. And Delphi isn't a very big island, Tom. There isn't a huge population over there, a couple of hundred at most. It might be easier than you think to keep a secret. Especially if whatever was coming up was, as they say, being reinvested in the local economy.'

I laughed, but there wasn't so much as a flicker in those grey eyes.

'You're serious,' I said.

'Shay's on Delphi right now,' he said. 'He's already gone public with the news about prospecting in Lough Swilly. And I know, because he's told me, that he's trying to track down a guy who was on that submarine. So yeah, I'm serious. Because someone needs to be.'

'So you've talked to Shay about all this.'

'There's no *talking* to him, Tom. His mind's made up. He doesn't seem to realize that if this gets out, just a whisper, then people are going to start asking questions. As in, why was he involved in the massacre? What did he get out of it? How come Shay arrived in the States with no arse in his trousers, like he says himself, and suddenly he's a millionaire? Next thing you know accounts are being frozen, assets seized.'

I took that all in while I sipped my coffee. If I read him right, Franco was suggesting that Shay Govern had bolted for the States with a stash of Nazi gold, a little start-up capital. Which was why, maybe, he was looking to clear his conscience with the book he'd commissioned, Sebastian Devereaux's story with a little segue into a sordid tale about kids burning to death in a church.

'Has he paid you yet?' Franco said. 'For this book you're writing.'

'An advance, yeah.'

'But probably not in cash.'

'A cheque.' A post-dated cheque at that.

'Right.' He shrugged. 'Well, we'll honour it, Tom. Can't say we'll stump up for everything he's promised you, but if he signed a cheque then we'll see you right for that.'

'This is presuming Shay doesn't come through himself.'

'And also presuming that you come through for us.'

'How so?'

'He's talking to you, Tom. Telling you about the massacre. So all you have to do is keep listening.'

'And then report back to you.'

'Tom, no one will be happier than me if we're wrong. You can trust me on that. But if we're right about the submarine, and why Shay's planning a gold mine on Delphi, then Shay needs protecting from himself.'

It sounded to me like a win-win scenario. If Franco was wrong, I'd be working on a hell of a book and getting paid handsomely to do it. If he was right, and the family pulled the plug on Shay's crazy scheme to smelt down Nazi gold, then I was getting paid to listen to Shay's ramblings. And by then I'd have signed the contract, which I figured the family would be happier to honour rather than have its breach contested in court, the details leak out.

A grubby way to make a living, maybe, but my living well involved spending as much time as I could with Emily, and I had a custody hearing coming up fast, and a position of financial responsibility to establish.

Emily took out one of her buds and tugged at my sleeve. 'Daddy? I'm bored.'

'I know, hon. Two more minutes and then we're done.'

I waited until she was plugged in again, then said, 'OK.'

Franco nodded. 'Delighted to hear it,' he said.

There was just one thing I needed to know. 'Gerard Smyth,' I said.

The grey eyes watched mine. He didn't so much as blink. 'Who's Gerard Smyth?'

'You said Shay's trying to track down a guy who was on the submarine. He hired a man I know, and he's found him. Gerard Smyth.'

'And this Smyth found the guy.'

'It's the other way round. Smyth is the guy from the sub.'

'He doesn't sound very German to me.'

'That's his name now. He's naturalized here in Ireland since way back.'

'Right. So who found him?'

'Jack Byrne. He used to be a cop but he works private security now, surveillance gigs. Sometimes he does investigative work.'

'You know him?'

'We've worked together a couple of times.'

'Would you trust him?'

'Jack? Christ, no.'

'So he could be feeding Shay any old shit.'

'He hasn't told Shay anything.'

'I don't get it, Tom.'

'Jack came to me. Heard I was writing a book with Shay. He reckoned he had some dirt on Shay that might be worth a squeeze, wanted me to play along.'

'Fuck.' He winced then, glanced across at Emily and lowered his voice. 'So what did you tell him?'

'I told him he'd need to get his skates on, because Shay's telling the story himself, in this book.'

'What'd he say to that?'

'Not much. I haven't heard from him since yesterday morning.'

'Shit-shit-shit. So now he's gone to ground and we don't know *what* this guy Smyth is saying.'

'Yeah, well, there's good and bad news there.'

'What?'

'The good news is, he brought me to see Smyth, so I could hear his story.'

'And?'

'This is an eye-witness account, OK?' He nodded. 'Well, Smyth says nothing about any gold on the submarine. I mean, he seems to know everything else, the spies, the massacre, the works. But no gold.'

'That's not necessarily bad news, Tom.'

'Except that's not the bad news. The bad news is that Smyth drowned in a canal on Friday night, and—'

'He's dead?'

'He is, yeah, and the cops believe it was deliberate. Or that there's a strong chance it was . . .'

'The cops are involved?'

'They certainly are. And because I was talking with Smyth on Friday evening, I'm what they're calling a person of interest.'

'You're a suspect?'

'I'm helping them with their enquiries. Or supposed to be.'

'*Fuck.*' This time he didn't wince or glance at Emily. He said, slowly, 'On the basis that you're probably not the guy who put this Smyth in the canal, who did?'

'I don't know.'

'This Jack Byrne guy?'

'No reason why he would. Smyth was Jack's way of squeezing Shay. But listen, Franco – Smyth gave me his testimony, a typed manuscript, which was lifted from my apartment some time yesterday morning by people good enough to leave no trace of themselves. No signs of a break-in, nothing.'

'Christ, it's a nightmare.'

'It's worse. According to Smyth, he'd been on to the British and German embassies about this alleged massacre in 1940. A couple of months back, he got a visit from some guys telling him to keep his voice down, an official investigation was pending. The way Smyth tells it, they were spooks.'

Franco leaned in low across the table. '*Spooks?*'

'That's what he believed.'

I was expecting some spectacular collision of profanity and blasphemy but Franco, for once, was left speechless. Eventually he said, 'So this manuscript, Smyth's testimony – who's seen it?'

'Me and Gerard Smyth for sure, and whoever stole it from my apartment. And then . . .'

'Who?'

I'd been about to mention Martin, but there didn't seem to be any point in dragging him any further into the mess than he'd already volunteered for.

'I don't know how much Smyth said about the massacre when he contacted those embassies,' I said. 'For all I know he could have posted them copies of his script.'

'You think he might have?'

'I really couldn't say.'

He sat back and ran a hand across his buzz-cut skull. 'How much does Shay know?'

'Last I talked with him was yesterday morning, to let him know Jack Byrne had found Smyth, was planning to squeeze him about the massacre. It was later on that the manuscript was stolen, and then I heard Smyth had drowned.'

'So Shay knows nothing about all this.'

'He hasn't heard it from me.'

He thought it over, the tips of his fingers drumming a soft tattoo on the edge of the table. He said, 'Do the cops know Shay hired this Jack Byrne?'

'They do.'

'OK. So sooner or later they'll connect Shay to this Smyth getting drowned.'

'I'd plan for sooner.' I'd pretty much joined the dots for Kee there. 'What are you thinking?'

'I'm trying to figure out, Tom, if it'd look better that the cops catch up with Shay on Delphi, where he can play the innocent, or they stop him at the airport and arrest him as a flight risk.'

'Either way, he's in it up to his neck.'

'Sure. But if we play it right, Shay comes out the victim. He's been a bad boy but that was a long time ago and now he's being blackmailed by Smyth and Jack Byrne.'

'Says who?'

'Says *you*, Tom. Meanwhile, Shay's on Delphi trying to make this gold mine work for the locals. He's a good guy, a philanthropist like you said. Not the kind of guy, you'd imagine, who would run around tossing old submarine sailors into canals. Right?'

'I wouldn't have thought so, no.' Which was to say, I hadn't considered it until then. But Shay Govern had been in Dublin on Friday night, when Gerard Smyth drowned.

'I need to talk to some people,' Franco said, pushing his tea cup away into the centre of the table. 'We're going to get Shay out, get him home, then deal with this shit from there.' Lawyer up, he meant, pull out the injunctions and gagging orders, resist all attempts at extradition in the likely event of Shay becoming a person of interest in a foreign jurisdiction. 'In the meantime, Shay's expecting to see you on Delphi to talk about this book. Sounds like he trusts you, you've already come across about Jack Byrne's scheme. So maybe you could break it to him gently, how he's in the middle of a shit storm.'

Maybe I could. Once he'd signed the contract.

'Of course,' Franco said, reaching across to ruffle Emily's hair, 'that leaves us with the problem of this little lady. You'll hardly want to drag her into a crapfest like that.'

Emily glared up at him, then very deliberately took each bud from her ears. 'Please don't touch me,' she said. 'You are *not* my daddy.'

SIXTEEN

Franco paid for breakfast on the basis that he was the one who'd extended the invite but I dawdled on the way out, zipping up Emily's jacket and tucking in her scarf, so that he was right behind me when we left and caught the terse nod I gave Martin, who was parked diagonally across from Belle's Kitchen.

No harm in Franco thinking I wasn't alone. And if I had one guy backing me up, he couldn't be sure there weren't others.

Then I gave the street a scan up and down, looking for any non-Donegal registration plates that would let me know someone had trailed Martin to Rathmullan. Mainly, though, I was scoping for Jack Byrne, the ex-cop working more angles than a pool-hall shark.

Apart from Martin's Saab, every car I could see had Donegal registrations or the yellow plates that told me they were from over the border.

Franco took his time glancing away from Martin's car, letting me know he'd clocked him, then gave me a Belle's Kitchen card with his phone number scribbled on the back. Then we shook hands.

'I'll keep you posted,' he said.

I watched him walk away, then nodded to Martin again, directing him towards the pier.

Once Emily had given Martin a good hugging and then sprinted off to the swings, we sat on a yellow metal bench just inside the playground fence, huddled against the feisty breeze whisking in off the water beyond the pier. I was expecting the third degree and a short, sharp lecture about dragging Emily into a dangerous situation, but Martin, being an accountant, was battle-hardened when it came to damage limitation.

'I appreciate this,' I told him. 'I owe you a big one.'

'Put me in a book,' he said. 'Only make me taller.'

'No problem.'

'Who was the guy?' he said, inclining his head in the direction of Belle's Kitchen.

I brought him up to speed on Franco Govern. When I mentioned the Nazi gold he laughed, thinking I was winding him up. When I didn't laugh along his eyebrows flapped like he was sending out semaphore. 'You believe him?'

'You've read Smyth's account. It says nothing about any gold on the submarine. Shay Govern hasn't mentioned it either.'

'So where'd he get it from?'

'He didn't say. But it makes sense. I mean, as a motive for the massacre. And if Franco's right, it doesn't matter if the gold is there or not so long as Shay believes it's there.'

'So someone on Delphi, maybe Carol Devereaux, is telling Shay porkie pies to get him involved in this project.'

'Could well be.'

'You want my advice?'

'Always.'

'Take off *now*. Disappear. When it all shakes out the big guys'll survive, they always do. It's the little guy who'll get squeezed in the middle.'

'Sure, yeah. Except there's two things.'

'Is one of them Emily?'

'The first is that he's offered to honour the cheque Shay's given me. If I get a contract signed with Shay, they'll have to honour that too. They won't want anyone squawking.'

Martin the accountant was only slightly mollified by my pragmatic approach to financial liquidity. 'OK,' he said. 'But I sincerely hope that your second reason doesn't have anything to do with Gerard Smyth.'

'I should just forget about him?'

'Be serious, Tom.'

'Do I look like I'm having fun?'

By now Emily had moved to the climbing frame, was heaving herself up hand over hand. Not exactly a reassuring sight, especially as it was still early enough for the last of the dew to be gleaming slick on the bars. Not for the first time, and very probably not the last, I found myself consciously willing myself to stay put, crossing my feet at the ankles and tucking them away under the bench. Kids fall from climbing frames every day, earn their bumps and bruises and cuts like tiny badges of honour, and unless you want to go insane or drive them in the same direction, you have to let them take their own risks, conquer their own fears, allow them to grow on their own terms.

Assuming, of course, they're allowed to grow at all.

'Gerard Smyth's dead, Martin, and very probably because he wanted nothing more than the truth be told about those kids.'

It was perverse. A frail old man was dead before his time and most likely because he could corroborate a story Shay Govern wanted to tell the whole world. Maybe it was like Martin said, the big guys thrive and the little guys get squeezed. Or shoved into canals.

'That's all very noble, Tom. But I'm thinking you should worry less about those kids and think a little bit more about your own.'

'That's cheap, Martin. I'd have thought that you of all— Oh *fuck.*'

'What?'

But it wasn't a what. It was a who.

Strolling across the car park towards the playground like the Cheshire Cat, all menace and smile.

Kee.

She was still wearing the knee-length grey wool coat and her nose was every bit as interesting, although the bird's nest bob was a little more ragged than I remembered. The proofreading ruler was in her right hand, or what was left of it. She sat down on the bench with Martin between us and handed it across, mangled and just about hanging together on the thin metal strand.

'Careful you don't get a splinter,' she said. 'I'd hate to see you go down with blood poisoning.' She looked exhausted, drained and wan, which gave her smile a manic edge. 'So where are we?' she said. 'Someone bring me up to speed.'

'I'll just go grab Emily,' Martin said, standing up.

'Sit down, Martin,' she said. He hesitated and glanced across at me. 'Sit down,' she repeated, 'Martin Banks, chartered accountant, of fifty-seven Meadowvale Grove, Rathfarnham. Unless you want me to make a call right now, have you pulled in for aiding and abetting.'

'He's only here to collect Emily,' I said. 'He knows nothing.'

'Really?' She looked up at where Martin was standing, shading her eyes, still with the smile. 'So you didn't happen to mention at any point that the reason you needed to bolt with Emily was because you'd assaulted a detective in the course of her duties, in the process obstructing the course of justice and detaining her against her will.'

'Martin and me, we're not really that close.'

'No, I can see that. A purely professional relationship, accountant and client. And there's no chance that you might have given him Gerard Smyth's testimony, had him lock it away on your behalf, when you visited him the other night. Would that be right?'

'Couldn't be righter,' I said.

'So when we search Martin's premises, haul in his computer, we won't find any sign of the manuscript. Correct?'

'Not unless you plant one while you're searching, no.'

'Martin?' Kee said. 'Would you mind sitting down for a moment? I've had a long night and the last thing I need right now is a crick in my neck.'

Martin, looking a tad peaky, sat down again.

'Thanks,' she said. 'So you'll have heard of the Official Secrets Act. Yes?' Martin, uncertain, nodded. 'Great,' Kee said. 'So everything that's happened in the last couple of days, every interaction you've had with Tom here – physical, digital, emotional and psychological – it's all covered. Are we clear?'

'Not really,' Martin said.

Kee sighed, puffed out her cheeks. 'For now,' she said, 'just assume that anything Tom has told you is covered by said Act. Failure to comply, by which I mean talking about any aspect of this, to anyone, your lovely wife Jennifer included, will find you in breach. And once that particular shit hits the fan, and even if you don't see the inside of a cell, you'll never get the stains out. Am I any clearer now?'

'Yes.'

'Great. So I'll ask again – where are we now? You go first, Tom.'

'Anything Martin's done,' I said, 'he's done as a favour to me. The reason he's here is because I asked him to come collect Emily. So he gets to walk away, take Emily with him. Then we can talk.'

'Good,' Kee said. She closed her eyes and massaged them

with her fingertips. 'Standing up for your friend, I like it.' She opened her eyes again, blinking heavily. 'Where do you think we are, Tom? The fucking *play*ground?'

There was a moment's awkward silence, punctured by a gleeful '*Wheeeeeee!*' as Emily went careering down the slide. Then Kee said, 'Martin? I'd imagine Emily would love a push on the swings. What do you say?'

As soon as he was gone I said, 'Martin isn't involved. Yes, I asked him to hold the manuscript. Last night he emailed it to me, and now he's here because I need Emily gone. Once I know she's safe, you and me, we're good to go. I'll tell you what I know.'

'Martin,' she said, 'will piss off home when I tell him he can go. And he'll be going without Emily. As far as I can make out, she's about the only thing that puts manners on you.'

'Now wait a fucking minute. There's no *way* I'm—'

'I've already waited a minute, Tom. I waited three fucking *hours* locked in that wardrobe trying to kick out the doors. So I'm all done with the waiting. From here on in, I tell you what to do and you do it.'

'Emily's out of here. That's non-negotiable.'

'Is that a fact? Try this one, Tom. *You're* the guy who dragged your daughter into this mess. Not exactly the actions of a fit parent.' She leaned in. 'I make one call, Tom, and little Emily over there will be bounced into care so fast she'll be dizzy for the first six months. And you better believe she'll know all about how and why it happened, whose fault it is she can't see her mother any more.' She sat back, rearranged her coat and crossed her legs at the knee. 'So let's try this one last time. Start with the guy you met for breakfast. Who's he?'

By then the playground was starting to fill up, bleary-eyed parents and hyperactive kids, toddlers bumbling along, tripping up and sitting down hard on their padded diapers. The sun warm enough to take the edge off the breeze. Martin, bless him, played his part to the hilt, pushing Emily higher than she should have gone, then running around in front of her to play toreador as she swished past.

'I'm going to take a flying guess here,' I said, 'and say you already know who I was having breakfast with.'

She conceded that one. 'I just want to be sure *you* know who he was,' she said.

'He's calling himself Franco Govern. Shay Govern's brother.'

'So what'd he have to say?'

'Mainly he wants me to keep my mouth shut or Emily gets hurt.'

It was a gamble, but I was pretty sure Kee and whoever she was working with weren't so good they'd been able to overhear my conversation with Franco. Not that they weren't good – they'd been all over us from the start, tracking me from the meet with Gerard Smyth out to Martin and Jenny's house that night. But good enough to plant some kind of bug at the right table in Belle's Kitchen? Organized enough that they'd have a long-range listening apparatus in place in Rathmullan? I didn't think so.

'He made an explicit threat against your daughter?' Kee said.

'Not up front, the way you did,' I said. 'But it was there, sure.'

She didn't like that. Then again, she wasn't supposed to. She said, 'So what is it he wants you to keep your mouth shut about?'

'Are you serious? We're going to have this conversation here, where anyone can see us?'

'You're worried we're being watched,' she said. 'That's good. Paranoia can be a healthy early-warning mechanism. But what's worrying me is you're thinking about Franco, not me. Which leads me to believe that you think Franco's the dangerous one. That he can hurt you more than I can.' She spoke softly but the words were precise, hard and cold. 'Now, maybe I shouldn't take that personally; maybe it's just that he's a bloke and I'm a woman. Or maybe it's because you're kidding yourself that Franco's off the charts and I'm obliged to play by the rules. Is that it?'

There was no right or good answer to that question, so I just waited for her to make her point.

'Tom,' she said, 'you need to understand that you're in a very bad place here.'

'I didn't ask to—'

'Don't come the innocent with me, Tom. Maybe you didn't know what Shay Govern was letting you in for when you first met him, but you've had plenty of time since to think it over. And you've made more than a few bad decisions over the last couple of days, made choices and taken sides. Your problem being, right now, that you don't even know who the sides are. Or what they're capable of.'

'Yeah well, I'm all ears now.'

'What?'

'Feel free to put me straight, Kee. I mean, if you'd told me the score when you sat down in the coffee shop that time, we very probably wouldn't be having this conversation. Correct?'

'Do *not* fucking—'

'Whoa. Easy on the language there, Kee, we're in a playground.'

For a moment her face looked a lot like something that had ripped loose from a Picasso. She was already pale from exhaustion, but now her complexion turned milky with suppressed fury.

'Just before you start in again,' I said, shifting closer to her on the bench, 'let me warn you about making the same mistake Franco Govern made.' I extended an arm, pointing out Emily as she swooped and squealed on the swings. 'Franco took one look at my daughter and thought he saw a weakness, something that makes me vulnerable. Which was a little surprising, to be honest, because Franco, or so he says, has two girls himself. So Franco, providing he wasn't bullshitting, should know that Emily isn't so much of a weakness as she is a strength. Maybe,' I shrugged, 'the only one I have. Because there's nothing I can't do, and no one I won't do it to, once she's in the frame. No, wait,' I said, as Kee made to speak. 'The thing about that is once the misunderstanding was cleared up Franco became a totally different guy. Very chatty. Took me into his confidence.' Emily, spotting us looking over, took one hand off the swing chain and waved, sending herself into a parabolic wobble. Once Martin had rescued the situation and got her back on line, I said, 'So have a wee think about that. How your life and mine might be a little bit easier if we can come to some kind of arrangement about who we really are and what we really know.'

She had a good gnaw on the inside of her lower lip thinking it over. Then she said, 'One question.'

'Go on.'

'Did he mention salvage?'

'If you're talking about the gold, yeah, he did.'

'Fuck.'

A couple of heads farther along the chain-link fence turned, lips pursed.

'Sorry,' I said, wincing. I nodded at Kee. 'Tourette's. She can't help herself. I'll take her for a stroll.'

There was a sculpture on a grassy rise halfway between the playground and the beach, six or seven life-size but grotesquely thin figures cast in bronze and facing out to sea with their arms raised. At first I thought it was a Famine commemoration but then I realized they were waving off four other figures who were standing on a raised gangplank looking back, their own arms raised in farewell. It could only have been the Flight of the Earls, the O'Neills and the O'Donnells, the last of the ancient Gaelic aristocracy fleeing into exile, hounded out in 1607 by the marauding English, never to return.

It was hard to tell whether those left behind were begging passage, beseeching them to return, or bidding them a bon voyage and good riddance. Given that the Earls were abandoning their followers to the tender mercies of the English army following on, it was probably a combination of all three.

Not a great omen, if you were a man who set any store by omens.

'You're not a cop,' I said. 'I know that much.'

'Why would you say that?' Kee said.

A couple of thoroughbreds were being put through their paces on the hard-packed strand below, chunks of sand kicked up by their hooves, the dull drumming arriving half a second later. Directly across from us lay Delphi in bright sunshine, covered in forest and tricked out in at least half of the forty shades of green. There was something of the wild boar about its hunched back, the prickles of pines along the spine of its ridge.

'I'm saying it,' I said, 'because you're not a cop. Or not just a cop. If you were, you'd have arrested me as soon as you heard Gerard Smyth was dead.'

'Maybe I was planning to, once Emily was out of the picture.'

'Then,' I said, 'you catch up with me this morning, I'm a flight risk who's already assaulted you. Except you sit down and start making threats. Not exactly by the book, Kee. And then there's the fact that you were scoping me long before Gerard Smyth went into the canal, had me followed to Martin and Jenny's that night. Then, I disappear, I'm a potential murder suspect, but you turn up here running solo, no back-up, no uniforms. Organized enough to track me down but not making any fuss about it, not dangling the old handcuffs. Instead you're asking me about Franco Govern and gold bullion, trying to get me onside and giving it all this about the Official Secrets Act. All of which tells me there's more to you than meets the eye – not that what meets the eye isn't plenty in itself.'

She'd walked around to the other side of the sculpture, shading her eyes again as she stared up at the anguished faces. Now she squinted across at me, one eye closed, half amused. 'It's a bit late to start flirting now, Tom.'

'You never know. Let's start with a little honesty, see where that takes us.'

'See,' she said, 'this is my problem. I always assume people are being honest from the get-go.'

'It's my experience that they generally are, in a *quid pro quo* kinda way. So – you *quid* me, I'll *quid* you. But you'll need to start talking fast.' I pointed past her, out at the lough, to where the ferry was making for the pier. 'I'd say you have about fifteen minutes.'

She turned to look and watched it come. It had the look of a converted trawler, wallowing a little now as it battled the turning tide. She said, 'You're going over?'

'That's right.'

'To meet with Shay Govern.'

'I have a book to write.' Starting, I didn't add, with my signature on a dotted line.

'The book about the thriller writer,' she said.

'Sebastian Devereaux, yes.'

'So they'll be expecting you to poke around, ask questions.'

'I'd imagine they'd be disappointed if I didn't.'

She thought it over, chewing again on the inside of her lower lip. 'Shay Govern,' she said. 'Has he met your wife?'

'He knows I have an ex-wife. But no, he hasn't met her.'

'OK.' She reached into the pocket of her coat and took out her phone, brought up a number. 'Clearance,' she said, then turned her back on me and put the phone to her ear.

I strode around the sculpture, grabbed the phone out her hand and kept walking, pressed it to my ear.

'Hey!'

Brr-brr, brr-br – click.

'Code,' said a male voice.

I dropped the phone to the ground, stamped it with my heel. Then I turned to face her.

Bad idea. She was right there behind me, already swinging.

SEVENTEEN

I t was tough telling Emily she was going back to Dublin with her Uncle Martin for a sleepover with her cousins. What was tougher was that she said nothing, not so much as a token protest, instead channelling her disappointment into giving Kee a good long stare over my shoulder. I knew she was wondering if Kee was my version of Mommy's Peter, perhaps even a possible new mum. My heart went out to her, a tiny sun trying to map out the coordinates and orbit for a new and unexpected planet that had sailed into her solar system.

I tried to make a game of it, telling her Kee was a wicked queen and that she was a secret princess who had to be taken to safety by the noble knight Martin. She wasn't buying. As I belted her into the booster seat in the rear of Martin's Saab she did that thing she does, reaching up to squidge my earlobe between her fingers, and said, 'Are you still my daddy?'

'Of *course* I am, love. You know I'll always be your—'

'No.' An exasperated sigh. 'In the *game*.'

'Oh. Right. Well, I suppose I could be if you'd like me to be.'

The ferry had rounded the breakwater, was crawling in towards the pier. Kee, who'd wandered by to hurry me along, slipped a plain band off her middle finger and handed it to me. 'You'll be needing this,' she said, taking my left hand and easing it onto my ring finger. Then she ducked out of a thin silver chain she wore around her neck, opened the clasp and allowed a diamond ring to slip into her palm. She pressed it to her lips, then slid it on to her finger and fixed the chain back in place around her neck.

'You're married?' I said.

'To you, Tom, and just the other day. So try to look happy about it.'

When I glanced into the rear of the car to wink at Emily, let her know it was all part of the game, she was staring out the window beyond us, a glassy gleam in her eyes, the faintest of tremors in her lower lip.

*   *   *

The ferry steamed out into the lough on a heading that looked to be taking us about two miles north. At first I presumed we were bound for Buncrana on the far shore and would divert to Delphi on the return journey to Rathmullan, an entirely endurable prospect on what had bloomed into a glorious spring day, warm and fizzing with the promise of summer. I wedged myself in at the rail for the trip, the ferry's bow climbing and plunging, spray exploding into salty mist.

Once we'd crossed the central channel, though, we began curving sharply around to the south, picking up speed as we ran with the current and came around parallel to Delphi's western shore. The coastline was unforgiving, a high rocky bluff crowned with thick forest, and I began to wonder if we'd need to anchor offshore and take a tender to the island. Then, as we were passing a stubby promontory, the pilot pulled a ferry's equivalent of a handbrake turn, throwing the wheel over and dragging a dull bellow of protest out the engines as he rammed them into reverse. For a moment we hung suspended in the current and then we slid easily into a tiny horseshoe bay surrounded on three sides by sheer cliff. The harbour was so calm that for a second or two, as we steamed towards the village tucked into a crevice in the cliffs, I believed we were going to ram the outlying buildings. It wasn't until the first few houses began to waver and dance that I realized they were a reflection, the mirror-still surface unsettled by the wake pushed out under our prow.

Kee stood behind me, huddled into her coat despite the warming sun. On edge as she scanned the waterfront, eyes cold above a fixed grin.

'Why don't you just get out a flag?' I said. 'Or a bullhorn, let them know we're coming.'

'You think they're not watching for you?'

'Who, the spooks? Here?'

'You were supposed to take a hint, Tom. Walk away. Except you've walked away and somehow wound up on Delphi.'

She made a good point. Still, I found it hard to believe that the break-in crew, however smooth they might be, were sufficiently resourced and prepared that they'd be able to track me all the way to north Donegal, and have people already in place when I got there. I said as much.

'And anyway,' I went on, 'if they'd wanted to hit me, they

could have done it last night, or this morning. Unless you think they held off because of Emily.'

She didn't answer.

'No,' I said, 'probably not. So if they are here, then they'll be waiting to see what happens next.'

'Which is?'

'I sit down with Shay Govern and get his story on record. Then I bang it off into the ether in an email, CC-ing a couple of people I can trust, including Father Iggy Patton. Anything happens to me, it all tumbles out.'

'That's your plan.'

'So far. And lose that smile, you look deranged.'

'I'm on honeymoon, remember?'

'With me, though.'

She switched off the smile, looked me up and down. 'I've been on honeymoon with worse,' she said.

'Atta girl.'

We hadn't had the most auspicious start to our shotgun coupling. Kee was sturdier than she looked, could throw a proper punch, and there was a swelling below my left eye that was throbbing now and would be a juicy dark plum later on. Still, she'd been entitled, and besides it was the kind of detail that would confirm that we'd recently been in the vicinity of an Irish wedding.

The ferry tied up and Kee rolled the car down on to terra firma, up on to the pier. There she paused. On our left, tucked in under the sheer headland, was a large car park sparsely populated by cars, some of them under tied-down canvas coverings, along with a couple of small trucks and a handful of camper vans. At its entrance we found a topographical map informing us that Delphi boasted no more than a single road that was navigable by car, which encircled the island and hugged the coast all the way round. Otherwise the interior was essentially a steep-sloped pine-covered mountain accessible only by footpaths and hiking trails, with a single donkey path leading straight up from the rear of the village to a viewing point high on the cliffs above.

The village itself, we discovered as we strolled back from the car park, was a jumble of houses and B&Bs, one hotel and a few pubs, with some cafés and restaurants lining the seafront. The narrow streets had been laid down when the ass and cart was the height of vehicular sophistication, and while there were signs announcing that delivery vehicles were allowed access during business hours, the streets were pedestrianized from six in the evening until nine in the morning. The house fronts were all whitewashed, with doors and window frames picked out in reds, greens and yellows. The street was so quiet that we could hear our footsteps above the murmurs of conversation inside as we passed.

The young receptionist at the only hotel – Nuala, from the name tag on her bottle-green waistcoat – greeted us *as Gaeilge* and made an appropriate fuss when Kee flashed her ring and announced we were taking an ad-hoc honeymoon, wandering wherever the wind and the mood took us. We paid for two nights, cash advance.

I put a bit of a dent in her brisk bonhomie when I asked if she'd put me through to Shay Govern's room.

'I'm afraid we don't have a Mr Govern staying with us at this time,' she said after checking the computer, although I was pretty sure, this early in the season, she'd know the few guests by sight. 'Might he have checked in under another name?'

'Possibly,' I said. 'He's an elderly gentleman, American, very dapper.'

She was shaking her head as I spoke. 'We have no one with us like that at the moment.'

'Is there another hotel? He might have gone to the wrong place.'

'We're the only hotel,' she said, 'but there are B&Bs. Would you like me to ring around and see if I can track him down?'

'No, that's fine. I have his number. I'll ring him myself.'

But when I rang, strolling over to the display case on the other side of the lobby that stocked leaflets and flyers advertising the island's points of interest, the call went straight to his answering service.

I left a message telling him I was on the island and looking forward to seeing him again and gave him our room number.

It all seemed a little odd. Sure, there could have been innocent reasons for his not taking my call. He might have been taking a nap, or switched off his phone for a meeting. But why would he avoid the hotel? Shay Govern didn't strike me as a man who'd eschew the relative luxury of Delphi's only hotel for the homely comforts of a B&B.

Had he been intercepted or abducted before he made it this far? Possibly, but why? The man was on his way to Delphi to announce funding for the biggest investment the island had ever seen. Who'd want to screw around with that? The only likely candidate I knew of was Franco Govern, who'd already told me that he knew his brother was on Delphi. Except that would mean Franco had taken breakfast with me as some kind of elaborate and entirely unnecessary double-bluff, which didn't seem to be Franco's style.

So, yes, it was all a little odd.

We'd asked for a room overlooking the harbour. It was on the second floor, which was also the top floor, and came with a tiny balcony with wrought-iron railings. The balcony only really worked as a balcony if you opened back the double windows and sat inside looking out, but the view – sight lines, according to Kee – was across the seafront to the harbour, the pier and the dog-leg breakwater built from those massive stones. To our left, when I leaned out over the railing and craned my neck, the village ran out along the shore like awkward pearls nowhere joined but invisibly strung.

The room was small and warm, low-lit, the bed too big for the space but soft and piled with duvets and plump cushions. Which was the first problem, because it meant Kee and I would have to share or someone would have to kip on the hard-backed chair.

The second problem was that Kee seemed to think she was running the show, laying down ground rules about how we'd behave when out and about.

When she'd finished I said, 'Kee, you need to get your head around the fact that they already know we're on the island. Or if they don't now, they'll know it five seconds after I touch base with Shay Govern.'

'Humour me,' she said. 'You'll live longer.'

There was a mocking edge to her tone, but it was an edge all the same. When she went to the bathroom to freshen up, I lay out on the bed with my arms behind my head and offered up a silent prayer of thanks to the noble knight Martin Banks as he escorted my secret princess very far away from the island of Delphi.

I must have dozed off. A harsh click brought me back fast.

The kind of dry grating you associate with a gun. A hammer cocked, a slide racked.

Kee was sitting at the desk, the laptop pushed to one side to make room for one of the bathroom towels. A small plastic bag with the logo *Toher's Chemist* to one side. She was slipping the magazine out of a gun, checking there was nothing in the chamber. Then she eased off the slide and placed it on the towel, went rummaging in the plastic bag. She gave the slide and the barrel a clean with a baby wipe, coming up with a faint oily residue, and went after the corners very gently with a Q-Tip. Then she produced a small can of three-in-one oil, squeezed in four separate drops, slid the barrel back into place and clipped home the spring. She gave it all a minute or so to dry. Once the gun was re-assembled she racked the slide three or four times and stuck it into the belt at the small of her back, squirming a little until she got it comfortable.

'Not ideal,' she said, cleaning her hands on another baby wipe, 'but it'll hold for now.'

'You really know how to kill a honeymoon buzz, don't you?'

'Try a gun jamming when some bastard's trying to blow your head off. That'll kill your buzz all right.'

Sounding bitter, like she'd been through it. I eased myself off the bed, padded across the room to the kettle. 'Coffee?' I said.

'I'll take a tea if there's one going.'

I filled the kettle in the bathroom and knocked it on, got the coffee sachets and teabags organized.

'Go on,' she said. 'Ask.'

'Ask what?'

'To hold it.'

'The Glock?'

An amused shimmering in the grey eyes. 'You know it's a Glock?'

'Standard issue, isn't it?'

'I'll give you that one. But the answer is no.'

'Fine by me. I wasn't asking.'

'Sure you weren't.'

'Guns aren't really my thing.'

She got a bang out of that. 'So if I was to take us up into the hills, set up a few tin cans and tell you to take three shots, you're saying you wouldn't do it?'

'No thanks.'

'Strike one for Kee,' she said. 'I had you down for the homo-erotic type.'

'Those hunches ever work out for you?'

'I'm usually right, yeah.' A wry grin. 'Which means they rarely work out. Anyway,' she said, 'Shay Govern.'

'What about him?'

'Just a couple of things for when you sit down with him. You've used the Record function on your phone before, right?'

'You want me to tape the conversation?'

'Of course.' Kee took another sip of tea, wrinkled her nose and set it down on the desk. 'Look, Tom, don't start with the ethical bullshit, or whatever it was kind of bullshit you were about to get cracking on with. OK? You are where you are, and we need you to do this. And besides, all we're asking is that you have the exact same conversation you were going to have with him anyway, except you'll be recording it.' She shrugged. 'I mean, you could probably get his permission to record the conversation if you wanted, tell him it's all for the book. Except then, he knows the tape's running, he'll be a little more cautious about what he's saying. You *don't* tell him, then he feels free to say whatever he wants. He's thinking, worst-case scenario, if he says something he shouldn't, incriminatory, it's all deniable, your word against his.'

'We already have Gerard Smyth's word,' I reminded her.

'Sure thing. Except Gerard Smyth isn't in any position to testify in court, is he? Also, and unless you've been playing silly buggers, Smyth never mentioned any gold.'

'Exactly. I mean, that's what I'm asking. How come you're chasing this gold when the only eye-witness account doesn't say anything about it?'

'Alleged eye-witness account.'

'Split hairs all you want, there's still no one talking about any gold.'

She got up from the chair and went to the window, opened it and stepped out onto the balcony. Leaned forward, gripping the rail, inhaling deeply. Then she turned and folded her arms, talking back into the room, so that she was dark against the sky, her face in shadow. 'You heard Smyth's story first, right? And then Franco Govern wades in with this story about missing bullion.'

'Sure.'

'It came to us the other way round.'

She named no names, partly for my own safety, partly because they'd mean nothing to me. Sloggers from the Long War, who'd done their time, still had the whiff of cordite in their nostrils. 'Let's just say they watched the pie being carved and got fed up waiting for their slice. Or with a few crumbs, when other people were buying holiday homes in Donegal or the Algarve, and setting themselves up in business with start-up capital delivered in sacks of cash.' An edge to her tone now, although shadowed as her face was, I couldn't make out her eyes, her expression. 'Or getting themselves boosted on to the gravy train in Brussels, say.'

Whispers and rumours and anonymous calls. The Revenue passing along allegations of a corner cut here, a shell company there. 'Nothing anyone might be jailed for, yeah? But enough, once in a while, for CAB to clean out a bank account or freeze some assets, maybe force a repossession. Not putting anyone in the poorhouse or starting a war, but, y'know, keeping people on their toes. Letting them know the rug could be pulled out any time.'

The word about the Delphi gold had wafted down the line one fine day, and flagged as a maybe. When it popped up again a couple of months later, it was upgraded to possible.

'Next thing we know, Shay Govern is sniffing around Delphi talking gold mines. So Govern gets a background check and we discover that he's donated his fair share to Noraid and whatnot back in the day. It might be a coincidence, they happen all the time, but we have to take a look, don't we?'

'And then Gerard Smyth pops up.'

'Seems a little off, doesn't it? This massacre no one has ever heard of on an island about ten people knew existed. And yeah, it just pops up out of nowhere.'

'You don't believe it.'

'I'm not *not* believing it. For now everything's on the table until it's not. But it feels wrong, yeah. Like someone's trying to force it.'

'Force what?'

'I don't know. Draw attention to Delphi, get people talking about it. Get a couple of journalists up here,' she nodded at me, 'poking around. Maybe even a TV crew. All of which would make it a lot harder for anyone to pull up the gold.'

'Except Smyth doesn't mention any gold.'

'Would you?'

'Me?'

'If you were Smyth, I mean. Or whoever's behind Smyth. Like, say you were inventing a story about some German sailor and a submarine on a secret mission. It'd be a bit much if he knew all the ins and outs of the operation. Right? And once he starts waffling on about all the bullion stashed in the hold, you'd be thinking, Really? They told the *sailors* about it?'

'So the fact that he doesn't reference it makes it more probable that it was there.'

'I'm saying that it makes the story more plausible than if he does mention it. That's all.'

'Except he's dead. And if it was a con, why would anyone want to tip him into a canal?'

'That we don't know. We also don't know that it wasn't a tragic accident.'

'It'd be a bit of a coincidence, though. A very convenient coincidence.'

She shrugged, and came forward off the balcony rail, stepping into the room. Her face, her expression visible now. 'It's like I said, Tom,' she said with that bittersweet smile she'd very probably be wearing when the priest arrived to give her the last rites, 'coincidences happen all the time.'

EIGHTEEN

I t was just after two thirty when we strolled out of the hotel and turned up a side alley, away from the seafront. A pleasant afternoon, still warm and sunny, with a hint of briny tang on the breeze whisking in off the lough. The whitewashed houses and shop fronts reminded me of Greek villages I'd been to over the years, the narrow streets winding back on themselves and intersected by alleyways, the apparently chaotic planning designed to confound pirates and sundry other seaborne attackers. There had been Greeks on Delphi back in the day, according to the tourist literature available in the hotel lobby, traders who had sailed around from Cornwall via the Cork coast, drawn by rumours of the copper mines on the north coast. They'd had plenty of foreign visitors since – Celts and Vikings, the English, and even some Spanish, swimming ashore from the sinking remnants of their ill-fated armada, wrecked in the storms off the unforgiving Donegal coast.

And then, if Gerard Smyth was to be believed, there was the handful of Germans who'd turned up on the night of 4 April 1940.

There were enough tourists around for us to blend in. The pubs and restaurants were quiet at that hour of the day, but there were three or four cafés, two art galleries that seemed to specialize in seascapes by island artists, an antiques shop that also offered sculptures hand-carved from sea-bleached wood, a visitors' centre, a couple of ice-cream shops, and an outlet that sold tapestries hand-woven on the working loom in the back room. It was a tourist trap, certainly, but the atmosphere was congenial, and the smiles and welcomes were either genuine or brilliantly faked.

The mood lent itself to aimless sauntering, and the layout made it very easy – as per Kee's instructions – to pause and glance into a shop window and check the street behind in its reflection, or abruptly about-turn for no good reason other than to peer again at a galleon tossed on a stormy sea, or double back down a cobbled alleyway in the spirit of exploration. All of which we did without seeing the same face behind us twice, or anyone ducking out of sight into a doorway. Which meant we wasn't being followed, or whoever was following was much better at their job than we were at catching them out.

We took a table outside one of the cafés on what they called the village square, even though it was a balloon-shaped cobble-stoned plaza that narrowed in a gentle incline to the steep steps of the tiny whitewashed church, one of the few buildings in the village not shouldered about by its neighbours, the gravel-chip paths on either side allowing it some breathing space. To its left was a small bakery, on the right a hostel with an Alpine-style balcony running the full width of the second storey. The bell tower that rose over the front door was small enough to seem humble, or even apologetic, in its domination of the square, perhaps because the church appeared to have been built into the base of a sheer wall of striated rock that loomed high over the church, the tower and the village itself.

We ordered some sandwiches and coffee, and then I strolled across the square and up the steps for a closer look. By the time I got back Kee was already tucking into her soda bread sandwich, wolfing it down. I guessed she hadn't eaten too regularly in the last twenty-four hours. I gave her time to finish, then said, 'OK, you're up.'

She'd been preparing a speech of sorts, I guess, because she went straight into it, pausing only to brush some crumbs from the corner of her mouth. 'Do I need to mention the Official Secrets Act again?'

'No, but well done, you've mentioned it anyway. Crack on.'

'I'm serious, Tom. You need to understand that no matter what happens from here on in, it's all under wraps. There will be no published account about anything that has happened in the last four days.'

'What about Gerard Smyth?'

'If he's lucky he'll get an obituary.'

'Where do I stand there? Am I still a suspect?'

'You're still a person of interest, yes. While we're waiting for the results of the autopsy.'

'That'll tell you how. Not who, or why.'

'Depends on the how. If it involved violence, and the assailant left behind traces, we get an angle on the who. Then, maybe, the why. Unless you have any ideas, after reading his testimony, that could save us some time.'

I sucked down a mouthful of latte. It was good, sharp and bitter. 'First tell me a little about you,' I said. 'More to the point, tell me about this "us".'

She took her time, hedging this and qualifying that, context-ualizing everything, but eventually she got it out. She was a cop, all right, with the SDU, the Special Detective Unit, which special-ized in counter-terrorism and counter-espionage. She almost choked on the word espionage, and needed a couple of sips of Americano to soften the blockage in her throat.

Once that was out of the way, though, it was plain sailing. A couple of years back she'd been seconded to a working group, an intelligence-aggregating unit that functioned as a kind of spider's web composed of operatives – a little hiccup over that one – drawn from the ranks of the SDU, the Criminal Assets Bureau, the Departments of Finance and Foreign Affairs, the Coastguard, and G2, aka the Irish Army's Directorate of Intelligence. Known to those involved as – *cough* – EirTel, the group didn't officially exist. There was no structural hierarchy, and all intelligence received was filtered back through the web to the appropriate authority. The group received no direct funding, and no records or minutes were kept. EirTel, she said with only the faintest of blushes, was the ghost that kept the machine honest.

She sat back then, waiting for my reaction. The moment was crying out for *Quis custodiet ipsos custodes* but I've never been sure of the pronunciation, so instead I settled for, 'Black ops?'

'If called for. But more shades of grey than black.'

'So if an old guy was running around shouting about a massacre, say, and then conveniently fell into a canal, that'd be more shades of grey than black.'

'More black than grey, I'd say. But that wasn't us.'

It was Jack Byrne they'd been watching, ever since he'd hacked into the Department of Social Welfare in pursuit of Gerard Smyth.

'It raised a flag; he wasn't particularly clever the way he went about it. And Jack Byrne, his reputation precedes him.'

'So you go after Jack.'

'Go after,' she said, 'is probably putting it a bit strongly. It's not like we have infinite resources. But yeah, the hack was traced back to source, and one of our guys data-mined Jack's email accounts, his online searches and so forth. Anyway, long story short, Gerard Smyth was one of the names that popped up. When that went back into the mixer, red flags were popping up all over.'

'Because he's contacted the embassies.'

'His submissions were officially logged, sure. Standard practice.'

'Logged and ignored. Well, officially ignored. Except Smyth got an unofficial visit from our friends the spooks.'

'Which we knew nothing about, obviously.'

'Obviously. So why the red flags?'

'I told you. Nazi submarines and Delphi Island.'

'I know *that*. I also know he made his allegations eight months ago. So how come people are suddenly taking him seriously?'

She used the tip of her forefinger to dab up three or four chunky crumbs from her plate and popped them in her mouth. 'This is still covered by the Official Secrets Act, Tom.'

'Go on.'

'OK. So you know Smyth made three submissions, to the Department of Foreign Affairs and the British and German embassies. Making, like I said, serious allegations of unprovoked aggression by a foreign power.'

'The Germans, yeah, back in 1940.'

She nodded. 'Right now isn't the best time for us to be squealing about German aggression.'

'I wouldn't imagine they'd be pleased to hear about it any time. But Smyth's story checks out. So far I have one witness who corroborates his—'

'*This*,' she said, 'would be a particularly bad time.'

'How come?'

'What do you know about international banking, Tom?'

'Not a lot.'

'Yeah, well, you're about to learn more than you'll ever need. Between you and me, and according to our friends in the Department of Finance, we're fucked.'

'I don't follow.'

'The country, Tom. The economy. We're running on empty and about to blow a gasket. That soft landing the politicians keep talking about? It's not going to happen. We're on our way down fast and this time there's no parachute.'

She gave me the bullet points, some of which I was vaguely aware. Sub-prime mortgages and the US property bubble. The credit crunch. An Irish economy wobbling on a foundation of sand, spit and next year's hopes. Irish banks leveraged to the hilt and beyond to German lenders, Fritz and Karl already calling in their markers. The bods in Finance on their knees with the bowls out, begging for credit extensions. The IMF on speed dial.

'So the last thing we need right now,' she said, 'is some kind of diplomatic incident about Nazi atrocities giving Karl and Fritz the hump.'

'You're serious.'

'Why don't you try asking Gerard Smyth,' she said, 'if I'm serious.'

It made sense, of course. A perverse kind of logic. The kind that fuels your most convincing nightmares.

I sat there in the sunshine outside the café with the remains of our lunch on the table and tried to wrap my head around how normally the world went on. The tourists wandering around the square. The fly mooching along the handle of the spoon in the saucer. Watched, as if it were a movie, as Kee caught the eye of the waitress and ordered another brace of coffees. I should have been feeling something on behalf of Gerard Smyth, that most pathetic of pawns. But all I felt was stunned. No – stunned and useless, and relieved that Emily was long gone.

'Can I take it,' Kee said as she cupped both hands around a fresh cappuccino, 'that we're not flirting any more?'

She was needling me, sure, reminding me of how far out of my depth I was, and had been from the start. But if it was petty insults she was after, I was game.

'So brass tacks,' I said, 'with all this crap about EirTel and shared intelligence malarkey, what you're really telling me is that you're working for the German banks.'

She didn't flinch. 'Suck it up, Tom. In six months' time we'll *all* be working for the German banks. If I was you, I'd been doing a little work on my umlauts, finding out where they go.'

I'd have plenty of spare time in which to do it, too. Given the delicacy of the situation, there was no way Shay Govern would be allowed to tell his story.

'He can build as many gold mines as he likes,' she said, 'and the more the merrier. Christ, if he can find a way to tow the whole country across the Atlantic, anchor it off New York, the guy'll be a hero. But that story stays buried. The massacre, submarine, the gold, the whole shooting match. For now, anyway.'

'Until our new German overlords say otherwise.'

'Until,' she said, 'it no longer has the potential to disrupt any possibility of preventing the country going bankrupt and millions of lives thrown into chaos, yes.'

'And what if he tries?'

'We're hoping he won't. That he'll be reasonable when presented with the new political paradigm.'

'And if he isn't reasonable?'

'Then someone he trusts,' she said, inclining her head at me, 'will need to persuade him otherwise.'

'Me? I hardly know the guy.'

'You're his link to Gerard Smyth, Tom. You have Smyth's testimony, you're the man he told his story to.'

She didn't have to join the dots. 'You want me to discredit Smyth.'

'Well, you could be less . . .' she searched for the word '. . . emphatic, for example, when representing the story Smyth told you. Let it be known that you might have doubts about Smyth's mental health, or the accuracy of his memory. That you have questions you need answered, like you told me yesterday morning, that Gerard Smyth is no longer in a position to provide.'

Black ops in shades of grey.

'So I go back to Shay Govern,' I said, 'and tell him sorry, it just occurred to me that Gerard Smyth was a senile fantasist.'

'You might want to be a bit more subtle than that,' she said. 'But yeah, we're talking about undermining Smyth's story so it doesn't stand up. At least for now.'

'Won't work. Govern only wants Smyth's story to corroborate his own eye-witness account. I mean, the guy's already told me he's doing all this to clear his conscience.'

'I understand that. But there has to be a good reason why he needed Smyth's corroboration. Why he went to all the trouble of tracking him down in the first place. Which means, without it, he's back to square one.'

'Without it?'

'Sure. You haven't given him Smyth's testimony yet, right?'

'Not yet.'

'Great. So all he has is your word that Smyth's story backs up his own. And if you're telling him that you can't stand behind Smyth's version of events, that you need more information, then he's stuck. Right?' She dabbed up a few crumbs on the tip of her forefinger, sucked it dry. 'Look, Tom – we're not stupid. We know something like this, if Shay Govern really wants it to come out, it's only a matter of time. Especially given what happened to Gerard Smyth.'

'It didn't just *happen* to him, Kee. The guy was drowned.'

'Right now we don't know that for sure. And you really shouldn't be shouting the odds about it either, because you're still in the frame. No, wait.' She held up a hand, palm facing me. Earnest now. 'This is an incredibly sensitive time, Tom. We're looking at the worst crisis this state has ever faced, and between you and me there's serious people already talking about economic treachery, certain prominent individuals being hauled in to face charges. Trust me, it's going to be a shit storm and you don't want to get caught up in that, even in a minor way. This story, we know it's going to come out. Something this juicy, there's no way it can't. Right?' I nodded. 'So what we're engaged in is damage limitation, delaying it until after the worst is over. I mean, think about it. The country goes to the wall, held to ransom by German banks, and in the middle of it all this story surfaces about a Nazi atrocity? It'd be carnage.'

Again, it all made sense. Except the last thing I could afford to do was obstruct Shay Govern. Franco was already putting the wheels in motion to get Shay out of the country, and the longer the book was delayed, the less likely it was that I'd get paid. And if what Kee was saying about economic collapse and the IMF wandering in was even remotely close to the truth – it all sounded a bit far-fetched to me – then it sounded like I needed to bind myself to Shay Govern rather than blow him off.

I explained as much to Kee. 'If I go fucking with this book,' I said, 'I'd be shooting myself in the foot.'

She shrugged. 'Better that than a double tap to the back of the head,' she said. 'I mean, they've already taken out Smyth. And if they think you're stepping up to take his place . . .'

'Christ.'

'Be smart, Tom. You want to do this book because of Emily?

OK, I get it, she's a sweet kid and she's the only one you've got. But if you ask me, I'd imagine Emily would rather a father she didn't get to see all that often to one she had to visit in prison. Or, for that matter, a cemetery. Wouldn't you?'

I didn't answer. She took that as an affirmative. 'Martin has a copy,' she said. 'Of Smyth's testimony.' I nodded. 'And there's the copy taken from your apartment yesterday morning, the original. And you have a copy, the one Martin emailed you. Is that all of them?'

'Far as I know.'

'Great.' She reached behind her, into a pocket of her coat. Came up with a USB drive, slid it across the table. 'What you're going to do now is put your copy on to that, then delete the file. Then, when Shay Govern gets in touch, you're going to tell him that you've had a good scan through it, come up with some anomalies.'

'Like what?'

'I don't know, Tom, I haven't read it yet. But you'll think of something.' She patted the table. 'Tom? Let's go. We don't have all day.'

I did what she said. When I'd copied Smyth's testimony on to her USB drive – for some reason she'd encased it in a little plastic yellow tiger – she watched as I deleted the file from the hard drive, then emptied the trash basket.

'I'll see you back at the room later,' she said. 'I need to get this into the system, see how they want to play it. And call me if you hear from Govern.' She dug into her pocket, came up with a twenty, tossed it on the table. 'There you go,' she said. 'Lunch on the taxpayer. I hope you enjoyed it, because there won't be many more of those unless you're thinking of emigrating to Berlin.'

Then she leaned in. I drew back, half-expecting another right cross to the jaw, but she took my face in both her hands and kissed me long and lusciously. 'Sorry,' she said, 'but we're supposed to be on honeymoon.' She straightened up, reached across the table to unhook her bag from the back of her chair, and strolled away across the square.

NINETEEN

I sat for a few moments, stunned in an entirely different way. Kee knew her way around a kiss, that much was for sure. Everything else, for those few moments, was a little hazy. The faint taste of a slightly sticky mint gloss and the lingering scent of a delicate citron perfume didn't help.

I could only imagine it had been for the purpose of cover. Or maybe Kee was the kind of woman who, once she'd bludgeoned her man into submission, couldn't resist trying to revive him. I tasted the mint gloss again while I thumbed the swelling beneath my eye and acknowledged, with no more disappointment than was strictly called for, that Kee was in the business of black ops in shades of grey: confusion, diversion, distraction.

Thank Christ Emily hadn't been around to see *that*.

To get myself back on track I rang Shay Govern again, and got his voicemail again. This time I didn't leave a message.

I killed time scribbling a few notes, descriptive material about the square and the church, the cafés and shops. It seemed bizarre to me, literally incredible, that this sun-splashed plaza had once been a place of torture and murder. And yet, if Gerard Smyth was to be believed, this was where it had taken place.

Just before four o'clock the church bell began tolling, a deep and resonant tenor amplified to something portentous by the cliff face behind, and the square grew busier. Older folk mainly, emerging from the side streets and alleyways, shuffling up the church steps, greeting one another with the easy diffidence of people who meet every day, here a hand laid softly on a forearm, there a peck on the cheek. A quiet, gentle people. Grandparents, probably, or most of them at least. I wondered how quiet and gentle their own grandparents might have looked as they were driven up those steps by the awful imperative of searching the smouldering ruins for their dead children. It was even possible that some of the grey-haired grandmothers and stooped grandfathers were survivors of that night, children who had been shoved into coal cellars or hoisted into cramped attic spaces, who had lain there in deathless silence, hardly daring to breathe, quailing at the piercing screams.

I tried to picture myself in one of those rooms, pushing an uncomprehending Emily under a bed, shushing her with a finger to my lips, then barricading the door. The terror when the banging came. The horror of not being able to protect your child. And then the unimaginable grief of picking your way through those smoking ruins and seeing something small and human and charred curled up on its side just—

The phone rang. I went scrabbling after it through the detritus of lunch, the caller ID flashing a number I didn't recognize.

'Mr Govern?'

'It's me, Tom. I'm on Peter's phone.'

'Oh. Hey.' Rachel. *Shit.* 'How are things there?'

'Grand. Or as grand as can be expected, anyway. How's Emily?'

'She's fine, yeah.'

A pause, and then it all came in a rush. 'Listen, Tom, I need to ask a favour. The funeral's been delayed for twenty-four hours, Peter's sister is flying in from Hong Kong and there's some issue with her flight. So I'll need you to take Emily for an extra night. Can you do it?'

'Sure. Not a problem.'

'Really?'

'Absolutely.'

'That'd be great, Tom. Really, really great.'

'Seriously, don't worry about it.'

'Brilliant.' I could hear faint sounds of traffic in the background at Rachel's end. She'd obviously stepped outside to make the call.

'Hey, Rach? I'm expecting a call, so I can't stay on too long.'

'No problem. Just let me say hello to Emily.'

'She's not here right now.'

'How do you mean?'

'I mean, she's not here. She's with Martin.'

'Oh, *Tom.*'

'It's complicated, OK?'

'When is it not?'

'Let's not get into it. Not now.'

Silence, and the faint sounds of traffic. 'Text me Martin's number, I'll ring her there.'

'Will do. Only don't panic if he doesn't answer straight away, he's driving.'

'Driving where? Tom, what's going on? Where *are* you?'

Contrary to popular belief, honesty is rarely the best policy. Lying now, though, would have serious consequences down the line. 'Donegal,' I said.

'*Fuck*. Tom, seriously?'

'It's not what you think.'

'Marvellous. So now you're a mind-reader too.'

'Rachel—'

'Or wait, maybe you are. Maybe you can already tell that I think you're a selfish bastard because you had the chance to spend the weekend with your daughter and instead you ran off to Donegal to clear his name and dumped Emily on your ex-girlfriend's husband.'

'That's not what's going on.'

But she wasn't listening. 'Let it *go*, Tom. The man's dead. Guilty or innocent, he's *dead*. And if you don't start thinking about the living, and specifically your daughter, then you're going to wind up having these conversations with *her*. You know that, right?'

She was wrong, this time at least, but I couldn't help but admire her priorities. A lesser woman would have been storing up this latest manifestation of my irresponsibility, to place it in front of the judge at the custody hearing, but Rachel's instinct was to preserve my relationship with Emily. She was doing it for Emily, sure, but it was still good to hear.

Even if she was totally wrong. 'You're jumping to conclusions, Rach. This has nothing to do with my father.'

'I find that hard to believe, Tom.'

'And I can understand why. But you need to trust me on this one.'

It was my father who had driven the first wedge between us. I'd brought it up, his disgrace, during one of our earliest dates, because I wanted her to hear it from me. To hear his side of it, the version in which he wasn't stickered with lurid labels: patriot, bagman, traitor. That he'd been nothing more than a civil servant doing his job in the Department of Finance who'd had the bad luck to be seconded, early one September morning in 1969, as financial advisor to an Irish Army intelligence officer who was flying to Berlin later that day. A go-between with a cheque book, he said. There wasn't even time to go home and pack. The arms, he was informed on the flight, were originating in Split and destined for the newly formed IRA units in the Nationalist areas of Northern Ireland besieged by Loyalist mobs, said arms to be sailed from the eastern Med all the way to north Donegal, and onwards to Derry. All of it organized and overseen by a charismatic and ambitious young cabinet minister who, my father later learned, could teach Pontius Pilate a thing or two about personal hygiene.

The meeting never happened. My father and the young intelligence officer flew home and went their separate ways. The next time they saw one another they were in court, listening to allegations of subversion, criminal negligence and treachery. One particularly inventive theory went under the heading of attempted military coup. When it all fell out, nothing was proven. By then it was long forgotten that my father, and that young intelligence officer, were witnesses for the prosecution. But the shit stuck. My father's reputation was vindicated in the short term, but when the charismatic young cabinet minister came riding back into power some years later, my father was one of the first to be purged. By then, he said, he was glad to go. By then he was isolated and vilified, a traitor not to his country but to the system, a man who had blown the whistle by testifying in his own defence.

My mother always claimed that the seeds of the cancer were sown then, that the stress of defending his name had poisoned him to the core. Maybe she was right. But there was a more insidious element to it too, the shame of being patronised in public as a minor civil servant, of being dismissed as a dupe, a patsy, a hapless pawn in some great game.

I'd told Rachel all this and she'd listened, fascinated, and then told me she'd never heard of him. And later, when his cancer took hold and my obsession with proving his innocence began to shape my own career, keeping me freelance so that I could devote any spare time to what we called 'The Project', she would ask, as patiently as she could muster, how I intended to clear the name of a man who had been publicly vindicated three decades before.

She was right, of course. What I was attempting wasn't revisionism, to force a reappraisal of the historical facts. What I was trying to do was alter the public's perception of those facts. A Sisyphean struggle at the best of times but especially, as Rachel frequently pointed out, when the public simply didn't give a rat's ass.

I think she'd believed that Emily, when she was born, would change a lot of things. That I'd recalibrate, and realize that I needed to leave behind my old toys and obsessions. That it was the baby that now mattered, not the old man. A reasonable expectation, according to biology and psychology and even the most cursory application of common sense. Except by then he was a widower and a jaundiced stain seeping into his bed sheets. How could I slough him off? How could I not at least go through the motions of pretending that his obsession was mine too?

Rachel understood that, and held on, and held on. What she couldn't cope with was how, three years after he'd died, I was still refusing to let it go. That I was clinging to the impossible hope of clearing his name as a way of assuaging my guilt for not truly believing it had been possible while he was alive. At first she'd accepted that my novels were an attempt at catharsis, the necessary inventions of unresolved conflicts. But as book followed book, and the book-buying public remained resolutely unimpressed by the increasingly bleak scenarios and downbeat endings, she realized that I'd simply diverted the obsession into a different but equally unrewarding channel.

Eventually, being not only a good mother but a fully functioning human being, she'd decided that Emily needed more than the basics of food and warmth and a roof over her head, and that living month to month at the whim of commissioning editors was a recipe for little more than the heartache of breadline economics. So we separated, and began the slow torture of ripping Emily in half.

If it wasn't for the fact that Peter was still married, and failing miserably in his bid to get his wife to sign the appropriate papers – the last I'd heard, she was living on an ashram somewhere north of Goa – then she'd have pushed through the divorce a year ago.

'Sorry, Tom,' she said, 'but you ran out of trust tokens a long time ago. Send me Martin's number. We'll talk when you're back in Dublin. And Tom?'

'What?'

'You need to think very seriously about what's best for Emily. My thoughts are that a guy who dumps his daughter on some stranger in the middle of a crisis probably isn't it.'

'Martin isn't a—'

'He is to me, Tom. More to the point, he is to Emily. Have you even stopped to think about what she's feeling right now?'

She's safe, I wanted to say. She's safe and she's with a good man she calls Uncle Martin, a solid guy who drove 300 miles to take her out of the dangerous situation I'd dragged her into.

'There's a bigger picture, Rach.'

'For you, maybe. But I'd imagine Emily's looking at a totally different picture.'

She hung up.

I sat there staring at the phone and wishing I was Martin. Or at least, wishing I was sitting where Martin was right now, motoring for Dublin with Emily in the back seat, cheating at I Spy.

Where did it end? When did I become the man my daughter deserved?

The temptation to stand up and simply walk away was a trembling in my legs. To stroll down to the pier and take the next ferry out, head for home. Gather my little girl up in a hug and tell her I'd never let her go again.

I could do that, sure. Turn my back on Gerard Smyth and Shay Govern, and my own conscience. Just walk away, and wave goodbye to the forty grand that might persuade a judge I was worth taking seriously as a father.

I could do all that, for the sake of a priceless hug and a promise I'd know was a lie.

Or I could dig in, suck it up like Kee advised. Tell Shay Govern the truth, about Gerard Smyth's story and how he died. About Kee's investigation and the threat of a double tap to the back of the head.

If he wanted to go on from there, well and good.

If not, I had enough story to tell it myself.

TWENTY

Kee was smart and she threw a fair punch, but she was nowhere as tech-savvy as she seemed to believe. Or maybe watching me dump Smyth's file into my trash basket was a test, to see if I'd let it lie or if I'd call up my Gmail account as soon as her back was turned, find the attachment Martin had sent me.

I copied the document across on to the hard drive, opened it up and scrolled down to where I'd broken off earlier that morning. Richter bursting out of the house, livid with rage as the villagers gave voice to their defiance in song . . .

But it is not his manic energy that is terrifying: behind him the second masked man drags the Tommy into the square, the pair of them trailing a stench of sweat and blood and singed flesh and fresh shit. One look at the prisoner, before I turn away with bile surging hot and bitter into my throat, confirms that whatever will follow will be terrible beyond my most perverse imaginings. The Tommy appears alien. His face has been pounded to a bloody concave bruise. Most of his nose has been torn away. The ears too, gone. The mouth a dark maw. Eyebrows ripped out. Strips of flesh razored from his chest and stomach, so that he looks scourged. His left arm dangles from the elbow, whitish shards protruding from the joint.

Richter strides across to the man behind me and shouts an order. The man, his hands shaking, fumbles as he cocks the Schmeisser. Richter snatches the gun away and points it at the church and looses a burst. Pandemonium ensues when chunks of plaster rain down on the children, their screams matched by shouts and oaths from inside the church. When the echo of the harsh chattering dies away, Richter announces that any further singing will result in the immediate slaughter of the children. Then he orders the adults from the church.

When they are out, and harried into a ragged bunch in the centre of the square, Richter sends my masked shadow and me up the steps to ensure no one has tried to hide themselves away. Inside it is a gloomy, cramped space that barely affords standing room, with five or six pews either side of a narrow aisle. The rear wall behind the tiny altar is roughened plaster, the corrugated contours of the cliff face starkly visible. The windows are no more than narrow slits high up beneath the eaves. The only light comes from the sanctuary lamp, a dim flickering that casts a ruddy glow.

We find no one. As we leave, I turn to shut the church doors but as I do so a hand is laid on my arm. The school-teacher. She meets my eye and where I might have expected to see hatred or terror or pleading there is only calm. She gives the tiniest shake of her head as she exerts a little pressure on my arm, then inclines her head back and down to where the children huddle behind her, and I understand. I leave the church doors open and walk down the steps and go straight to Richter, telling him that it is my duty to inform him of the men's mood.

'The men will do as they are told,' he says. His eyes are caves, unreadable. 'I advise you to do the same.'

By now he has had the Tommy strapped to a wooden chair and positioned so that he faces the group of adults, or would have were his head not lolling forward on his chest. He is to be executed, of course, in full view of the villagers, as a punishment and a confirmation of the totality of Richter's power. As a warning, to be spread far and wide, about the consequences of defying the German Reich.

Then I notice that the Tommy's right hand has been left untied.

Now Richter calls for the mayor to come forward. When he does, Richter informs him of his conditions. Time is becoming increasingly precious, he says. If the village will not give up the spy Morrigan, or otherwise confirm for him the time and place of the U-43's rendezvous, they will pay the price of one villager executed for every fifteen minutes that passes.

Stunned, the bearded man protests that the villagers know nothing of a spy Morrigan, or anything about the movements of a submarine. Richter tells him that he can inform the villagers of his conditions or allow them to die in ignorance. The man has ten minutes to consider his proposal.

The mayor goes down on his knees, clasps those huge rough hands together and tells him they can tell him nothing because they have nothing to tell.

Richter places the barrel of his Luger against the mayor's forehead and says that he is interested only in facts.

When the bearded man protests again, Richter cocks the Luger and asks if the mayor has volunteered to be the first victim. At this an older man steps forward from the group, shabbily dressed but with a snow-white beard. He shuffles forward and places his hand on the mayor's shoulder. When he speaks, the words quiet but curt, the mayor's head falls forward. Then he gets to his feet and embraces the older man, kisses the top of his head, and walks back to the centre of the square.

Now Richter stands behind the Tommy. He makes a final appeal to the Englishman's conscience, telling him that the death of civilians will be on his hands if he does not volunteer the whereabouts of Morrigan. As he speaks he is ejecting bullets from the Luger's magazine. He palms the magazine back into the gun, and tells the Tommy that because he is the one responsible by his presence for creating the situation in which the villagers find themselves, it is only logical that the Tommy, and not any of Richter's men, should conduct the executions, which will continue until such time as the prisoner or the villagers provide him with the information he requires. For this purpose, and for each villager, the prisoner will be provided with the Luger and a single round. As the Englishman is unable to stand, each islander will kneel before his chair.

All of this is announced aloud, the words ringing out clearly in the deathly silence, but now Richter bends to the Tommy and whispers something in his ear. The words register, and a shadow seems to flit across the dark bruise of the Tommy's face. There is a barely perceptible slumping, some final reserves of spirit or hope evaporating of their own accord, and then the Tommy's chin comes down to meet his chest so slowly that I understand it to be a nod,

that he is acquiescing to Richter's proposal. Richter claps the
prisoner companionably on the shoulder, checks the Luger
and places it in the Englishman's right hand. Then he speaks
to the old man, telling him to kneel.

The old man's response, though brusque and given in
Gaelic, needs little by way of translation.

Enraged, Richter orders the man's legs be kicked out
from beneath him. Then he orders the Tommy to shoot the
old man where he lies sprawled on the cobbles.

But the Tommy appears to have slipped into shock, his
entire body heaving in gentle, irregular spasms.

Richter beckons to my shadow for the Schmeisser, wrap-
ping the leather sling around his forearm and boring the
muzzle into the side of the Tommy's neck.

Half-blind, his hand shaking, the Luger a tremendous
weight, the Tommy raises the pistol until it is pointing at
the back of the old man's head.

But still he does not shoot. Maddened by frustration, his
face contorted into the delicious agonies of a sadist denied
on the brink, Richter rants at the prisoner until phlegm flecks
his lips that he will have a massacre on his conscience if
he does not pull the trigger.

A sob, and then the sharp crack and the old man's head
explodes.

There is an eruption like that of a coven of banshees.
All around the masked men step back a pace or two,
some dropping to a knee to adopt a defensive position. Were
those soldiers in the villagers' position, I knew, they would
have charged despite the hopelessness of the situation and the
futility of the gesture – better to die on your feet than wait to
be dragged out and slaughtered like so many animals. But
the men are soldiers and the villagers are not; and the men
have no children to protect, nothing more infinitely precious
than their own lives to give.

Deranged now, Richter forgets about his fifteen-minute
period of grace. He tosses the Schmeisser back to my shadow
and forces another round into the Luger as he orders another
of the group forward. Another old man steps out, tall and
no less venerable than his predecessor despite the comically
baggy black trousers tucked into knee-high boots. As he

crosses the square he makes a point of searching out the eyes of every one of the masked men, or trying to, their faces turning away from his fierce gaze.

He too refuses to bow the knee, and stands towering over the prisoner.

'Where is the spy?' Richter demands, and for an answer receives a thick gob of phlegm.

Richter taps the Tommy's shoulder, directing him to shoot, but before the prisoner can raise his hand there comes the sound of smashing glass from the church.

Afterwards I concluded that it could only have been the sanctuary lamp. But in the moment there is no time to think. A scream is heard from inside a church, a full-blooded woman's scream, and a second later a tinny chorus of children screaming too. Then, at the high slitted windows, the ragged shadows of flames.

As one, the guns forgotten, the adults surge across the square and up the steps. There they pound on the church doors, the men shouldering and kicking. The doors give but do not give way, and I realize the schoolteacher, anticipating the worst, has barricaded them from the inside.

By now the flames have taken hold, an angry glow visible at the slitted windows, smoke beginning to seep through. Inside the woman continues to scream, although the children have fallen silent. The adults outside claw at the doors, and some of the men slip around the side of the church, desperately searching for another entrance they already know does not exist. I am dimly aware of Richter's bawling as he instructs his men to restore order, to force the parents back from the church doors, all the while thumbing bullets back into the Luger's magazine. Finally he rams the magazine home and sets off towards the church, leveling the Luger and taking aim at the milling crowd.

A harsh chatter. Richter jerks and seems to break into a run, but then stumbles on the cobbles and pitches forward. He lies still for a moment, then attempts to force himself forward and up, his left foot scrabbling for purchase. Then he slumps and is still.

What happens next seems to happen very slowly. I look to my masked shadow, who loosed the burst at Richter. He looks to be vibrating with tension, his shoulders shuddering, but in his eyes I can see a kind of stunned horror. Did he intend to shoot Richter? Was it meant as a warning? I step towards him and ram an elbow into his gut, and as he lurches back and goes down on one knee I grab for the Schmeisser. Winded as he is, his instinct is to hold on. We are face to face, snarling and grunting, until I relax my grip for a split second. As he pulls away and topples back, I follow through, smashing the butt of the gun into his face. Perhaps the mask softened the blow, but he goes down with an abrupt groan, then lies silent.

When I turn around the rest of the masked men are staring, some at the prone Richter, others at the church. By now the tinder-dry pews are crackling and popping, and even through the walls the heat is so fierce that it drives the adults back from the smoking doors. I shout across to the man nearest me, waving in the direction of the harbour, telling him that we need to retreat to the boat that brought them in. Hearing me, some of the parents at the top of the steps turn. They might not understand the words, but they immediately grasp the situation. With Richter down and with nothing left to lose, they charge down the steps, faces set hard in masks of their own.

They were unarmed, of course. And it was not courage that drove them on to the guns but madness, an unbearable grief harrowed into a desire for vengeance and blood – and, failing that, oblivion. For a split second the only possible outcome was slaughter, the villagers massacred until the masked men ran out of ammunition, and then they butchered in their turn, but then came a single hoarse roar, a 'No!' ripped from the very heart.

The Englishman. The Tommy.

In Greece they celebrate Ochi Day on 28 October, to commemorate the day in 1941 when the hated tyrant Metaxas suddenly covered himself in glory by responding to an ultimatum from Mussolini's envoy to surrender the country. Metaxas, or so the legend goes, gave a classically laconic Greek one word answer: *Ochi*.

No.

The truth, as always, is a little more prosaic. What Metaxas actually said was, 'Then it is war.'

The result was the same, and history records the consequences, but that *ochi* still resonates with the same power that hums in the word *thermopylae*.

No.

I can't say that the Tommy's ragged roar is due the same legendary status as the Spartans' final stand, or the gloriously doomed defiance of Metaxas. But in his own way, strapped to that chair, a bloodied husk of humanity tortured beyond human endurance, he managed to find something of the same spark. And, in his own way, he achieved what the Spartans and Metaxas also achieved: he bought time, just a few precious seconds, but enough for the masked men and the villagers to realize that they were bound for savage mutual destruction.

For myself I can only say that I behaved shamefully. My shadow, Richter's killer, still lay at my feet, moaning now, stretched out on the cobbles. A better man than I might have tried to save him, hoisted him on his back and carried him away. Instead I ran.

The rest is quickly told. I bolted into the nearest alleyway, hoping the darkness would swallow me up. I had no idea of how many, if any, bullets were left in the Schmeisser, or if I could have used it even had I been trapped. My only goal was the harbour.

I was too late. By the time I emerged on to the seafront, sixty yards or so from the pier, the masked men were already tumbling into their boat. They had shoved off, and were twenty or thirty feet out, by the time I made the pier. I called to them, loud enough to be heard over the engine but not so loud I might be heard from the village. Whether they heard or not, they did not turn back.

I heard a flat crack, a sharp whine. When I looked back the village was a hellish sight of shooting flames and twisting shadows. At the opening of the main alleyway stood a man with his legs apart and braced, a pistol – the Luger, I believed – pointed at me. His upper body jerked, and a split second later came a puff of white and another crack. A moment later the man was joined by two other men, who paused to assess the situation. Then all three came on, slow but sure.

It was swim or be shot. I threw down the machine gun
and tore off my boots and turned to the edge of the pier,
preparing to dive. That was when I saw the boat.

You will know, of course, that I escaped. By the time they
came to the end of the pier I was far enough out into the
lough for the pistol to be severely reduced in its effectiveness.
They fired, but I was an impossible target as the boat rose
and fell on the choppy swell. Soon I was caught by the current
and dragged away, and lost in the darkness.

It was shortly before dawn the following morning when
I beached to the north on the Donegal shore. I was exhausted
by then, and sickened, and gave myself up as a German
sailor, asking to be arrested and considered a prisoner of
war. I sat in the cell of a police station for two days, every
minute expecting to be dragged out and hanged by a mob,
but eventually I was handed over to a detachment of Irish
Army soldiers, who delivered me to an internment camp. I
stayed there for two months before being moved on to
another camp. I was never questioned about the massacre
on Delphi. No one ever asked what I knew about Richter
and his raiding party and the murder of those children. It
seemed impossible to me that the authorities would not
connect me with those events, but as the months went by I
began to realize that the authorities – or those in command
of the camps, at least – knew nothing of the atrocity.

You will assume that I wondered why, but perhaps you
can understand why I did not. At the risk of being accused
of washing my hands of the incident, it was something I
had been dragged into, and had no way of influencing. What
I understood was that my life was over, or my life as I had
once known it. I would be reborn or go mad, for no one
who witnessed what I saw could attempt to splice his actions
to any future existence, unless he was insane to begin with;
and if he wasn't insane, the attempt would surely drive him
mad. When I eventually heard, almost a year after it
happened, that my wife and children had died in an Allied
bombing raid in 1944, there was grief, certainly, a profound
sense of loss that I have never fully overcome; but as time
passed there was relief too, because by then I had long been
aware that I could never return home, could never again

look my own children in the eye, never again allow them to embrace me or kiss these lips.

Perhaps I will see them again soon. Perhaps by then I will have been cleansed. Believe me when I tell you that I would have taken my own life many years ago if it did not seem too easy, too disrespectful to those young souls lost that night.

Sometimes I dream of the Tommy, and see him suffer again. In the dreams he is faceless, not from his wounds but because he has become a blank avatar for the task God, or the gods, or a pitiless universe, sets every man, woman and child who has ever lived or ever will: the decision that must be borne, to kill or die.

Muss es sein? Beethoven wrote. *Es muss sein.*

In the dreams the massacre boils down to a contest of will between Richter and the Englishman, one representing death, the other life; and both prevail.

This is the testimony of Gerard Smyth, formerly Gerhard Uxkull, and I swear that it is true.

TWENTY-ONE

T he island of Delphi had a permanent population of just three hundred souls, its main sources of income tourism and fishing. Most of the islanders lived in the village, with tiny hamlets of four and five houses dotted elsewhere on the island, some of them now deserted or converted to holiday-home enclaves.

So said the *Visitor's Guide to Delphi*, a fold-out pamphlet of the kind I'd hacked together copy for on more occasions than I cared to remember. It had a map on the reverse with cartoon illustrations of the various tourist attractions. There was no mention of Sebastian Devereaux, thriller writer and fabled recluse. Neither, unsurprisingly, was there any reference to a Nazi war crime. None of the cartoon illustrations hinted at a secret cemetery or a place of private pilgrimage deep in the woods.

I checked my phone for the twentieth time, established that it had a signal, and decided that if I sat at that table any longer I'd turn into a coffee bean. Besides, I had credentials to burnish, as Sebastian Devereaux's biographer, and a legitimate excuse to go poking around in the island's quiet corners. So I packed up my laptop, slung my bag over my shoulder and got going.

I angled up through the village following the wooden signposts, out along a grassy track and across a rough pasture towards the forest. It was easy going until I entered the trees, and the path became a stiff incline. By the time it intersected with the trail winding up from the shoreline, I was maybe fifty metres above sea level and blowing hard. No breeze now. Here and there was a beech or alder, a clump of holly, but it was mostly pine, the trunks soaring overhead in a conspiracy to blot out the sky. The light had thickened faintly green, as if I was drifting along undersea, all sound deadened bar the soft crunch of the tinder-dry brown needles that lay carpet thick on the track. Whenever I stopped for a breather the midges swarmed.

The entrance to the sanctuary was marked by tall stone columns either side of the path, mossy on their lower halves and stained on the upper with the streaky yellow-white of guano. There was a double gate between the columns, a vertically barred rusting white affair that gave easily at a push, but no fence or wall either side. Soon the quiet grew livelier. Rustlings in the undergrowth, some *skrees* and *skwaus* from further up the hill. A trombone honk that was answered in kind. A fierce chittering from the far side of a dry stream bed gave me a start, and then five or six birds, partridge-like, went waddling Indian-file across the path at a fair old clip.

There came a dull boom that sent the partridge-like birds skittering away and then, a moment later, a spattering so light it hissed. A summer thunderstorm, I guessed, but when I craned my neck the sky was as clear as it had been all morning. I slogged on, flapping in vain at the midges, until I came to another fork atop a gentle rise. Here the sanctuary trail crested and meandered away and down to the left, following the contours of the slope. Another path led upwards, curving out of sight beyond the jagged roots of an ancient pine torn up long ago. A sign in English, Irish, German and French announced that this path was Private Property and that trespassers would be prosecuted. To reinforce the threat, or perhaps to protest it, someone had treated the sign to a shotgun blast, the tiny holes puckered and rusting.

Twenty yards further on a heavy wooden gate between two solid stone pillars blocked the way, five-barred again but this time horizontally, with another spar running diagonally down across the bars. Beyond the gate was a shallow incline that broadened out into a tiny valley, the far wall of which erupted almost vertically. Steep steps, steep as those of an Aztec pyramid and numbering well over a hundred, had been cut out of the rock, or had been laid in. As an engineering project it was as architecturally impressive and pointless as any Victorian folly, disused and forlorn, littered with leaves and needles and twigs. Beyond the last step hunched one last little peak of grey rock and then there was nothing but clear blue sky.

I sat myself down on a flat stone and sipped on a bottle of water and acknowledged that the prudent thing to do was to keep going along the sanctuary path and look to bump into some of the staff and introduce myself, Tom Noone, a freelance journalist researching the life of Sebastian Devereaux. Smile and shake hands and then return to the village and the hotel room and Kee, the justification for further snooping established and, hopefully, humming along the island's grapevine.

Except here I already was, and in exactly the kind of place I'd want to sniff around. If proof of Gerard Smyth's story was to be found – *if* it was to be found – then it wouldn't be anywhere near the village or the harbour, or lying offshore and fathoms deep in a rusting submarine. The islanders might have gone to great lengths over the years to keep the massacre buried, but I found it hard to believe that such a small community wouldn't have marked the death of so many young children for themselves. A memorial, a Celtic cross, say, or even a small cemetery, a long way off the beaten path taken by all the hikers and diggers and twitchers. A private and sacred place forbidden to outsiders, with its Private Property sign pocked by a shotgun blast to further dissuade the casually curious tourist.

I cut off the track and worked my way up the hill, east away from the Private Property sign, before cutting back north. Soon I was scrambling on hands and knees around vertical outcrops and sheer rock faces, the weight of the laptop in the shoulder bag not helping. Dirty, hot and sweating, I finally emerged on to a knife-blade ridge that curved around back towards the top of the steps. The breeze was refreshing but the stony path looked like it had been designed by goats with ambitions to join a circus high-wire troupe, and I felt suddenly exposed, acutely aware that I would be sky-lit from below. When the path finally opened out on to a crude table of rock I was tempted to sink down to kiss the grey stone. Instead I made my way across to a wooden bench that had been lashed together from salt-bleached driftwood and sat to get my breath back.

The island fell away on three sides, a fuzzy carpet of deep green tented on a crooked central ridge, the forest sweeping down on both sides all the way to the sea. Far below on the western flank, tucked into the curving embrace of the humped headland, the little cubes of the village were so many white diamonds fringing a turquoise mantilla. The sun was a-tremble directly overhead. I could almost hear the crackle of twigs shrivelling up dry. Even the midges had surrendered to the deathly heat. The breeze too had died away, leaving the air thick and druggy with sleep.

But it was the view behind that proved more interesting. What

I had thought was solid rock was two vast boulders, roughly thirty feet high, the right collapsed in on its twin at close to a sixty-degree angle to create a narrow cleft. Perhaps they had once been a single massive eruption, split aeons ago by a lightning strike, but maybe that notion was suggested by the sign nailed to the rock on the right-hand side. An old metal black tin plate of a white skull and crossbones with a pair of lightning flashes either side of the head. As was the case with the sanctuary sign further down, and for all I knew every sign on the island beyond the village limits, it had received a shotgun blast, its leering grin punctured with hundreds of tiny rusting holes. In the circumstances, the *Achtung!* above the skull and the *Verboten!* below the crossbones seemed superfluous.

The cleft beckoned, dark and cool, and I had come too far to be put off by a sign that was more than half a century old, but that wasn't what made me hesitate. The image, the words, seemed to undermine Gerard Smyth's story. Would a people that had suffered a massacre of their children at the hands of German soldiers really have employed such a sign anywhere on the island? I couldn't imagine them using it ironically.

Time heals, of course, even if it can't cure. Memories fade, generations come through, and World War II was as long buried on Delphi as it was everywhere else, an event as remote in time, as half-glimpsed in the lengthening shadows, as the Battle of Clontarf or the Flight of the Earls. You make your peace with history or you fight a pointless rearguard action, a losing battle, forever.

But somebody, at some point in the past, had had a good reason to tack that skull and crossbones sign to the stone, and no one had had a good enough reason to take it down since.

I ducked into the cleft in the rock. Not quite holding my breath but half-convinced, as I always am, that a structure that had stood for maybe half a million years would suddenly collapse. Once inside it grew cool, a faint breeze filtering through the gap at the far end, and it took a moment or two for my eyes to adjust to the gloom. The walls were coarse to the touch but the floor was smooth, the rock coming together a couple of feet overhead. The passageway was about forty feet in length and narrowed sharply near the end, which made my lungs constrict. When I emerged

into the sunlight, dazzled, I stood for a moment and breathed in
deeply, soaking up the heat. It was just as well I did. When my
eyes readjusted I was standing about three feet from the edge of
a precipice. Now I understood the warning sign on the other side
of the passage. There was no barrier. A stride or so more and
I'd have pitched headfirst off the cliff, gone windmilling down
into the valley below.

The valley was nowhere near as impressive as the view out
across the island – it lacked the sheer scale of the raw beauty
on the other side of the cleft – but it was easy to see why someone
might want to claim it as private property. It was a broad-bottomed
bowl, its wide floor and the gentle incline of its lower slopes a
patchwork, almost a chessboard, of low hedge, terrace and mani-
cured garden, with vivid splashes of yellow, red and violet blazing
either side of a wide and arrow-straight path that bisected the
floor from directly below where we stood to the foot of the steps
that rose towards what looked like a Georgian mansion in russet
brick set foursquare at the head of the valley.

The path down to the valley veered out around an abutting
shoulder of rock, then cut back sharply behind the cliff. When I
took a step forward to peer down from the precipice there was
a man sprawled on his back, basking, on a wide flat rock maybe
twenty yards directly below. Beside him, within easy reach, lay
a shotgun broken open. A pair of binoculars on his chest.

I was stepping back when the shrill ringing of my phone sawed
into the silence.

It took a second or two to locate the phone in the front pocket
of the shoulder bag, but once I had it I stepped to the edge of
the cliff again, answering as I did so. The man was scrambling
to his feet, the broken shotgun already in his hands.

'Hello?'

'Tom?'

'Mr Govern?'

'Where are you, Tom?'

Now the man was looking up, shading his eyes with one hand.
I raised my own hand, palm outward, a greeting and a sign of
peace.

'I'm somewhere in the bird sanctuary on Delphi. Where are you?'

Now the guy was snapping the shotgun closed, thumbing back
the hammers. I waved to distract him, to get his attention.

'I guess I'm not too far away,' he said. 'I'm at Carol's place right now. Can you come here?'

'Sounds good. Let me just – hey, *whoa!*'

This last to the guy below, who had jammed the butt of the shotgun against his shoulder and was aiming up the cliff face.

I turned and dived and heard the dull boom. A split second later came the tings and chips of ricochets as the load spattered against the rock overhead and the kick in the back that booted me into the dark cleft. The near wall reared up and cuffed the side of my head and then there was nothing much of anything at all.

TWENTY-TWO

I came awake slowly and not all at once. Rising and sinking, adrift in warm green depths.

'Ah, you're awake. Good.'

She might have been waiting there a minute or an hour or a week. Probably not a week, though. Or even an hour. No woman stands around looking at a sleeping man more than is strictly necessary and I don't know many women who'd think it necessary at all. Besides, the bowl on the tray was still steaming.

There was a jug of water on there too, a drinking glass and a straw.

It was a high-ceilinged room, thick with carpet and curtain in pale yellow or worn gold, an old-fashioned open fireplace taking up most of the far wall. The bed was a four-poster that lacked a canopy but the cotton sheets were white and crisp and warm.

She set down the tray on a bureau.

'How are you feeling?' she said. She produced a thermometer from the breast pocket of her shirt and shook it out. 'I'm Erin, by the way.'

I stared. She tapped the tip of the thermometer against my lips and waited for me to open up. When I didn't she said, 'If you want I can have someone come in and hold you down while I tuck this in somewhere else. So what's it to be?'

I opened up and she slipped the thermometer under my tongue. Then she took my wrist in a gentle but firm grip. All the while she kept her eyes on mine. She was close enough to count the cluster of freckles across the bridge of her nose. A pert nose and a jutting chin and a fleshy lower lip that seemed poised on the cusp of a pout or a smile.

She removed the thermometer and glanced at it, shook it again and laid it on the tray. 'So,' she said, 'one more time. How are you feeling?'

'Dizzy and nauseous,' I croaked, 'and parched for a drink.' The back of my head was throbbing and my back felt raw and prickling, like I'd been battered with a giant cheese grater.

She poured some water into the glass and warned me to sip at it through the straw, then sat on the edge of the bed and probed the lump on the back of my skull with her fingertips.

'You might have a mild concussion,' she said as I sipped. 'We'll keep an eye on that. Probably happened when you banged your head.'

'I was fucking *shot*.'

She nodded as she took the glass away. 'Sure, but the force of it slammed you into the rock. You were lucky.'

'Lucky?'

'Rock salt.' She'd been putting on a pair of surgical gloves while she spoke, and now she took a package from the tray and tore it open with her teeth, squeezed it until a pair of tweezers popped up. 'Turn over on to your front. I think we got it all, but I want to be sure there's nothing impacted under the skin.'

I was bare-chested, wearing only boxer shorts and a bandage that had been wound around my abdomen and halfway up my ribs. I tried to remember if they were the shorts I'd put on that morning.

'I understand you have questions,' she said, 'but let's just get the job done first.' She laid the purple-stained bandage to one side. 'Turn over on your front. Or do you want me to bring someone in to turn you over?'

Another dizzying rush as I turned on to my stomach, the room yawing off beam. That left me vulnerable, virtually naked and weak and ready to puke, my field of vision reduced to the blank white of the pillow. If anyone wanted to run in right now and put a shotgun to the back of my head . . .

But it made no sense. If they'd wanted me gone, disappeared, they'd had all the opportunity they needed. And they'd hardly tuck me up in bed, bring hot soup on a tray and go to all the trouble of removing salt shrapnel from my back, if they were planning anything lethal.

I shivered as she brushed the cold tweezers against my skin, then gently prodded. A pinch, a squeeze, and then a tinny *pik* as she dropped a fragment of rock salt on to the tray.

'Where am I?' I said.

'Bellapaix,' she said. 'Which is where, I assume, you were headed.'

'I've never even heard that name before.'

'Maybe not, but this is where you were aiming for.' The tweezers were cold where she brushed the skin, grazing it. 'Mr Govern was here when they brought you in. He was very upset when he saw you.' She paused then. 'It was a pity you didn't simply announce yourself, Tom. Take the boat around. Carol is absolutely distraught.'

'So it's my fault I was shot.'

'I wouldn't go so far as to say that.' A pinch, a *tik*. 'Carol tells me you're here to write a book about Sebastian.'

'That's the idea.'

'She's hoping you won't be put off by your, um, experience.'

'By this? Not at all. Being honest, I have problems with committing to a project until I've been shot at least once.'

'I'm glad to see it hasn't affected your sense of humour,' she said. Pinch, *tik*. 'You'll need it when you interview Sebastian. I presume you *are* planning an interview?'

'Sebastian Devereaux?'

She pinched some skin, gave it a playful twist. 'It's not like we get many Sebastians to the pound here in Donegal, Tom. So yes, Sebastian Devereaux. Unless you came all this way looking for some other Sebastian?'

'He's here?'

'Sebastian is here,' she said, 'and as it happens, very keen to interview you too.' She put the tweezers down on the tray. 'OK,' she said, 'that looks fine to me. I'm going to put some iodine on now, so stay still.'

'What does he want to interview me about?'

'One step at a time, Tom.' She dabbed in silence, then told me to sit up and face her. She wrapped a fresh bandage around my abdomen, focusing on the job, leaving me to stare down at the top of her head. When she was finished she sat back to examine her work, then nodded at the bowl on the tray. 'Chicken broth,' she said. 'You think you could feed yourself?'

She topped up my glass of water, put two painkillers on the bedside table. 'You've already had a couple,' she warned as she stripped off the gloves, 'so don't use them unless you really need to. Will I send in your wife?'

TWENTY-THREE

My clothes were folded on the bottom of the bed. I was stiff and aching and still woozy, so it took me about fifteen minutes to get dressed. They'd given me a new t-shirt, or at least a fresh one, but the waistband of the jeans was ragged from the rock salt.

Erin was right about my being lucky. There was no sign of my shoulder bag, presumably because it, and the laptop inside, had taken the main blast. Both were probably mangled. The skin on my lower back tingled at what might have been.

Bellapaix. *Good peace.*

Ironic, perhaps, but the place was well named. It felt like the room was muffled in wads of cotton wool. Or maybe that was just the concussion and the painkillers.

I took a turn around the room to stretch out and get my gyroscope back on its axis. Fresh air was a priority too. The sash window slid down easily enough, but then I made the mistake of looking out and down three floors of ivy-tangled stone to a crazy-paved courtyard. Dizzy again, I withdrew, and heard Kee drawl, 'Don't jump, you'll make me look bad.'

She looked fresh and pink-faced, recently showered, the hair still damp and looking a lot like a water-logged bird's nest. She wore the jeans and boots she'd been wearing yesterday, and a form-fitting peach t-shirt.

I sat on the bed and she perched on the bottom, asked how I was feeling.

'Ropey. How long was I out?'

'Since it happened, more or less. It's now,' she checked her watch, 'nearly nine in the morning.'

'Jesus.'

'They're saying you shouldn't have run.'

'I already got the message, yeah. It's my fault some fuckwit blasted me.'

A terrible misunderstanding, reported Lady Carol McConnell after consulting in private with Shotgun Sam. Possibly because

Sam, aka Eoin, was a little jumpy. After all, they'd had a security breach at the southern end of the valley earlier that day.

'A security breach?'

'Her very words. An interesting turn of phrase, no? Anyway, Lady Carol is accepting all responsibility, even if you were, as she pointed out a number of times, trespassing at the time.'

Hence the best medical care the island could provide, along with a private room in which to recuperate.

Kee, who'd realized I was hurt but not fatally, or even punctured to any noticeable degree by a blast of rock salt from twenty yards, had decided to play along with the hospitality routine, see where it might go. Gave it the whole hands-wringing honeymooning wife bit. Which was how she'd scored herself a room across the hall and one of the finest dinners she'd had in years.

'Pheasant, Tom. Marvellous stuff. Make you wonder about this bird sanctuary they're running, wouldn't it?'

Kee, Shay Govern and Lady Carol McConnell, aka Carol Devereaux, Sebastian's daughter, the three of them hunched around one corner of a table they could have used for indoor tennis. 'That's actual tennis, mind. None of your ping-pong nonsense.'

Kee playing her part, the newly married Mrs Tom Noone ('I hope you don't mind, but I told them I was keeping my own name') while Shay and Carol picked her brain with a little more verve than they brought to the pheasant. 'I mean, this was seriously good bird. But they didn't seem to have much of an appetite. Maybe they shouldn't have had the melon starter.'

They started easy, asking if she'd known of my books before she met me. 'We met at a book launch, by the way. Hodges Figgis, I couldn't remember the writer. Probably because I was so dazzled by you.'

'Probably.'

It wasn't long before they were asking, keeping it casual, whether I'd mentioned anything about the latest book, the biography of Sebastian Devereaux. If I'd talked about any research I'd managed to do, or sources I might have turned up in the last couple of days.

'So I say, sorry, no, Tom's a bit mental when he's working on something. Hates anyone to see his work until it's finished. And was there any source in particular they were thinking of?'

None that sprang to mind immediately, according to Kee.

Although Lady Carol did happen to drop the name Gerard Smyth during the banoffee pie.

'It wasn't Govern who mentioned him?'

'Nope.'

'Because I already told him about Gerard Smyth. That Jack Byrne tracked him down.'

'Well, he's obviously told the good Lady Carol that, because he wasn't remotely surprised that she knew the name.'

'So maybe they think I'm hooked up with Jack, trying to pull a scam.' I shrugged, which was a bad idea, because it sent shudders of burning pain through my lower back. 'Except I was the one who told Govern about Jack wanting to do a number on him.'

'OK, but maybe this isn't the first time Lady Carol is hearing about Gerard Smyth. It's possible, right? I mean, if the guy's firing off missives to Foreign Affairs and half the embassies in Dublin, it's likely he didn't stop there. For all we know Smyth came back here, tried to get them onside for his campaign.'

'He never said anything to me about travelling to Delphi.'

'OK, so maybe he wasn't here. Maybe he wrote to them instead. The point being, Carol seems a little sensitive about Gerard Smyth and what he might have told you. When you'd imagine, wouldn't you, that she'd be pleased to learn there was someone out there who could confirm the story.'

'Do they know he's dead?'

'Not from the way they were talking, no.'

'So maybe they're worried that Smyth won't just confirm the story, but add a little bit more that doesn't exactly sit straight with the idea of Sebastian as this hero. You got a chance to read it?'

'Yesterday afternoon.'

'Sebastian's the Englishman, right? The Tommy.'

'Has to be.'

'Doesn't exactly come out of it covered in glory, does he?'

'Not unless dead kids are your idea of glorious, no. But here's the thing,' she said. 'What we're looking at here is an open door. You want to push back against Shay Govern, tell him you think Gerard Smyth's testimony isn't rock solid. Meanwhile, they're edgy right now because you're the connection to Gerard Smyth, who's saying more than they might want about Sebastian, and they've only gone and pumped a round of rock salt into you. Maybe soured your perception a little.'

Now, she said, they needed to pamper me and get me well, feed me up on roast pheasant and make sure I was properly disillusioned and cynical about the dark fairytales told by old men craving one last moment in the spotlight before eternity folds in forever.

'I say let them do it,' she urged. 'Nod and smile and agree with their concerns. Then we walk away. Once you're back in Dublin, you drop Shay Govern a line letting him know that Gerard Smyth has drowned in a canal, the book is going to take a little longer than you thought. What?'

'Have you seen my laptop?'

'Not since the café yesterday afternoon. You think they took it?'

'It was in the bag that was blasted with the rock salt. It's probably in bits.'

'Probably, yeah. But that doesn't necessarily mean the hard drive is irretrievable.'

'What about your copy? The one on the memory stick.'

'Gone. They rang around, tracked me down at the hotel and told me you'd been shot. So I flushed the stick.'

'Nice priorities.'

'I like to think so. Besides, it was only rock salt.' She got up, clapped her hands. 'OK,' she said. 'I'm going to head down to the village, make some calls, get the wheels turning. Soon as you've had your chat with Shay, let me know and we're off this godforsaken rock.'

'It could take a while.'

'Just do it, Tom. You can work on your dying swan routine back in Dublin.'

'I mean, there's a queue.'

'A queue?'

'According to Erin, Sebastian Devereaux is quite keen to inter-view me.'

'Sebastian *Devereaux*?'

'Apparently so.'

'I thought he was dead.'

'So did I.'

'Shit,' she said, sitting down again.

'Kind of complicates things,' I said, 'doesn't it?'

'Oh, you think?'

It was bad enough, she said, when some old German guy was making allegations of Nazi atrocity. Now we had a bona fide living and breathing British spook who'd been operating in neutral Ireland and the reason six kids had been burned up in a church.

'It wasn't him who killed them,' I said.

'Maybe not by pulling a trigger, no. But he's why they were rounded up. Because he wouldn't tell Richter what he wanted to know.' She put her face in her palms, dry-washed her face. 'Christ, Tom. This could blow the lot sky high.'

But while she was talking all I could think about was the church in flames and children shovelled into the Moloch's maw.

TWENTY-FOUR

K ee departed in a hurry shortly afterwards, forgetting in her haste to bestow any additional luscious kisses. The soup had begun to congeal – besides, who eats soup for breakfast? – so I swallowed the painkillers and lay on the bed, wishing the water was coffee.

About half an hour later there came a cautious tappity-tap on the door, and Erin popped her head around the door.

'Are you feeling up to a wee chat yet?' she said. I said I was, the dull stabbing pains in my lower back notwithstanding. She led the way along a stone-flagged corridor, then down a broad and curving flight of stairs. It was the kind of place that generally boasted oil portraits of venerable ancestors on the walls, a modest chandelier or two, but Sebastian Devereaux – or Lady Carol McConnell, or whoever the hell was running the place – favoured the minimalist look. The hall was a vaulted affair soaring three storeys to oak rafters, the floor a chequerboard of black and white tiles, but other than a wooden chest against the wall to the right of the front door there was nothing to take the bare look off it.

She crossed the hall and opened a heavy door, ushered me in ahead. A fine room, high-ceilinged again, the walls lined with bookshelves and leather-bound volumes, a writing desk to my left. She directed me to the semicircle of leather couch and armchairs at the other end of the room, where a low fire glowed in a huge fireplace. The smell of turf hung heavy on the air.

The table in the middle of the room was littered with the remnants of breakfast.

'I thought she'd be here,' Erin said. 'She must have gone through to the kitchen. Back in a sec.'

I poured myself a lukewarm coffee and strolled across to the French windows. Outside was a wide terrace with potted palms at each corner, steps down to a lawn. Beyond hung an azure sky. It all put me in mind, for some reason, of *Tender is the Night*, although the guy sitting on the wall with his back to the house and tapping cigarette ash into the potted palm, a shotgun propped beside him, rather ruined the illusion. It was hard to tell, given that he was sitting rather than lying sprawled out, or pointing a shotgun in my direction, but I guessed it was my old friend Sam.

Then again, it was entirely possible that Bellapaix was guarded by roving gangs of tooled-up thugs, the shotgun their preferred weapon of choice.

From behind me there came a clearing of the throat that was meant, I guessed, as a politeness, a discreet way of letting me know I wasn't alone. What it sounded like was a cement truck going through the gears, the clutch long since burnt out.

The elusive Sebastian Devereaux.

But not yet. When I turned I found myself looking at a woman who was tamping tobacco into a clay pipe.

I'd been expecting an old man, something wizened and shuffling, so it took me a moment to readjust. I got the impression that she was anticipating a pause, that she tended to have that effect when she walked into a room, expected or not. The eyes a faded but glittering blue, the kind of blue you half-glimpse and think you might have imagined if you stare long enough into a diamond. She wore her hair loose and wild, an autumnal tumbling of russet and grey, and there was something in the imperious upthrust of nose and chin that suggested she was constantly defying the world to disappoint her. She had the look of a woman who hadn't been so much born as carved out of the void by a loving but crude hand.

She puffed a cloud of aromatic smoke from the pipe, the wide nostrils flaring. 'Tom, I take it?'

'That's right,' I said. 'Lady Carol?'

She stepped forward, the pipe clawed between the fore and middle fingers of her left hand. When we shook, her grip was strong, wiry. 'We don't stand on ceremony here, Tom,' she said. A bright smile, faintly yellowing teeth. 'We don't sit on ceremony either, for that matter. Or turn handsprings on ceremony, even if such were possible. At Bellapaix we prefer to simply go about our business with the minimum of fuss. Attracting as little attention as we can get away with. So please, call me Carol. How are you?'

'Fine, I think. A bit stiff and sore, but I'll survive.'

'I'm sure you will.' She had another draw on the pipe, studying

me. 'Will you accept our apologies for the unfortunate incident
last evening? It was unforgivable. Eoin can be, shall we say, a
little enthusiastic about defending hearth and home. Is your coffee
not cold? Never mind, Mary will be bringing through a fresh
pot.'

It was a disarming blend, the awkwardly formal words softened
by a thick Donegal brogue, the apology delivered and immediately
forgotten.

'Coffee would be good,' I said.

'It will be here presently.' She gestured out beyond the French
windows. 'Are you able to walk and talk,' she said, 'or would
you prefer to have your coffee first?'

Shotgun Sam stood up when we stepped out on to the terrace,
then sat back down when Carol said, 'That's fine, Eoin. We won't
be going far.' Then, as we descended to the lawn, she stopped
mid-stride on the steps, fumbling in a pocket for a box of matches.
When she got her pipe going again, a pungent blue cloud rising
on the breeze, she said, 'So what is it you want to ask me, Tom?'

'I'm sorry?'

'Erin tells me that you wish to conduct an interview with
Sebastian Devereaux. Or was she just flattering me?'

There was a devious twinkle, or a glint, in the diamond-blue
eyes.

'You're telling me,' I said, 'that you're Sebastian Devereaux.'

'Well,' she said, 'that all depends. Sebastian Devereaux was
my father. But Erin tells me that it's Sebastian Devereaux the
author you wish to interview.' The bright, disarming smile of a
cheeky child. 'And that would be me, yes. Do I disappoint you?'

There was a wooden bench near the end of the lawn overlooking
an abrupt drop into forest and beyond that the Swilly opening
up northwards towards the Atlantic. At both corners of the lawn
was a set of crazy-paved steps that curled into a central path and
then disappeared into the pines below. The breeze was stronger
now, so she abandoned her pipe, tapping it against the sole of
her shoe to loosen the dottle and slipping it into a pocket.

'This way,' she said, indicating the left-hand set of steps. Down
we went until we intersected with an unpaved dusty path
branching off, which opened up into a tunnel between the trees.
The breeze fainter now.

She had asked me to be patient, and that – the devious glint again – *all would be revealed*. So we strolled along in silence, Carol with a faint limp that appeared to originate in her hip, her left leg swinging out in a small semicircle. The pace was gentle, but already the bruising on my back was beginning to ache.

So I was grateful when she indicated another path, a short downhill incline that opened out into a small sloped clearing, a horseshoe space cleared from the pines. A tiny meadow dotted with daisy and buttercup, and a bench at the near end, two crude stones in the middle, and then wild grasses and flowers flowing on to a cliff edge. We were lower down now, but the view was more or less the same: the vivid blue of Lough Swilly, mountains rising either side, the paler blue of the North Atlantic shimmering in the far distance.

Carol eased herself down on to the bench, then indicated the graves. 'My parents,' she said. 'Margaret and Sebastian Devereaux.'

'May I?'

'Of course.'

The rough stones had been dug out rough rather than quarried. If it hadn't been for the smooth squares where the names and dates were chiselled you might have thought they'd been there for millennia, mossy and veined yellow. Grass and flowers flowed around them, swelling high against the foot of both, but there was no sense of neglect. Rather, the effect was to suggest that the stones were simply part of the landscape, their only notable feature the side-by-side symmetry and the few millimetres that didn't so much separate them as confirm their unity. The dedications were as minimalist as decency allowed.

Margaret Devereaux
1913–2004

Sebastian Devereaux
1915–1997

I went back to the bench, where Carol Devereaux was poking a matchstick into the stem of her pipe.

'I'm afraid Shay has brought you a long way,' she said without looking up, 'to interview a man who has been dead for more than ten years.'

'Well,' I said, 'I'd kind of assumed all along he was dead. My condolences, by the way.'

'You're very kind. And there is no reason why you should have known if he was alive or dead. Ah.' She dislodged the blockage, began tamping tobacco into the bowl. Now she looked at me. 'Whose business was it but our own?'

'He was a well regarded writer in his time. It seems a pity that no one noticed his passing.'

'Untrue. He was mourned by those who knew him.'

'I'm sure he was. What I mean is he—'

'I know exactly what you mean. But my father was an intensely private man, Tom. He would have been very pleased indeed to learn that he slipped away without being subjected to the usual vulgarities. Besides,' a match flared, and she puffed the pipe to life, 'what was there for anyone else to remember? He was not Sebastian Devereaux the well-regarded writer, as you put it. To celebrate him in such a way would have been the most horrible sham.'

'I suppose it would.'

'You suppose correctly. Now let's suppose that you ask me the questions you had planned to ask my father.'

'Well,' I said, 'it's not exactly that straightforward, is it?'

'How so?'

'Being honest, I'm still trying to get my head around the fact that you wrote the books.'

'The last two only,' she said. A bird came dipping through the clearing with a piercing *pee-wit*, and was gone. She watched it go. 'My mother wrote the others.'

'Your mother?'

She turned to me again. 'My mother was a remarkable woman, Tom.'

'It's my experience that most of them are.'

A faint grin. 'Nicely put. Ingratiating, but nicely put.' Her pipe had gone dead, so she took a moment to crack a match, cupping it in her palms until the blue smoke came again in ragged puffs. She put the dead match back into the box and fixed the diamond-blue eyes on mine. 'Just ask, Tom.'

'Ask what?'

'The one question you want answered.'

She made it sound so simple. Somehow, illogical as it might

sound, it felt as if I'd be betraying a confidence if I traded Gerard Smyth's name. Bartering his death for information. And yet, a small voice in the back of my mind insisted, Gerard Smyth had told me his story in the hope of having it confirmed. So that the truth would out.

Weasel words, of course. What it all came down to was *I wanted to know*.

So I told her. About Gerard Smyth and how he had decided to live beyond the law. How he had reminded me too much of my father in his own final days to ignore him. That he hadn't lived beyond the law very long, and was now prone on a slab awaiting autopsy.

'I'm very sorry to hear that, Tom.' A husky quiver in her tobacco-stained throat. 'Now be so kind as to tell me what he said.'

There was every chance she was testing me. That they had, as Kee suggested, retrieved the hard drive from the mangled laptop. So I kept to the basics. Once in a while those diamond-blue eyes glittered, and at one point seemed to glisten, but she heard me out in silence.

When I was finished she considered for a moment or two and then cleared her throat and said, 'Yes, that appears to be more or less it.'

'It's true then.'

'As your Mr Smyth saw it, yes.'

There was a cold kind of horror in her words. Or perhaps not the words themselves, but the detached way in which she spoke, as if reminiscing about a summer holiday when it had rained every day.

My stomach began to churn. Delayed shock, perhaps, although disgust played its part.

'What I don't understand,' I said, 'is why they didn't lynch him after.'

'My father?' She seemed amused. 'There were some who wanted to, certainly.'

'It never occurred to him to save them the trouble?'

'Apparently it did, yes. Many times.'

'But he didn't do it.'

'Sometimes it takes more courage to be a coward than a hero.'

'That's rot.'

'Is it though?'

There must have been a hive nearby. Bees hummed through the clearing on their solitary missions.

'Whose idea was it?' I said.

'Pardon me?'

'The book. The first one. Whose idea was it to write a *thriller* about the massacre of innocent children?'

A thin smile this time, one that seemed to slice her words. 'Would it have been more appropriate had the children been guilty, Tom?'

'Guilty of what? Don't be ridiculous.'

'Precisely. Why should we emphasize the children's innocence? All children are innocent, are they not? Your own daughter being a case in point. Emily, yes?'

'What are you talking about?'

'Your daughter. I imagine you had her baptised, Tom. To wash away her sin. Did you not?'

'That has nothing to do with this.'

'No? Then answer me this. Did you do it as a believer in the Christian values? Or was it social convention?'

I couldn't really blame her. If my father had been responsible for children being herded into a church and burned alive, I'd very likely have tried to dissemble too.

'If you really want to know,' I said, 'we had Emily baptised because it'd make it easier to get her into the village school when she was old enough to go. Happy now?'

'That you have admitted your hypocrisy? Yes.'

'There's a difference,' I said as evenly as I could. 'Having a child baptised is one thing. Writing a novel about a massacre of children and passing it off as fiction is another thing entirely, and that's putting it pretty fucking mildly. Especially when you bank the royalties and end up buying whole islands and calling yourself Lady Muck.'

'Let's not say anything we might regret, Tom.'

I almost laughed. 'Seriously? You're the one trying to equate a child's baptism with an atrocity.'

'I only asked about your daughter in order to tell you I was never baptised myself. Would you like to know why?'

'Go on.'

'My mother decided it would be inappropriate. Because there

was no miracle for my father that night. No divine intervention. Because those young children were simply abandoned to their fate. And please, I beg you not to suggest that the evening's events were devised as a perverse examination of faith and forbearance. The very idea that an intelligence capable of creating an entire universe would indulge in such petty games is laughable. No. Even as she watched the church burn my mother understood that if she was to survive then it would be by her own hand. That she could rely on nothing but her own—'

'Wait. She was *there*?'

'Yes.'

'That night?'

'Indeed. You have your eye-witness testimony, Tom. I have my own.'

TWENTY-FIVE

Margaret – more commonly known as Morag – Devereaux, née Rutherford, was indeed a remarkable woman. The first time she descended out of the Highlands, via Inverness, was to attend university in Edinburgh.

'She hated it,' Carol said. 'Not Edinburgh itself, she thought it a fine old town. Just the fact that she had to be there.'

A child of the heather, and an only child, Morag had grown up on her father's estate shooting and fishing and swimming and running wild. And digging, digging, digging.

She was the daughter of a laird who was rarely home and a mother, widowed at the first battle of Ypres and reluctantly remarried, who was a great-great-granddaughter of the Scottish Enlightenment. Laird Rutherford wasn't unique in the House of Lords for his support of the Suffragette cause – this when he was younger and rather more vital than the man Morag came to know – and he was by no means the only man from north of the border to be told he wore a kilt because his wife was at home parading around in his trousers. Unusually, there was an element of truth in this particular slur; even more unusual was the fact that the laird, a man partial to fine wine in excess and something of an evangelist on behalf of the Laphroaig distillery on the Isle of Islay, never tired of repeating it, or was unaware of the repetition, on his infrequent forays home.

Morag grew up on her mother's stories of the Great War and the Highland clearances and the brutal suppression of the Suffragettes. Her understanding of men, as gleaned from her mother, was that they were not exactly a necessary evil – which was to say, they were not necessarily evil, and not necessarily necessary. Which meant they were not to be trusted in any matter of importance, a phrase that grew, as Morag grew, to incorporate anything from war and politics to philosophy and fashion. Most important of all, of course, was her unswerving belief that no man should ever have a right to make any decision that might impact on any aspect of any woman's life.

'An unsustainable credo,' Carol observed dryly. 'But you couldn't fault her for lack of ambition.'

Morag went down from Edinburgh University in the spring of 1935 – her mother deigned to attend, her father sent flowers and a bottle of 10-year Laphroaig – with a first in the History of Archaeology. By October of that year she was battling the flies in southern Egypt, serving a penitential apprenticeship at Tell el-Amarna under John Pendlebury, although by then the dig was in the convulsive throes of its final months. When Pendlebury moved to Crete early the following year, Morag found herself on the south coast of the island, working on what they hoped would reveal itself as one of the summer palaces of the Minoans.

It was in Heraklion during the Easter recess ('Easter was late that year. Doesn't it always seem that Easter is always *late*?') that she met Peter Kingsley. 'Tall, beaky and sallow.' An older man, of course, married twice and twice divorced. He'd been through Eton, Cambridge and the Somme, worked under Evans and Petrie, and somehow survived them all. His field now was the Old Religion, the pre-Greek worship of goddess and matriarch glimpsed through the veil of the Eleusinian Mysteries. 'A passion for dead women,' observed Carol, 'that cost him two wives.'

He came and went from Crete all that year, on occasion venturing to the south coast. For the most part their rendezvous were in Heraklion and Chania. That Christmas he told her war was in the wind, that he had no intention of fighting another, and that anyone who could decently absent themselves from that particular kind of hell should take the opportunity to do so. He suggested a thesis that might overlap with his own, which was that the pre-Greek colonisers who came marauding down out of Central Europe into the Mediterranean shared a common heritage – and not incidentally, a penchant for fierce goddesses – with the Celts, who had spread west and north.

'He duped her,' Carol said, 'although I can only be grateful he did.'

Kingsley introduced her to Mórrígan, the Great Queen of the Celts, the Supreme Warrior Goddess. The shape-shifting mother of war and death, goddess of magic and prophecy, fertility and revenge. 'His theory was that Mórrígan shared a common root with the Erinyes, the Furies. In some variations she keeps

company with Hateful Fea, Badb the Fury, and Macha of Battle.
A trinity to be reckoned with, Tom, wouldn't you say?'

I would, and did. What I didn't say, so as not to interrupt
Carol's flow, was that I'd come across Mórrígan before, as a code
name in Gerard Smyth's account of the atrocity.

'Kingsley offered to pull strings back in London and secure
a commission. He knew of a site associated with Mórrígan, a
monastic Irish settlement of beehive cells built on a much older
place of worship. If she was agreeable, he believed he could get
the permissions and enough funding to allow them to excavate
together.'

She agreed. Kingsley sent her on ahead to Delphi Island in
Donegal, via the Highlands, where Morag saw her mother for
the first time in two years. It wasn't needed or even asked for,
but she was nevertheless pleased to receive her mother's blessing
on what she called her 'arrangements' with Kingsley. She stayed
a week, then left for Delphi.

By the time Kingsley arrived the following month, Morag was
fully at home. She'd hired islanders for the dig, established a
rapport with the local priest, Father Cahill, who initially resisted
the idea of excavating beneath the beehive cells, and discovered
that the Scots Gaelic she'd used in her youth had much in common
with the Irish language many of the islanders still spoke. 'Her
accent was on the peaty side, but not so different from the Donegal
brogue that a frightened young German sailor might notice.' With
little to do in the evenings, and with the consent of the priest
and the island's mayor, she began to teach English and history
and geography, even some archaeology, although, as she insisted
the lessons be conducted through the local dialect, the teaching
was as much for her own sake as it was the children's.

Kingsley didn't stay long. He stepped off the boat trailed by
a younger man – younger than Morag by four years – and introduced him as Sebastian Devereaux, Cambridge graduate and
archaeological neophyte. With war on the way, and non-essential
budgets being slashed, Kingsley had much by way of string-
pulling to attend to in London. Satisfied that Morag had the
Delphi dig in hand, he left a week later, promising to return as
soon as he could get away. She never saw him again.

Sebastian, she said, was a difficult man to like. Tall, blond and
awkward were her first impressions, awkward physically and

socially. A polite Viking, she said. He announced himself a pacifist and a conscientious objector. Those islanders who didn't translate the concepts as 'coward' and 'traitor' thought the idea of a pacifist Englishman hilarious, although they waited in vain for the punchline.

Sebastian, in his self-deprecating way, accepted their judgement. If he was a coward, he was at least an honest one.

He was infuriatingly clumsy on site, so much so that it took Morag a number of months to realize his awkwardness was a kind of spiky cloak he draped over his hesitancies, his uncertainties and what she called an unfocused gentleness. He'd spent eight years in a boarding school, which didn't excuse but certainly explained.

Even so, on such a small island, it was inevitable that they would gravitate towards one another. Morag had always been fonder of Peter Kingsley than she was in love with him, but there were some aspects of their arrangement she missed more acutely than others. She spent long and late hours in Sebastian's company as they pored over their few finds, and plotted to persuade Father Cahill to allow them to expand the dig. It wasn't inevitable that she would become pregnant, but she did.

She told no one. Not even Sebastian. By then Germany had invaded Poland and informing her employers of her condition would have risked compromising the dig, or at the very least her position, on practical as well as moral grounds. But her concerns were less for herself than for Sebastian. Far better he be laughed at in neutral Ireland for his conscientious objecting than find himself, should this latest war follow the pattern of the last, shamed, jailed or conscripted.

The secret couldn't stay hidden forever. They wintered quietly, suspending the excavations for three months, and Morag told Sebastian on Christmas Eve. By early spring, the entire island knew. The news broke as a three-day wonder that might even have constituted a scandal if Sebastian had made a local girl pregnant, not least because he'd very likely have been drowned for his troubles, or at the very least keelhauled. But the islanders considered the pair half-mad to begin with, cooing over bits of stone and slivers of what might have been bone, and Father Cahill was secretly pleased, now that their long-suspected immorality – and by contrast, the islanders' virtue – had been confirmed for all to see. 'Actually,' Carol said, 'he proved very useful. A pragmatic man, when you got past all the theory and down to the nitty-gritty. Gave the midwife his blessing and so forth.'

Their plan was to wait until the baby was born and then apply for political asylum. 'It was actually Father Cahill's idea. He offered to write a letter, based on how important Morag was to the island as a teacher. A long shot, of course, but the idea was to string out the process for as long as they could and hope the war would be over before the process was.'

'Except then Gerard Smyth washes up on the island and Rheingold gets arrested in Derry.'

'Indeed.' The ghost of a smile. 'Not the first time they were overtaken by circumstance.'

'He guessed, you know,' I said.

'He guessed?'

'Gerard Smyth. At the time. He knew straight away that Sebastian was a British agent. The Morrigan the Germans were looking for when they came ashore.'

'Is that so?'

'It was Smyth who identified him. To Richter, the German leading the—'

She waved it aside. 'You don't need to explain Richter to me, Tom.'

She tapped the pipe against the bench's leg and began scraping dead dottle from the bowl with a matchstick. I sat back and basked in the sunshine, listening to the *twee-whips* of the birds behind us in the trees. The lough glittering blue, hypnotic in its ceaseless glimmering.

'I do understand,' I said. She was tamping tobacco into the bowl with the ball of her thumb.

'Do you?'

'Emily,' I said.

'Yes?'

'What a man might do,' I said, 'to protect his own child.'

'Or a woman.'

'Or a woman, of course.'

'You would have done the same?' she said.

'I'd like to think that I would.'

The match scratched and burst into flame and was nipped out by the breeze. She tried again, cupping her hands, but another flared and died. I sat forward and cupped my own hands to form a windbreak. She gripped my wrist.

'You would *like to think*?' she said.

'What I mean,' I said, 'is that I believed all along Sebastian shot that old man and allowed those children to burn to death for the sake of whatever was on the submarine. Because he was a spy.'

She puffed a bluey cloud from the pipe and released my wrist. 'But if he was protecting his pregnant lover . . .'

'It's different.'

'And all those other lives are worth that of his unborn child?'

'All I'm saying is, in his shoes I'd have done the same.'

'And what if he simply didn't know?'

'I don't follow.'

'The information Richter needed. What if those children died not because Sebastian wouldn't tell, but because he couldn't?'

Sebastian suffered irrevocable damage that night. He never spoke about it to Carol. What she knew had been handed down by her mother.

'His mind was never the same. He was crippled, shell-shocked, by survivor's guilt. Sometimes, just sitting at the dinner table, he would begin to shake, and then weep for hours.'

Richter had emptied his Luger of all but one round, then whispered in Sebastian's ear, telling him that he, Sebastian, would now begin to execute the villagers one by one until he gave up the information. If Sebastian refused, Richter would kill them all in one fell swoop.

'So the old man died,' I said, 'for the sake of all the others.'

'He was shot dead,' Carol said, 'because my father didn't know.'

Sweet, awkward Sebastian was no more a British agent than he was a polite Viking. A cut-out, she said. A sacrificial lamb.

'Protecting the identity of the real spy,' I said.

'Yes.'

'Are you telling me,' I said, 'that the spy, Morrigan, was your mother?'

'That is correct.'

It was a lot to take in. My mind went scrambling for connections, riffling back through Gerard Smyth's account.

'Smyth mentions her trying to help him,' I said. 'The pregnant teacher. He thought she was a local.'

'Why shouldn't he?'

'He remembered her because she tried to speak to him in German.'

'He was alone and frightened and far from home. I would imagine she sympathized with his plight.'

Not quite. What was it he'd written? *Blue eyes devoid of compassion.* And no wonder.

She'd been recruited on Crete by Peter Kingsley, Carol said. Posted to Donegal to dig and sift and report back on the fishermen's gossip.

Last seen by Gerard Smyth disappearing into the church, heavily pregnant with her unborn daughter, and locking the doors behind her.

'I don't qualify, exactly, as an eye witness,' Carol said in that dry tone. 'But you might well agree that my account is the more compelling.'

Mined from ancient times, the island was a honeycomb of tunnels and crosscuts and shafts and passages. Morag had taught the children history and geography and they'd taught her a little in return.

They'd smashed up the wooden pews and torn down the few hangings. Once the children were safely in the tunnel behind the altar, Morag set the pile alight.

'They made it out?'

'*We* made it out, Tom.'

TWENTY-SIX

G erard Smyth saw the church burn, heard the children
screaming.
Heard them his whole life.

'You can't imagine the scenes,' Carol said, 'when my mother
reappeared with her sooty brood.'

She'd waited a couple of hours, to make sure the Germans
weren't regrouping. Long enough that grief and despair had taken
hold. The children exhausted and filthy, pale behind their smoke-
blackened masks. The first women to see them thought they were
ghosts.

I tried to picture it. Emily dead, then suddenly wandering into
the village square, tottering with tiredness but alive again.

It didn't work. My mind wouldn't let me see Emily dead.

'There was no massacre,' I said.

'You seem disappointed.'

'Just trying to adjust. It's a lot to take in.'

'You're wondering,' she said, 'why the story took hold. Maybe
you're even trying to decide whether it would be better, for the
book, that the atrocity never happened.'

She was right on both counts.

'I can help you with the first,' she said. 'As for the second,
that is between you and your conscience.'

The children were quickly shepherded away from the square.
Shielded from the sight of awkwardly hunched corpses and blood
congealing black on the cobbles.

The old man Sebastian had shot was called Rory McGinty. A
demon fiddler and a good man for a wild story late at night in
the pub, he kept goats at the back of the mountain. He'd never
married, although whether that was down to the stink of goat,
Carol couldn't say.

'No one *blamed* Sebastian, exactly. They knew Richter had forced
him to shoot. But Rory was dead and Rory was one of their own.'

Morag had tried to speak with Sebastian and turn him away

from the dead man. It was as if she wasn't there. He simply stared, his right hand flexing.

'Something slipped that night,' Carol said. She tapped her temple. 'A cog or a gear. Left his clockwork jumpy, erratic. He'd be fine for weeks on end and then,' she snapped her fingers, 'gone, just gone.'

'I'm not surprised.'

'He never forgave himself. My mother tried to persuade him that if he hadn't pulled that trigger then the consequences would have been far worse. And even before they'd buried Rory, the islanders understood that Sebastian had bought my mother time, provided the distraction that allowed her to get the children into the church.' She puffed on the pipe, which had long gone out. 'It never took. With my father, I mean.'

'He was a hero, then.'

'An honest coward.'

Gerard Smyth saw the church burn, heard the children scream. He wasn't the only one.

'It was decided it would be best to allow the story to be believed. Richter was dead. His men might consider he should be avenged.'

The Germans hadn't invented the idea but they were particularly ruthless when it came to reprisals.

'This was the fear,' Carol agreed. The burning of Cork by the Black and Tans was still fresh in the memory, although a few of the islanders mentioned Cromwell too.

One of the German raiding party still lay unconscious in the square. Those who wanted to toss him into the harbour were persuaded otherwise. When he woke the following day, and Morag tried to question him in her rudimentary German, he only stared at her. Concussion, she believed at first, and then she realized he simply didn't understand.

'He was no more than a boy,' Carol said. 'Fifteen years old, if that.'

When his own gun was cocked and pointed at his face, he began to cry.

He hadn't understood Morag's German because he wasn't German. He came from Castlemartin, a small town not far from Magherafelt across the border in Derry.

It was his first time out, he told them.

A family tradition. His uncle the area's IRA O/C.

He knew very little about Richter, he told them, a Belfast man he'd met for the first time only three days before. What he did know was Richter wasn't long returned from Berlin, where he'd been for two years.

The submarine, he said, was carrying a consignment of gold. It was intended to fund an IRA campaign aimed at destabilizing industrial targets, the most important of which was the Belfast shipyards. The unit responsible would operate across the border, out of the South. The idea was to force Britain to stretch its already meagre resources to keep open the crucial North Atlantic shipping lanes. Ideally, and ultimately, the hope was that a successful campaign would provoke Britain into invading neutral Ireland to protect its back, an act that would not play well in Washington.

When Richter's contact, Klaus Rheingold, was blown in Derry, Richter was left twisting. He knew the submarine was in Lough Swilly, and that the rendezvous was planned for Delphi Island. What he didn't know – the finer details were subject to weather conditions and tides – was the exact time and place.

He'd been ready to abandon the mission when word reached him that a German sailor had washed up on Delphi, and that the sailor had been interrogated by an Englishman. An archaeologist who went about declaring himself a conscientious objector. A man so shameless in his cowardice that when some of the locals mockingly dubbed him 'Morrigan' for the goddess of war, he pronounced himself delighted, and thereafter introduced himself to visitors and strangers as such.

Richter, desperate, made a new plan.

'The rest you know,' she said.

But there was a lot I didn't know.

'According to Smyth,' I said, 'it was the man guarding him who shot Richter.'

'So it would seem. At the time they only knew Richter was shot in the back. It could only have been one of his own men.'

'A cowardly act.'

'A noble kind of coward.'

'It wasn't one of his men, though, was it? It was the boy from across the border. Smyth knocked him unconscious with his own gun.' *His masked shadow*, Smyth called him.

'Apparently so.'

'Who was he?'

'You know who he was, Tom.'

It had to be Shay Govern.

When he had told the villagers all he knew – the blow that knocked him unconscious played havoc with his mind; the last he remembered was the Englishman shooting the old man on his knees – they took him out and showed him the smouldering ruins of the church. He thought they would kill him but they sailed him across to the mainland and cut him loose, to report back to his comrades about the dead children, the blood on their hands.

Months later they heard he had stowed away on a merchant ship bound for New York.

Morag began writing the book that became *Rendezvous at Thira* as a therapeutic exercise. 'A catharsis,' Carol said, 'as much for her as for my father.'

But Sebastian wanted nothing to do with it. The very thought of dredging up that night was horrifying. To put it down on paper, record it for posterity, was an obscenity too far. When she insisted that it would stand as a record of heroism he threatened to throw himself from the cliff. She let it go, put it away.

Years later she took it up again. She changed the names, the setting and the ending. Now it was set in the Greek islands, and the children burned to death in the church. It ended with a wounded young German soldier – no more than a boy, really – being set free by the islanders and coming to terms with his evil deeds from the sanctuary of America, where he'd fled once the war was over.

She typed up a manuscript and posted it to Shay Govern in Boston, by then a multi-millionaire already legendary for his reputation for employing young emigrants from Derry, Donegal and Tyrone. In her covering letter she said that she was a Donegal-based writer – she used her mother's maiden name, but announced her intention of employing 'Sebastian Devereaux' as a pseudonym – who was having trouble getting her story published in Ireland, possibly because it climaxed with the murder of children in a burning church. If he knew of any American publishers who might be interested in her story, she would be very grateful indeed.

'Blackmail,' I said.

'The island was dying, Tom. The young were leaving in their droves. My mother did what was needed to keep the place alive.'

It was discreetly done. Shay Govern endowed a foundation with a remit to foster Irish-American cultural links, with a boutique publishing house at its heart. The young Irish author Sebastian Devereaux was one of the first recipients of a surprisingly handsome advance. It and all subsequent monies earned over the next two decades, royalties included, were paid to the newly formed artists' cooperative established by Morag Devereaux on Delphi Island.

It was entirely incongruous, in that sun-dappled meadow high above the sparkling blue sea, to think now of the Moloch and children sacrificed to the flames.

The children hadn't burned to death in the church that night. Even so, Delphi was built on their blood.

They'd been bleeding Shay Govern for the best part of five decades. Letting him believe, all those years, that he'd played his part in a massacre of innocents.

'A transfusion might be a less crude way of putting it,' Carol said. 'You can see how the island thrives. And Shay gets to salve his conscience in a very practical way.'

'Except he's not really guilty of anything.'

'He made his choice, Tom, when he stepped on to the island with a gun in his hands.'

'I'd imagine, if you were to tell him the truth, he'd argue it was more important that he killed Richter. Christ only knows how it'd have gone if he hadn't.'

She accepted that, and further acknowledged that even if Shay Govern had refused to join Richter's raiding party – if he had ever been in a position to refuse – his place would have been filled by another man. A man more loyal to his leader, or the cause, or both.

Sebastian had found himself in an impossible position. Shay Govern had cut the Gordian knot, giving Morag time to spirit the children away and saving who knew how many more lives in the process.

By any measure, a hero.

That he had guilt thrust upon him was perverse, disgusting.

'My mother was of more or less the same opinion,' Carol said. 'And, being a woman, she tended to blame herself. She was after all the one Richter came looking for, the one Sebastian killed to protect. Nonsense, of course.'

'Is it?'

'I believe so, and I tried my very best to persuade her. Unfortunately, my mother was very much her own woman, in this as in everything else. She suffered with it her entire life, believing that Rory McGinty's death was on her head, as was Sebastian's, shall we say, withdrawal from the world. Was her conscience clear when she allowed Shay Govern to believe he was complicit in an atrocity? No. Was it necessary? Yes.'

'And necessary explains everything, does it?'

'I would fault her, Tom, if she did it for her own benefit. But what she did was done on behalf of the community. For the sake of Delphi. Once he was on the hook she could have taken Shay Govern for millions, but she only ever asked for what was necessary. She had a phrase she was forced to use more than once in the committee. "What needs and no more." Shay had what Inish needed. She never desired any more.'

It was Shay Govern, ironically, who needed more.

'I think he might have fallen for you,' I said, and for the first and only time she had the good grace to appear discomfited.

He had arrived on the island the previous July, unannounced. Just another American tourist, albeit slightly unusual in that he travelled alone. A little on the frail side to be hiking the hills. When he began straying off the established trails and poking into odd corners, they'd had him watched. One afternoon, as he was prowling the fringes of the bird sanctuary, they'd slipped into his hotel room and opened the safe.

'He was calling himself Charlie McGettigan. His passport and travel documents, of course, said otherwise.'

'Who knows?' I said.

'Who knows what?'

'About your mother blackmailing Shay Govern all these years.'

'The committee. One or two others.'

'The committee?'

'The cooperative's board.'

'And how do you get elected to this board?'

'By invitation, but the decision must be unanimous. The board acts as one.'

'Is that right? And did it suffer a collective heart attack when it realized Shay Govern was sniffing around?'

Not far off. It was decided that one of the committee would bump into Shay Govern in the hotel lobby and make a fuss, having recognized him as the famous Irish-American philanthropist. An invitation to dinner with Lady Carol McConnell was quickly issued.

'Naturally we believed he had uncovered the truth. It was something of a relief to realize that this was not the point of his endeavours.'

It seemed that Govern, recently widowed and brooding on his life's work and legacy, had come to the decision that he needed to make his expiation a more public affair.

'Not that he ever mentioned the massacre directly,' she said. 'It was all in the context of his philanthropy, the foundations funded and the endowments bestowed. He wasn't boasting, you understand. He was simply talking about the generalized nature of his giving. And what he wanted, the reason he had come to Delphi, was a more specific, what he called intimate, connection. Delphi, as far as he could tell from his explorations, was a close-knit and thriving community. If he had grown up in such a place as a boy, he might never have had to leave.

'I told him I was very pleased he'd had to leave. He was a little startled by that, until I explained that Delphi only thrived as a result of his largesse. The consequence of the endowments that had begun with Sebastian Devereaux were visible everywhere he went on the island.

'I brought him out here to see the graves. Gave him to understand, without being so coarse as to be explicit about it, that Sebastian and Morag had taken their secrets to wherever it is they have gone.'

Gave him to understand . . .

'A lesser man,' she said, 'believing us ignorant of the truth, would have left it at that and gone away. Shall I tell you what Shay Govern did?'

'I'm guessing he told you everything.'

She nodded. 'It was almost as if the bench were a confessional.

He sat where you are sitting now and spoke for an hour. I was very impressed, Tom. He is an unusually honourable man.'

But not impressed enough to repay his honesty with the truth. Instead she, or they, had allowed him to continue believing that he was guilty, at least in part, of a horrific act. A sin of omission that silently offered him the opportunity of purging his conscience in perpetuity.

'While you,' I said, 'get to absolve yourself of that nasty old taint of blackmail.'

She considered that while she fussed with her pipe, and then informed me that I was as impractical as I was sentimental. She had, prior to her dinner engagement with Shay Govern, been quite prepared to inform him that if he attempted to disentangle himself from the various endowments and grants that helped fund Delphi, she would be forced to go public with his disgrace. Naturally, she would have delayed destroying his name and reputation until after his death, so that he would be in no position to defend himself, or sue.

'A dirty business,' she said. 'So you can imagine how relieved I was when he made a clean breast and pronounced himself willing to maintain the old arrangements.'

'Did it never occur to you to tell him the truth?'

She had wavered, yes, during his long and painful confession. But her personal sympathies were irrelevant. She had the entire island, and its generations to come, to put before her own feelings.

'The first time he stepped on to this island,' she said, 'he came masked and armed. Everything else flows from that.'

She'd had decades to build it up in her mind. Maybe she even believed he'd been some kind of dark angel invading Eden with a burning sword held aloft.

'And please,' she said, 'spare me the part where he was only obeying orders. That kite no longer flies.'

The gold mine was Shay Govern's idea.

'There was some talk, initially, of his changing his will,' she said. 'Shay was quite fond of the notion of buying out the estate, and becoming Lord McConnell.'

Too tricky, apparently. It ran the risk of his children, all of whom were non-executive directors, and their lawyers, asking difficult questions about why their father was suddenly so intrigued by Lady Carol McConnell of Delphi Island.

'Unfortunately, I am no one's conception of a pneumatic blonde,' she smiled. 'Had I been so blessed, they very likely wouldn't have questioned it at all. Blocked it, yes. But certainly there would have been no need to investigate any further.'

His investment in Delphi, they decided, needed to be a commercial venture. The old copper mine, of course, had played out long since. Carol, wanting Shay to believe that it was all his own work, told him she had conducted her own research, and discovered that gold was often found in close proximity to copper. Given his expertise, and the latest developments in technology, might it be worth their while to prospect for gold?

'In a way it was almost comical,' she said, although there was no humour in her eyes or her tone. 'He seized on it like a child.'

It was the symmetry, she believed, that appealed. That preliminary explorations for a subterranean seam would accidentally discover the German submarine and its lost hoard of Nazi gold, at a stroke uncovering a source of income for Delphi and in the process hauling to the surface the very reason Shay Govern had first come to the island, masked and armed, all those years before.

The secret exposed for all to see. Shay Govern's conscience bleached clean. And good luck to anyone who tried to figure out where the submarine had come from, or why it had gone down.

The historical record would be picked over, of course. Certain connections made. 'But unless someone conducts an unusually productive séance with Klaus Rheingold, their efforts are likely to achieve very little.'

'You're not tempted to keep it all?' I said.

'Keep it?'

'The gold mine. You could declare a new seam and then smelt the gold bars.'

'Much too complicated, Tom. And really not very practical. It would require too big an operation, too many outsiders.'

Better instead to simplify matters. Announce the discovery, hand it over to the State and be content with the salvage reward.

What needs and no more.

'Which brings us to Tom Noone,' she said, after giving me a few moments to pull the threads together.

'What about me?'

'You do appreciate, I'm sure, that I am not telling you all this for the sake of my health.'

I hadn't snuck on to the island in the early hours with a Schmeisser in my hands. But I'd come masked and armed all the same, operating under false pretences and carrying with me the information, courtesy of Gerard Smyth, that could blow the cosy existence of Delphi sky high.

'All of which puts us,' she said, 'in a rather awkward position at a very delicate time.'

'That's the thing about the truth, though, isn't it? It's rarely delicate or awkward. It's all a bit blunt and straightforward.'

'Well, perhaps it is,' she said, amused. She could fully understand, she said, why I might want to tell Shay Govern the truth. 'The moral obligation and so forth.' That I might feel Shay Govern, having lived his entire life with the guilt, was entitled to know that he was a hero rather than a killer.

'Or perhaps your obligation is to truth itself. That you have a duty to reveal it wherever it is found, regardless of whether the world is interested or not.'

It was her opinion, she said, conceding her bias, that when it came to the truth and a good story, the world has always tended to prefer a good story.

'A human failing, perhaps. But the failing, one could argue, that made us human.'

This was the conclusion of a study that began with her mother's novels, the thrillers published under Sebastian's name, but had broadened out, as Morag encouraged her daughter to continue the family tradition, to include the books that lined Morag's shelves. 'She was partial to Christie, of course, but also Tey and Highsmith and McInnes. Not that she only read women. She did believe, though, that while men left behind bruises and scar tissue and corpses by the pile, women cut through to the living heart. She found Austen terrifying.'

It was her theory, and one Carol subscribed to, that great literature consisted almost entirely, in one guise or another, of the cautionary fable. 'We find it in the Brothers Grimm and Charles Perrault, or, if you are classically inclined, in Aeschylus and Sophocles and Euripides. But my mother believed its roots go much deeper, all the way back beyond Cain and Abel to the ancient savannah and the tales told around fires at the mouths of caves. The tales language evolved to tell. Of the darkness lurking beyond the shadows, the shadows outside and the shadows in men's hearts, and what must be done and said and believed in the tribe's name if the darkness was to remain at spear's length.'

'Nice theory.'

'It doesn't ring true?'

'We'll debate it another day. Right now I'm more interested in what it has to do with Shay Govern.'

'Isn't it obvious?'

'Not really.'

'You came here, Tom, with the stated intention of writing Sebastian Devereaux's story. Shay wants his own story tied into it. I am offering you the opportunity of doing just that.'

'To write the story or tell the truth?'

'I think you already know the answer to that question, Tom.'

'So, what – a story about how Sebastian saves the day and his unborn child from a Nazi atrocity and goes on to become a bestselling author by recycling his own heroism. Something like that?'

'Something very like that, yes. Even allowing for my personal bias, it's a fascinating story. And it will be written,' she leaned forward to tap my wrist, 'by the newly appointed director of the Delphi Writers' Retreat.'

And there it was – the juicy carrot to go along with the stick.

'A wonderful opportunity, Tom, wouldn't you agree? Can you truly afford to turn it down? A handsomely remunerated permanent position in an idyllic setting that could not be more conducive to the creative process. And a beautiful place, if I may be so bold, for your charming daughter to visit for her holidays. I've seen pictures, of course. My apologies if you find it intrusive, but you'll understand that we felt it appropriate to conduct some research into your background when Shay proposed you as the ghost-writer. She really is a most beautiful child.'

'You're not tempted?' Carol said after waiting a minute or two for my reply.

'Who wouldn't be?'

'But you have . . . qualms.'

'With bribes? Not at all.'

'So it's the material you object to.'

'Not the subject matter, no. It's what you plan to do with it.'

'Is it really so reprehensible,' she said, 'to want to tell a story that allows people to believe in the greater good rather than remind them of how cruel the world really is?'

'In theory, no. If it's fiction you're writing. But if you're presenting it as fact . . .'

'Now you're confusing facts with the truth.'

'They do tend to collide every now and again.'

'Yes, well, even a stopped clock tells the correct time twice a day. Be sensible, Tom. If you won't think of yourself, think of Emily.'

'Why, because she loves fairytales too?'

'And why shouldn't she, Tom? A child understands the fundamental truth of a happy ending.'

'Even if it's a lie?'

'Because they are so exceedingly rare.'

'Like unicorns, say.'

'Perhaps dodos might be a more appropriate metaphor, but I take your point. Does Emily believe in unicorns?'

'For now.'

'And you will not be the one to disabuse her.'

'No.'

'Why?'

'Because she's innocent and that's too precious to destroy when I don't have to and you can wipe that smirk off your face because none of that has anything to do with rewriting your father's story and pretending he was a great hero when he was just some guy who shot an old man because he didn't know the answer to what he was being asked.'

'I disagree, Tom. Did he forgive you?'

'What?'

'Your father,' she said. 'When he realized he was dying and that you had failed to clear his name. Did he forgive you? Was he able to look you in the eye?'

'My father has *nothing* to do with—'

'Doesn't he? Be honest with yourself, Tom. You, who are so fascinated with facts and truth.'

'My father did the right thing and was punished for doing it. He was nothing *like* Sebastian.'

'No? My father did the right thing too, and suffered a ruined life for his troubles. Were they really so different?'

'My father was an honourable man, Lady McConnell, who was systematically destroyed by allegations and lies so that others might thrive. He died knowing that those who had trusted in him believed him a fool at best, and at worst a coward and a traitor. There was no happy ending for my father, Lady McConnell. Believe you me, heroes were every bit as rare as unicorns in the vicinity of that particular hospice facility.'

'I believe you, Tom. But it's not me you need to convince.'

'What do you mean?'

'It's posterity you need to persuade. The wider world. And yet here you sit, turning up your nose at the offer of a position that would allow you to write whatever your heart desires.'

'You think I haven't tried? There isn't a sane publisher who'd touch that story with a barge pole.'

'We'd publish it, Tom.'

'Aye, and get yourself sued out of all your Nazi gold.'

'Well, we wouldn't necessarily have to present it as literal fact, would we? What I mean to say is, the facts are important, but they are utterly irrelevant if no one reads about them.'

'You're talking about a novel.'

'Of course.'

'So you want me to write a biography of your father's fiction . . .'

'. . . and a novel of your father's facts. Yes. Do we have a deal?'

'I'll need some time to think it over,' I said.

'Certainly. Take all the time you need. You will excuse me, I hope, but I must return to the house. There are contracts to be signed, and Shay is due to return at any moment. In fact, he is very likely already here. Do join us when you are ready. I'm sure Shay is extremely anxious to hear your decision.' She paused. 'There is a contract waiting for your signature too, Tom.'

'One last thing,' I said.

'Yes?'

'Gerard Smyth.'

'What about him?'

'Will I be using his eye-witness account?'

'It would be useful, certainly, to have some aspects of the story confirmed.'

'Then I'll need to know how he died.'

She didn't flinch. 'I am given to understand that he fell into a canal and drowned. Is that not the case?'

'I don't know. They're still waiting on the results of the post-mortem.'

'Ah.'

'But I think they're worried about the timing. That he fell into the canal the day after he handed over his testimony. A canal he knew well, a path he'd walked along for years.'

'It does seem rather a horrible coincidence,' she said. The diamond-blue eyes glittered. 'A tragedy, really, for a man to have lived so long and then die so cruelly. A lesson to us all, I suppose, to never take anything for granted. Least of all life itself.'

Then she turned and limped away up the slope, her left leg swinging out from the hip in a crooked *demi-rond*.

I strolled down through the meadow, past the graves and on to the edge of the cliff. A short mossy incline, then a sheer fall to the rock-fringed beach far below. The headlands on either side curving around in a pincer movement, trapping a calm harbour. A small boat bobbing in the cove. Beyond, the lough was sapphire blue and white riffles, the low, lush hills of Donegal marching away north either side.

Idyllic, she'd called it. Well, she was right about that much.

You're not tempted?

I was. Who wouldn't be?

And all I had to do was mind my manners, avert my eyes and leave that solitary apple on the tree.

TWENTY-SEVEN

I n the end they made the decision for me. I sat on the edge
of the cliff and watched a small boat come throbbing around
the western headland, buffeted by the swell as it came around
in a crude arc, aiming for the bay. I could sympathize with the
pilot, even though it was the person huddled in the bow that was
taking the worst of the spray. Or maybe it was the boat I was
sympathizing with. Either way I felt smacked around, no control
over where I was going.

There were a lot of ifs and buts to negotiate if I was to play
along with Carol Devereaux's plan. The big one being Shay
Govern. He was the man putting his money down, funding it all.
And he deserved to know the truth.

If he still wanted to go ahead with the book after that, then
great. The rest would work itself out.

By then – an omen – the little boat had turned into the calm
bay and was making for the stony beach. I stood up and patted
my pockets for my phone. Better to speak to Shay Govern alone,
before he sat down with those contracts Carol Devereaux was
so keen for him to sign.

Except the phone's screen was dark, the battery long since
dead, and I realized that there was no way Carol Devereaux
would have told me what she had about Shay Govern if I'd had
any way of contacting him in advance.

Which meant I needed to get to him before he sat down with
those contracts.

I was turning away, the muscles in my lower back already
screaming in anticipation of the stiff hike back up to the house,
when I noticed the little boat had reached the shore, the person
in the bow standing up now – something familiar in the stance
– to step down into the shallows and haul on the boat to drag it
up on to the stony beach while the pilot, up to his waist in water,
shoved on from behind.

And then, the boat secured, the person on the beach reached
back towards the pilot with both arms out, as if inviting a hug,

and I was reminded of the sculpture in Rathmullan, the flight of the earls and those left behind on the shore with their arms aloft, beseeching . . .

But it wasn't the pilot she was calling forward. The little lump in the middle of the boat came to life, stood up and turned unsteadily, wobbling as she put one foot in front of the other, eventually collapsing into those waiting arms.

Unmistakable, even from that distance.

Emily.

They came trudging up the path through the woods, Kee in front and murmuring over her shoulder to Emily, who was slumped in the piggy-back position. Jack Byrne five or so yards behind, what looked like a small black automatic dangling in his hand.

I waited until they had gone by and stepped out from behind the pine.

'Jack,' I said.

He came around fast, the gun coming up. Then he saw who it was and relaxed a fraction, just as Emily screamed, 'Daddy!'

'It's OK, love. I'll be with you in a second. I just need to talk to this man.'

'There's nothing to talk about, Tom.'

'Where's Martin?'

'Martin, ah, had a bad accident.'

'Fall into a canal, did he?'

'Not exactly. But something along those lines, yeah.'

'He's dead?'

Jack nodded. The dread came seeping up from my gut, but right then I couldn't afford to waste time mourning Martin Banks.

'And I'm next,' I said.

'Daddy?'

'Just hold *on* a minute, Emily.' I hadn't taken my eyes off Jack. 'Is that it, Jack? Anyone who's seen Gerard Smyth's story, they're being taken out. Yeah?'

'You had your chance, Tom. You were asked nicely.' He gave the automatic a little twitch. 'Where is it?'

'Where's what?'

'The laptop.'

'It was destroyed, yesterday. When I got shot in the back.'

Jack flicked his eyes at Kee, then grinned. 'So I hear. Rock salt, right? Burns like a bitch.'

'Language, Jack. There's a child over there.'

'Sure, yeah. Language.' He shook his head. 'So where is it?'

'I don't know.'

'Not sure I believe you, Tom.'

'That's up to you.'

'Not really,' he said. 'I mean, your kid's right there. So I'd say the onus is on you to persuade me.' He glanced again at Kee. 'Am I right?'

'Who are you working for, Jack?'

'What?'

'I asked who you're working for.'

'If I was you,' he said, 'I'd be more worried about—'

'The reason I'm asking,' I said, 'is he's the guy who told you to take Emily. So I'm going to kill him once I've buried you.'

He studied me for a long time. 'The idea,' he said, 'is nothing happens to the kid. But between you and me, that's not the way it has to play.'

'Daddy,' piped Emily, half-muffled against Kee's shoulder, 'I'm scared.'

'I *know*, love. But just listen to Alison for—'

'Let's cut the shit, Tom.' Jack took a step forward. 'Tell me where you've stashed the laptop, or what's left of it, and then we'll go from there. I tell Franco you played along, maybe we can work something out.'

'You're working for Franco now?'

'Jesus, Tom. It was Franco all along. Franco was the one who found me, pushed Shay in my direction.'

'I get it,' I said. 'And I know why. Franco's looking to protect Shay, cut out anyone who's trying to blackmail him about those kids getting burned to death.'

'The kids?' Jack grinned. 'You think Franco gives a shit about any *kids*?' He was shaking his head now. 'Franco wants it all buried, Tom. *All* of it. But especially the bit about his father.'

'His father?'

'Christ, you know nothing, do you?' Along with the gun he held all the aces, had nothing to lose. 'Peter Govern, Tom. Known to his friends as Pedro, apparently. Also known, back in the day, although not to so many people, as the officer commanding of the South Derry IRA.' He gave me a lazy grin. 'All the reading you've been doing lately, you might know him better as Richter.'

'Dad?'

I was still staring at Jack, that lazy grin. The last few pieces slotting in.

'Daddy!'

'Just *wait*, Emily.'

'But Daddy, I want a—'

'Oh, for the love of *Christ*!' I roared, and went charging towards Kee and Emily. Kee already, instinctively, swinging Emily away from me, that rage. Jack stepping back as I surged past him.

Except I didn't surge past.

Jack had made the same mistake they'd all made when it came to Emily. He'd presumed I'd be so terrified by their threats and guns that I'd be cowed, helpless. He didn't realize that when you point a gun at a man's child you strip away all the human decencies and lay bare the animal instinct.

He didn't stand a chance.

He was still stepping back when I lunged to the side and drove my shoulder into his chest, his momentum carrying him back and down, and once he was down, winded by the impact, with my weight on top, he was never getting up. I scrabbled around and clamped one hand on the wrist of his gun hand and my forearm across his throat. Began the kill.

He bucked and thrashed and spat and gouged, and Jack Byrne was a big man, a heavy man.

It took him a long time to die, but by then I was in for the long haul.

Like he'd said, the onus was on me to persuade him.

TWENTY-EIGHT

I dragged Jack off the path, dumped him behind a fallen tree. Relieved him of the little black automatic – so confident had he been that he hadn't even slipped off the safety – and found Kee's Glock tucked into his waistband in the small of his back.

Then I took off up the path in a shuffling jog, my back screaming in pain, calling Kee's name.

She hadn't made it very far, no more than a couple of hundred yards, before she'd had to step off the path into the woods, Emily a dead weight.

'Over here, Tom.'

A little depression, a dry stream bed. She'd hidden Emily behind some rocks and then found a dead branch for a weapon, taken up the best position she could.

When I went to Emily and held out my arms, she hesitated.

'It's OK, love. The bad man is gone.'

'Are you still cross with me?'

'I was never cross, hon. I was just pretending so I could fight the bad man.'

'You were very stern.'

Stern. 'I'm sorry. I'll never do it again.'

She came to me then, and clung fiercely. Over her head I said to Kee, 'What did she see?'

'The fight.'

'Nothing more?'

Kee shook her head. 'He's gone?'

'All the way gone.'

She whistled.

'Daddy?'

'Yes, love?'

Talking into my shoulder, Emily's voice was muffled. 'Where's Martin, Daddy?'

'I'm not sure, Em. But we'll find him.'

'The bad man said Martin is gone to heaven.'

She was shaking now, as if she was suddenly cold. I tried to

shush her but she erupted, bawling. 'I was so f-frightened, Daddy.'
A huge gulp. 'And *you never came.*'

'I'm sorry, love. I'm so, so sorry.'

The shudders subsiding now. 'D-don't ever leave me again.'

'I won't. Once I do this one last thing.'

'Tom,' Kee warned, but I was kissing Emily on the top of her
head, disentangling from her fierce hug.

'Daddy?'

I handed the Glock to Kee. 'If anyone except me comes back
down that path, blaze away.'

'I can't allow that, Tom.'

'You'll need to use that,' I nodded at the Glock, 'if you want
to stop me.'

'Don't *go*, Daddy.'

'I have to, love. But don't worry, I'll be back soon.'

'*Please* don't go.'

She cried and begged as I limped away, out of the trees and
up the path, each word a scourge driving me on.

I found them on the patio under the shade of an awning, the
champagne already fizzing in an ornamental ice bucket that served
as the table's centrepiece. There was coffee too, and plates of
sliced fruit. The contracts on creamy parchment in leather-bound
folders.

Shay and Franco were on one side of the table, Shay with his
chin cupped in his palm as they listened to Carol's plans for
expanding the nature reserve, which appeared to involve building
an artificial breakwater around one of the bays on the island's
western side to create a kind of polder.

'Tom,' said Carol, breaking off. 'So good of you to join us.
Are you ready for that coffee now?' Then, shading her eyes, she
recoiled. 'Good Lord,' she said. 'Are you hurt?'

The cuts and scrapes on my face, she meant, where Jack
Byrne's free hand had scratched and gouged.

'I'm fine,' I said. 'Lost my balance and fell in the woods.' I
touched a hand to my back, indicating where I'd taken the blast
of rock salt. 'It's nothing. I'll clean up once this is done.'

'Are you sure?'

'Really. It probably looks a lot worse than it is.'

'Very well,' she said, then nodded to Eoin as I sat down, taking

the seat across from Franco. Eoin came forward and reached the
bottle from the ice bucket and began pouring the champagne. I
was last. I thanked him and followed everyone else's lead in not
commenting on how absurd it was to be waited upon by a man
with a shotgun strapped to his back.

When all the glasses were charged, Carol picked up a spoon
and tapped a *tink-tink*. 'I somehow feel,' she purred, 'as if I
should begin by saying, "We are gathered here today . . ."'

Shay grinned. Franco, poker-faced, sat forward and propped
his elbows on the table.

'Joking aside, I do feel that it is an appropriate way to begin,'
Carol went on. 'Because what we are celebrating here today is
a mutual commitment to a long-term relationship that I, for one,
dearly hope will be more than financially beneficial to both
parties.'

'Hear-hear,' Shay muttered.

'We all understand, of course, that every relationship represents
something of a gamble. Nothing is guaranteed. Every venture,'
and here she glanced at Shay, 'commercial or personal, is fraught
with risk. And yet we are all familiar with the idea of nothing
ventured, nothing gained.'

'No guts,' Shay said, 'no glory.'

'Precisely put. I found myself humming a tune this morning
as I dressed, a tune you will all know – indeed, it was so familiar,
as sometimes happens, that it took me a moment or two to place
it.' She began, embarrassingly, to hum again, the opening bars
to 'Amazing Grace'. She cleared her throat. 'That hymn, as some
of you know, was written by a man notorious for his profanity,
a slaver whose ship was wrecked out at sea and who found safe
harbour, and enlightenment, right here in Lough Swilly. "I was
lost but now am found, was blind but now can see." How simple
are those words, and how profound.' She reached for her glass,
held it up. 'John Newton did not set sail on his slaving ship with
the intention of inspiring millions of people, and yet his sordid
venture was transformed by the power of grace into something
so beautiful it will no doubt remain with us until the end of time.'

She was laying it on a bit thick but the message was clear:
with one stroke of his Montblanc, the wretch Shay Govern was
about to be saved.

She stood and held out her glass. There was a dull scraping

as Shay and Franco pushed back their chairs and stood too. Then they all looked at me.

'Tom? Won't you join us in a toast?'

'In a minute, sure. I'm just trying to remember how the rest of that hymn goes. Isn't there something about the Lord promising good?'

'I'm impressed,' Carol said, although by now there was a slight strain on her smile. 'I wouldn't have thought you were a religious man.'

'If I was religious I wouldn't be trying to remember, I'd know it by heart. But there's a bit in there, I think, about hope, and a shield.'

'"The Lord has promised good to me,"' Shay said. '"His word my hope secures. He will my shield and portion be, as long as life endures."' A self-deprecating grin as heads turned towards him. 'Beaten into me as a child,' he said. 'You never forget the rote learning.'

'That's the bit right there that's bugging me,' I said. '"His word my hope secures."'

'Tom,' Carol said, a dull edge on the word.

'I'm happy to sign that contract,' I said, 'once Shay signs off on what the book will say.'

'How d'you mean?' Franco said. 'Signs off on what?'

I looked into those grey, lupine eyes. The man who'd had Gerard Smyth and Martin Banks killed. And Christ only knew what he'd planned for Emily once he knew I was out of the way.

'Now isn't the time, Tom,' Carol urged.

'Except it'll be too late once Shay signs on the dotted line,' I told Franco. 'If we know anything about Shay Govern it's that he's a man of his word.'

'Never mind his *word*,' Franco said. His gaze shifted as he glanced past me. Then he came back, locked on. 'What is it we should know?'

'You expecting someone, Franco?'

'What? No.'

'Because Jack won't be joining us. Jack's been delayed.'

'Delayed,' he said, and there was recognition in those grey eyes now.

'Jack who?' Shay said. 'Jack Byrne?'

Eoin was nobody's fool. He'd been sitting on the patio's low wall until he heard the tone of the conversation change, the tension in Carol's voice. Now he was on the move, prowling in behind the table, the shotgun in his hands with the barrel nestled in the crook of his elbow. I wondered what it was loaded with today.

'Jack Byrne,' I said. 'The very man.'

'Why was Jack coming *here*?' Shay said.

'Tidying up loose ends,' I said. 'As in, anyone who'd seen Gerard Smyth's testimony. Which I'm guessing included Jack himself,' I said to Franco, 'so I suppose I've done you a favour.'

'Are you sure you're OK, Tom?' Shay said. 'Because you're not making a lot of—'

'The kids never died,' I told him. 'In the church that night. It never happened. They all escaped. Carol's mother got them out through a tunnel. Ask her yourself, it's a terrific story.'

Carol closed her eyes, then exhaled long and slow. When she opened them again she was staring at me with a hatred so cold I half-believed she was about to smash her champagne glass on the table and set about me with the jagged shards.

Instead she lowered it to the table with a shaking hand and sat down. 'Christ, Tom,' she whispered.

Except it was clear from his expression that I wasn't telling Shay Govern anything he didn't already know. I'd expected him to dispute what I'd said, that he would need to be cajoled into accepting that he hadn't had to live with a terrible burden of guilt his entire life. And then, belatedly perhaps, tears of relief, of joy, as the realization of what it truly meant began to seep in.

Instead he simply put down his glass and reached for the Montblanc, sat down and pulled the contract to him.

'Shay?' Franco said. 'What the fuck are you doing?'

'Is that it, Tom?' Shay said.

'There's more, yeah. But you might want to hear it in private.'

He took a firmer grip on the fountain pen, signed the contract with a flourish and laid the pen down. Then he slid the leather-bound folder across in front of Franco.

'You don't think,' Shay said, 'that my brother deserves to know?'

So Shay knew. Had known all along.

'Know *what*?' Franco demanded.

'I shouldn't be the one to say it,' I said.

Shay acknowledged that with a brief nod. 'Sit down,' he told Franco, 'and sign the contract.'

'Not until someone tells me what's going on.'

So Shay told him. The words coming easy, a brook babbling over smooth pebbles. As if he had been rehearsing the speech in his mind for many years. How he'd always known the children hadn't died that night. How it had seemed simpler in the beginning to exaggerate the effects of his concussion and allow people to leach off his ignorance. That he was happy to pay a blood debt that didn't exist if it meant the truth stayed buried.

Or the lie, rather.

He'd told the islanders the truth when he'd said the man known as Richter wasn't long returned from Berlin before that night, and that he'd lived there for two years, an IRA man plotting with his enemy's enemy.

Where Shay had lied was in saying that he knew very little about Richter, a Belfast man he'd only met for the first time three days before.

Richter, also known as Peter McGovern, IRA commander and Shay's father.

'I didn't *mean* to kill him,' he said. 'The church was burning and he was running towards it with his gun drawn. It was madness, and all I wanted to do was make him realize that.'

He'd planned to loose a burst over his father's head. But he had never fired a Schmeisser before. A heavy weapon, far heavier than he was familiar with from shooting rabbits in the hills. It bucked in his hands and damn near broke his wrists.

He had no memory of being struck. The next thing he remembered was coming to and seeing his father sprawled on the cobbles and the full horror dawning.

The rest we knew.

'You have my blessing, Tom,' Shay said. 'To put it all in there.' He picked up the Montblanc and handed it to Franco. 'Sign it,' he said.

'You knew all along?' Franco said. His voice was a rasp. The eyes were ghastly, bright and dry.

Shay nodded.

'And you never *told* me?'

'It was my burden, Franco. How could I ask you to carry it?'

Franco seemed to have trouble swallowing. He picked up the pen, then stretched out an arm and clasped Shay around the neck and drew his brother into a hug that was almost brutal in its intensity.

'Jesus, Shay. Jesus fucking *Christ*.'

A sob broke from Shay Govern, a cry that had been buried for seventy years and came out bellowing, a wordless wail.

Franco closed his eyes. 'I know,' he shushed. 'I know.'

It was all over in a heartbeat. Franco clenched his arm around Shay's neck and drove the Montblanc so far into his brother's eye that the titanium barrel buckled and snapped in two.

Eoin gaped and began to swing the shotgun around but he was slow and he was clumsy and my hand was already in the small of my back, the automatic there with the safety off.

Franco was no more than a yard away across the table, his eyes closed, chin resting on the top of his brother's head.

I put two in Franco's face.

One for Martin, one for hate.

TWENTY-NINE

I heard the boat before it appeared, a dull throb beyond the western headland. Shaded my eyes and watched it turn in a slow wide arc into the bay. Skeletal and black coming out of the sun.

'Emily? Rikki-tik, love. Let's go.'

Rikki-tik was our new code word – do it *now*, upstairs, no questions asked.

She'd grown taller, or at least leggier, in the past five months, tanned by the breeze that swirled up the Swilly and scoured the little bay huddled beneath the cliffs. Now she sprang to her feet, tossing away the shells she'd been gathering, and ran lightly up the wind-warped steps on to the wooden gallery, past me and into the cottage. Exactly as rehearsed, every day for the past five months or so.

I put down the plane and blew some sawdust from the slab of driftwood that would, I was hoping, reveal itself as something useful one of these days. The plane went into the toolbox at my feet and out came the stubby automatic. I stood and went down the steps on to the beach, watching the boat come, standing sideways on with my left shoulder to the breeze, as Kee had instructed, this to present a thinner target and to hide the gun in my right hand and flush against my thigh.

'He'd need to be a hell of a shot *and* Lotto-lucky to hit you from a moving boat,' she'd said. 'So don't panic. Let him come. By the time he's close enough to do any damage you'll have a fair idea that that's his plan. And you'll be the one standing on solid ground.'

Good advice, provided he arrived in daylight, by boat, and came alone.

'Anyone tries to come down there in the dark,' she'd said, craning her neck to stare up at the craggy black cliffs, 'you'll probably find that a spade will be more useful than a gun.'

Now Kee raised a hand from the stern, throttled back on the outboard and allowed the boat to drift into shore. She threw me

a line, watched me weigh it down with a flat rock, then stepped
out into the water barefoot with her jeans rolled up to her knees,
and trudged up on to the sand.

'Still here,' she said.

'Still here.'

'Girl Friday?'

'Inside.'

'Good.'

We scuffed up the beach through the soft sand, up on to the
wooden gallery. Kee took a seat at the table and I went inside
to put the kettle on, called Emily out from the bedroom. When
I got back outside with a couple of mugs of piping black coffee
and a cold apple juice, they were staring at one another across
the table like a lion tamer facing down a new lion, although
which was which was hard to say.

'Do you want to stay and chat with Alison, love?'

'No thanks.'

'All right. Off you go.'

She went, taking her juice-box with her, sucking on the straw
as she headed back down the beach to her precious collection of
shells. Kee reached into her shoulder bag and took out a newspaper, the *Irish Times*. She laid it on the table already folded
back to page nine.

A coroner's report into the death of Mr Francis Govern, an
Irish-American businessman from Boston, Pennsylvania,
has returned a verdict of death by misadventure.

The body of Mr Govern washed ashore on a beach south
of Buncrana on Lough Swilly on 19 August last.

Mr Govern, an experienced sailor, went missing with his
older brother Shay Govern, the CEO of Govern Industries,
last April, during a short holiday in which they were tracing
their family tree in Donegal. The pair rented a boat on
Delphi Island and went fishing, and the alarm was raised
when they failed to return that evening.

Letterkenny's Coroner's Court was informed that decom-
position was so advanced that Mr Francis Govern's skeletal
remains were identified from dental records.

Mr Shay Govern is also presumed drowned.

Mr Francis Govern is survived by his wife and . . .

'Drowning *again*?' I said. 'You'd want to be careful; you'll wear out the motif.'

'It's a coincidence, Tom.'

'Right. I hear they happen all the time.' I wondered who'd been given the job of battering in Franco Govern's skull so badly that the bullet holes didn't show. 'So what now?'

She shrugged. 'I don't have to tell you there'll be no book on Sebastian Devereaux. Or do I?'

'You just did.'

'Of course, if you were to write it as a novel, change a few names, a few dates . . .'

'I'll bear that in mind, thanks.'

We sipped our coffee. Kee watched Emily play. 'She's grown,' she said.

'All that fresh air and healthy living.'

'Shouldn't she be back at school by now?'

'That's next week. First Monday in September. Rachel's coming up for a long weekend, taking her home.'

'What'll you do then?'

'I don't know.'

'If you're going to be at a loose end . . .'

'Go on.'

She hummed and hawed and hedged it around with so many ifs and buts that by the time she was finished I reckoned I needed a machete to get at the truth of it. But what it sounded like was a proposal for some kind of keyboard-warrior *agent provocateur*, an electronic coat-trailer prowling the wilder fringes of the Web to see if I couldn't raise a banner or two, and draw out some like-minded lunatics and fellow despoilers of the Constitution. Black ops, although in this case the shades would be rather more lurid than grey.

I let it lie for a while and drank my coffee, then said, 'Why me?'

'You write spy thrillers, Tom. Think of it as a never-ending novel.'

'No, that part I get. What I'm asking is why you think I might give a shit.'

'Well, we thought, y'know . . .'

'What? That I'm *blooded* now?'

'I wouldn't put it as crudely as all that, no.'

'Think again. I did what I did because Franco put Emily's life on the line. Because if he got away with it once, he might feel like he could try it again.'

'There's plenty more Francos, Tom.'

'I'm sure there are.'

'Not your problem, right?'

'Not unless they come after my daughter.'

'Which is highly unlikely.'

'I'd imagine so. And the less time I spend flushing crazies out of the electronic undergrowth the less likely it'll get.'

'Can't say I blame you,' she said. 'But it was worth a try.' She gestured at the copy of the *Irish Times* on the table. 'You want to hold on to that?'

'Sure. I need to catch up on the football results.'

I walked her down the beach to the boat, hauled it in and held it steady while she climbed aboard. She got herself settled in the stern, and only then, when it was clear she was leaving, did Emily come trotting down the beach.

'Bye, Alison,' she said, giving a shy half-wave.

'See you later, Emily. Take care of your dad.'

'I will.'

'Tell him he needs a holiday, he looks exhausted.'

'All right.'

'If he needs any ideas of where to go, tell him Cyprus is lovely in September. Especially Turtle Bay, it's not too far from Kyrenia on the northern coast.'

'Are there really turtles?'

'Loads of them. I'll send you a postcard when I get there in a couple of weeks, OK?'

'OK.'

Kee brushed her fringe from her eyes, gave Emily a big smile and waved goodbye. Emily waved goodbye too, perhaps a little too enthusiastically to qualify as polite.

'See you, Tom.'

'You take care, Kee.'

I tossed her the painter and shoved her off, and when she'd drifted far enough she tugged on the outboard's rip-cord. The motor roared to life, the boat arced around, and two minutes later she was turning out of the bay and around the western headland again.

'Daddy?' Emily said as we trudged back up towards the house.
'Yes?'
'What does exhausted mean?'
'Tired, love. Very, very tired.'
'Are you exhausted?'
'I am, yeah.'
She found my hand, gave it a squeeze. 'Maybe you should go to Cyprus. To see all the turtles.'
'Maybe I will, love. Maybe I will.'